THE BLIZZARD BRIDE

This Large Print Book carries the
Seal of Approval of N.A.V.H.

THE DAUGHTERS OF THE MAYFLOWER

WITHDRAWN

THE BLIZZARD BRIDE

SUSANNE DIETZE

THORNDIKE PRESS
A part of Gale, a Cengage Company

GALE
A Cengage Company

Thorndike Press® Large Print Christian Romance.
The text of this Large Print edition is unabridged.
Other aspects of the book may vary from the original edition.
Set in 16 pt. Plantin.

LIBRARY OF CONGRESS CIP DATA ON FILE.
CATALOGUING IN PUBLICATION FOR THIS BOOK
IS AVAILABLE FROM THE LIBRARY OF CONGRESS

ISBN-13: 978-1-4328-7599-2 (hardcover alk. paper)

Published in 2020 by arrangement with Barbour Publishing, Inc.

Printed in Mexico
Print Number: 01   Print Year: 2020

Daughters of the Mayflower

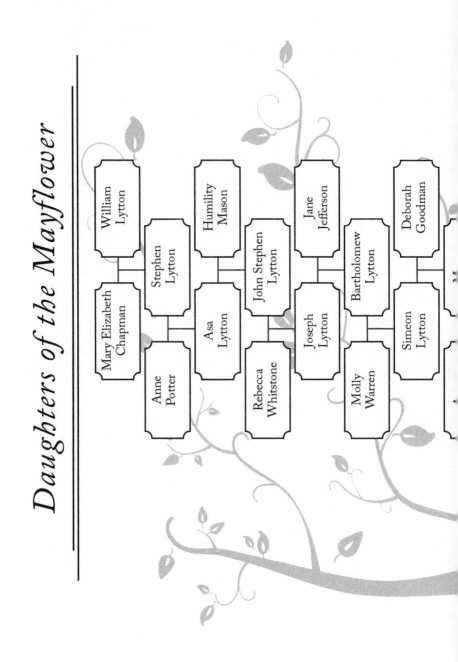

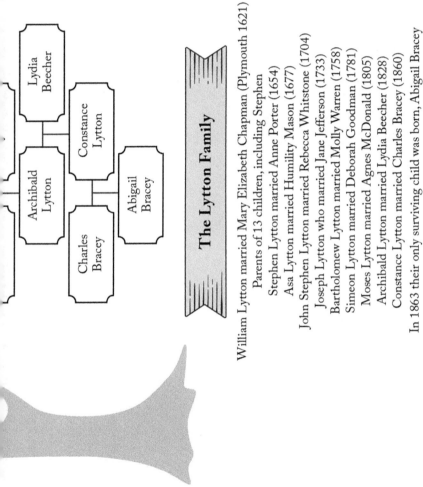

The Lytton Family

William Lytton married Mary Elizabeth Chapman (Plymouth 1621)
Parents of 13 children, including Stephen
Stephen Lytton married Anne Porter (1654)
Asa Lytton married Humility Mason (1677)
John Stephen Lytton married Rebecca Whitstone (1704)
Joseph Lytton who married Jane Jefferson (1733)
Bartholomew Lytton married Molly Warren (1758)
Simeon Lytton married Deborah Goodman (1781)
Moses Lytton married Agnes McDonald (1805)
Archibald Lytton married Lydia Beecher (1828)
Constance Lytton married Charles Bracey (1860)
In 1863 their only surviving child was born, Abigail Bracey

BRIEF GLOSSARY OF TERMS

- **Boodle:** counterfeit notes in bundles
- **Boodle carrier:** those who sell or transfer counterfeit currency
- **Capitalist:** the person behind a large-scale counterfeiting operation
- **Coney:** confidence man, con man
- **Dealer:** person who issues counterfeit notes to his patrons
- **Shover:** person who passes counterfeit money publicly — in a store, for example

DEDICATION

In memory of the
two hundred thirty-five.

And who knoweth whether thou art come
to the kingdom for such a
time as this?

ESTHER 4:14

CHAPTER 1

Chicago,
December 3, 1887

"Forgive my cryptic invitation to lunch, Miss Bracey, but I dared not go into detail on the chance your post was intercepted."

Abigail Bracey was not the sort of person whose mail was intercepted. No one showed the least bit of interest in her monotonous life, but Mr. Welch, the balding gentleman seated across the white-draped table from her, was probably accustomed to others attempting to intercept his correspondence. She made a sympathetic noise and closed her menu. She'd scarcely looked at it. Despite going out for a late lunch, food was the farthest thing from her mind.

"I was pleased to hear from you after so long, Mr. Welch. Have you news about my father's mur—"

Mr. Welch flinched. "Miss Bracey, we are in public."

She clamped her mouth shut. They had to be careful in public, and they couldn't exactly meet in private, could they? Mr. Welch might be several years her senior, but his calling on her, a maiden who lived alone in a rented room, would certainly give her landlady something to talk about. Meeting for lunch in a restaurant was his way of protecting her reputation. For that, she was grateful.

But she was also impatient.

"Forgive me, but I am eager for any scrap of news, and I do not think we can be overheard." Abby glanced at the only other patrons, an elderly couple several tables away, and three women in fur-trimmed mantles sipping tea at the window table. None of them had given Abby and Mr. Welch a second glance.

Mr. Welch scrutinized them with narrowed eyes, as if they could be spies. "Yes, well, I'd hoped we'd be alone, dining at this hour. Let's order before we chat. What would you like?"

"Soup is fine."

"But they have an excellent beefsteak here."

What a kind way to tell her she looked like she could use a heartier meal than a bowl of consommé. She didn't take offense.

14

They'd known one another too long not to be honest. Their relationship had never been social or casual. How could it be, when it was birthed in blood?

He first called on her and Mother four years ago, a few weeks after Father was found murdered on the steps of the bank he managed. Mr. Welch had offered them condolences, shown them his shiny, five-pointed star badge, and introduced himself as the Assistant Operative of the Chicago District Office of the United States Secret Service.

It had been her and her mother's last moment of sweet, oblivious ignorance.

Mr. Welch beckoned their waiter, a slender man with eyebrows that seemed to be permanently raised in expectation. "Steaks for me and the young lady, medium rare."

The waiter offered a half bow before returning to the kitchen. Mr. Welch twisted his neck to look behind him, a casual move that didn't fool Abby. Satisfied they couldn't be overheard, he met her gaze. "I'll not keep you in suspense any longer. As you may recall from our last meeting, your father's, er, assailant, the counterfeiter we know as the Artist, has been in the environs of Kansas City for a time."

She nodded. That was the last bit of

information Mr. Welch had given her.

"Rather than investigating his present activities, the assistant operative in Kansas City decided to look into the Artist's past. We knew he began his career in New York, before moving about and adopting pseudonyms, so our operative traveled there, made inquiries, and so forth. It is a long and winding tale, but he found a woman who rented a room to the Artist as a young man." He paused for effect. "She called him by a particular name, and when our operative used it to search public records, it yielded fruit. That name she used was the Artist's given, legal name."

Now that was indeed good news. All this time this counterfeiter had been sought by the Secret Service, but the pursuit had yielded few results beyond rabbit trails and dead ends. How could it, when no one knew what he looked like or knew his real name? The reign of terror he'd cultivated made him more myth than man, and therefore, untraceable, untouchable.

But now, he was no longer a shadow. He was flesh and blood, a person who was once a baby named by a mother and father who undoubtedly had hoped for more for their son than for him to become a counterfeiting murderer.

"What is it?"

Another quick peek over his shoulder. "Fletcher Pitch."

Abby mouthed the name of her enemy.

You're not supposed to have enemies, you know. The Good Book says —

She ignored the voice in her head. "He's in custody, then?"

"No, the wily creature is a master at eluding us, and as you know, he has assumed numerous names these past several years for his day-to-day undertakings. But knowing his birth name has allowed our operative to glean a fascinating bit of information —"

Mr. Welch stopped short at the appearance of their waiter carrying two steaming plates on a silver tray. He set them down, sending a waft of savory aromas around their table. Bone-in steak, roasted carrots, and mashed potatoes swimming in butter, garnished with tomato relish and a yeast roll. Abby hadn't seen anything so gorgeous in eons, much less eaten it, but she determined to ignore the noisy growls emanating from her stomach. The instant the waiter left them to their food, she leaned over her plate. "What information?"

Mr. Welch selected his knife and fork. "The most useful tidbit is that he married nine years ago."

"What sort of woman would marry *him*?"

"An honorable sort, apparently. When she realized the truth about him, a year after their marriage, she abandoned him, even though she'd just given birth to a son."

"Oh, that poor woman." Deceived by a man like that, and with a tiny baby too. Abby knew a thing or two about men not being who they appeared to be. She consumed a carrot — oh my, it really was delicious — and then speared another, this time swirling it in the butter spilling over the side of the mashed potatoes. "Can she be persuaded to tell tales about him?"

"She cannot. I'm sorry to say she died shortly thereafter."

Pitch was responsible for that death too, just like he was for Father's. And Mother's, because his cruelty killed innocents by breaking their hearts. "Where's the baby?"

"Disappeared in the care of the wife's sister, Katherine Hoover. She never met Pitch." His gaze flickered around the restaurant. The elderly couple had slipped out when she wasn't looking and the ladies by the window rose from the table, donned their wraps, and made their exit into the snowy afternoon, leaving Abby and Mr. Welch alone in the restaurant.

Nevertheless, Abby kept her voice low. "Disappeared, you say?"

"Like chaff on the wind. She told her friend goodbye in a dramatic, forever-like fashion, saying she'd promised her dying sister she'd ensure the baby's father never found them — but she showed her something extraordinary. A wedding tintype of her sister and Pitch, so her friend could recognize Pitch if he came sniffing. The friend couldn't tell our operative anything beyond saying he was decent-looking." He sighed. "At any rate, Miss Hoover vowed to protect that boy."

"She's a brave woman."

"I'll say. Left everything, changed her name for a child that wasn't hers. I wish we could leave her be, but she's got something that'd sure help us out in our investigation. That tintype of Pitch."

"That would be a valuable clue, to be sure." She sliced her steak. "But if Miss Hoover is in hiding under a false name, how can you find it? Find her?"

"Not easily, but we have reason to believe we aren't the only ones looking."

A shiver ran from her neck to her toes. "Pitch wants the baby. No, not a baby. He'd be, what, eight years old now?"

"Pitch wants to control everything that

concerns him. His image as a mysterious, violent, unknowable 'Artist' is carefully cultivated to intimidate. Everything he does is executed with the greatest care, from his engravings to his, well, God rest your father's soul, but Pitch's, er, dealings with those who cross him. When he engages in that sort of activity —"

"You can say *murder.*"

"I'm trying to be delicate, Miss Bracey. But yes. When he does *that,* he makes a statement of it, intended to frighten. He's controlling, for sure, and if I were the wagering sort I'd bet a thousand dollars, genuine currency, of course, that Pitch is furious to have been without his boy near on a decade, unable to mold him as he wishes."

A boy raised by a man like that? What a horrifying thought. "You must find Miss Hoover, then, and warn her." For the boy's sake. For Miss Hoover's sake. And for the sake of all of Pitch's victims. "And get that tintype, of course, but I'm not sure how to find a person who's so careful to hide her past."

His lips turned up in a smug expression. "I told you our operative in Kansas City's a good one, didn't I?"

"He found her? Goodness, how? Never

mind. I'm sure you would tell me 'confidential sources,' which is most unsatisfying when I want to know every detail. But in this case I shall leave it for the sake of expediency and state how impressive this operative is. I should like to shake his hand."

The waiter approached, bearing steaming mugs of aromatic coffee. The moment he vanished into the kitchen, she poured two dollops of cream into her cup. "So you have the tintype."

Mr. Welch took the cream pitcher from her. "Ah, no. Miss Hoover spooks like a feral cat. But the operative spoke to the bank she used in New York and learned she'd transferred her money to another bank, which in turn transferred it to another bank to be used by a woman with a different name — her new pseudonym, of course. He visited a few months ago and found out she was still using it, but to make a long story short, when she learned someone was asking questions about her, she ran away again. A wise woman, that, because how was she to know the fellow poking around was an operative and not Pitch or one of his cronies?"

"Months?" Abby repeated, hopes deflating.

"Of course, months. Takes time to do this sort of work, as I told you four years ago.

But you think I'd invite you to lunch to tell you all hope is lost? I've got more heart than that, Miss Bracey. The bank received a request to transfer funds to another bank in Nebraska. Big enough town for her to find employment. Small enough to know your neighbors, at least until the railroad line through there is finished. Farming community in Buffalo County called Wells."

The amused spark in Mr. Welch's eye told her he was enjoying stretching the tale for all it was worth, even if Abby didn't think her pounding heart could take any more. "So the operative will introduce himself this time rather than ask nosy questions that scare her away?"

"The problem is we don't know what she looks like. We only know that wherever she goes she pretends to be a widow with a son. And wouldn't you know it, she's settled in a town that boasts three widows with eight-year-old boys who've moved there within the past six months. One of them is Katherine Hoover, but which? Rather than visit and ask pesky questions that'll get her dander up, our operative planned to take up his former trade and move into the community so he could observe these families, but an opportunity has arisen, and I think you might be the perfect person to help us, if you're willing."

She dropped her fork. Her? How? Who cared? She could participate in bringing down Father's killer. "Yes. I'll do anything."

Mr. Welch grinned. "I thought so."

"What do you want me to do?"

"Finish your lunch." Mr. Welch pointed his knife at her plate.

"This is intolerable." But she shoved a bite of steak into her mouth anyway.

"The local schoolmaster's got a lung inflammation and is leaving for dryer climes right before Christmas. That leaves an open position, and what better way to find a child than to send a teacher to look for him? And you, Miss Bracey, are not only qualified to teach, but you have the desire to see Pitch brought to justice. There is no one better to take the task. Why, it seems providential."

Providence hadn't answered Abby once during the past four years. Not the way she expected or needed, at least. Could this turn of events be the answer to that long-ago uttered prayer?

Maybe, maybe not. But she would be on the train to Nebraska, regardless. "I must terminate my post, but they will not balk." Last week, a pupil's father learned who her scandalous father was and lodged an official protest about her family's moral turpitude.

The school board would be relieved if she slipped away.

"You can't start until the second of January, anyway. We'll pay you on top of your teaching pay, of course. Can't say it's much. The Treasury Department doesn't compensate as well as some of us think it should, not that it's a polite topic of conversation to have with a lady, but it cannot be helped in this situation. Forgive me."

Murder was a far less polite topic than finances, but she'd broached it already today. Oh well. "How many children are in the school?"

"I'm not sure." Mr. Welch consulted his brass pocket watch. "The operative in charge will be here shortly. You'll get to shake his hand after all."

"Excellent."

"He's to be your official contact, since he knows the intricacies of the case far better than I. And no, young lady, he will not be watching you work in Nebraska. He'll be close enough for you to summon with a quick tap of the telegraph, but we don't expect it to be necessary until you've found sufficient evidence to identify the boy. Otherwise, you'll have no need of law enforcement. You're in no danger. Pitch may want his son — and that tintype, if he knows

24

she has it — but there's not a single indication he's anywhere near Nebraska."

The restaurant door unlatched, and a frigid gust curled around Abby's nape. The Kansas City operative was here. She spun in her seat.

A tall man in a snow-dusted gray coat paused in the threshold. He dipped his head to remove his hat, revealing mussed dark blond hair curling over his ears and collar. She shifted, preparing to rise and shake his hand. But then the man looked up at her and she couldn't stand, much less breathe.

"Here he is, Miss Bracey. Meet Dashiell Lassiter."

She didn't require the information. The name Dash Lassiter was as familiar to her as her own, but one she hadn't expected to hear ever again. The instant she regained the ability to move, her molars ground together.

His light eyes widened, then narrowed as he joined their table. "Abby? Is it really you?"

Had he forgotten what she looked like in six years? Bile filled her throat. "Yes."

"What are you — I mean, how are you?"

She could not give him an honest answer and remain civil at the same time. Instead she rounded on Mr. Welch. "You said there was no one better than I for this teaching assignment. I agree. I will find that boy and that tintype. But I cannot work with *this man*, so I respectfully insist you assign someone else to me. Anyone else."

CHAPTER 2

"Someone else," Dash repeated, unsure he'd heard Abby correctly. But her spine was stiff as a flagpole, and she stared at Welch like her existence depended on it. Yessir, he'd heard her, all right.

He couldn't help it. He started to laugh.

"Is something amusing?" Abby's face was pink.

He couldn't answer, for laughing. His summons hadn't included the name of the teacher the Secret Service would be using. He never dreamed it would be her. Of course, being back in Chicago, he wondered if she still lived here. He assumed she'd be married by now, with a child or two. It had been six years since he left. Six years since his heart — that part of him that felt things, not the organ of the same name — had stopped beating.

Seeing her again, he had to laugh or cry, and frankly, it wasn't just her reaction to him that was hilarious. He'd always been an idiot when it came to Abigail Bracey.

He swiped a single bead of moisture from his right eye — a stupid response that happened when he laughed. Abby used to swipe away those single teardrops with her soft little thumb and say they were diamonds of joy.

Well, that memory sobered him up. "Nice to see you too, Abby."

"Have a seat." Welch indicated with a dip of his coffee cup that Dash should pull out a chair. Probably because they were being observed. By the delicious aroma of fresh-brewed coffee meeting Dash's nose, the waiter lurked behind him, pot in hand.

Dash lowered his too-long frame into the chair at the too-small table. His knees knocked Abby's and she shifted away from him.

"Would you care for a menu, sir?" The waiter's brows arched like upside-down U's.

"Coffee's fine, thank you."

The waiter filled his cup and topped off Welch's and Abby's. She took a dainty sip. The color had receded from her cheeks, leaving her face pale, a stark contrast to the study in serviceable brown she made. Brown hair pinned at the nape beneath a brown bonnet. Brown jacket buttoned to her chin.

Brown eyes studiously avoiding him. "As I was saying, I'd like to work with a different operative."

"No," Dash stated.

"No." Welch's tone was kinder. "This is Lassiter's case, Miss Bracey, and his orders come from Washington."

She gave a dainty shrug. "I cannot work with him."

He gulped his coffee and scalded his tongue. That'd hurt later. "Perhaps you don't understand, Abby, but I'm the one whose sources risked their lives to give me information. I am the one who traveled a thousand miles to learn our subject's given name. I am the one who has studied his habits longer than anyone in the service. I am the *only* one to be worked with, so I suppose we must find a different teacher to go to Nebraska to locate Pitch's boy. One with more experience."

That got her to look at him. "Why? I'm a fully qualified teacher, I assure you."

"I figured, or Welch wouldn't have asked you to do the job. I meant you're not trained."

"At what?"

"Lying, for starters."

Her brow arched as if to say, *like you?* "I shall be a teacher on a new assignment.

29

That's no fib. I want to become acquainted with my students and their families. That's no fib either."

"But you don't know what the man we're seeking is like. Any who cross him aren't given the benefit of the doubt. They're, well —"

"Dead, like my father."

Dash's vision darkened. "What?"

"Father passed thousands of dollars in Pitch's bogus currency through his bank. His conscience apparently got the better of him, though, because he wanted out of the mutually lucrative arrangement, according to Mr. Welch." She glanced at him. "But as Mr. Welch told me and Mother, no one stops doing business with Pitch. Pitch killed Father on the bank steps. Four years ago."

There weren't sufficient words to express his sorrow. "I'm sorry."

"Thank you for your condolences." She sipped her coffee.

These past four years had not been kind to Abby. Her round cheeks had hollowed, and there was a hardness to her now. Her lips used to be soft and pink, not this thin line of pain, and her eyes, well, they could always blaze fire when she was angry. He'd just never seen so much anger in her before.

"How's your mother?"

30

"She succumbed to pneumonia a year ago. Natural causes, but I blame Pitch regardless. He broke her heart and stole her will to live. She was not the same person after Father's death."

Ah, no. Mrs. Bracey was a kind woman with soft eyes and a ready smile. An ache hit him under his rib cage.

Abby had lost so much. She deserved better than to be thrust into the middle of this mess.

Yet the middle was precisely where she seemed to want to be. "Dash, I know what kind of man Pitch is, but Mr. Welch assured me I would be safe because Pitch isn't in Nebraska."

"That may be, but I don't know that it's wise that you go." She was capable, surely, but what if something went wrong?

"Ahem." Welch's tone drew both their gazes. "I do not know how you know one another, nor, to be frank, do I care, but if you cannot work together, I shall find others who will."

"I'm not walking away from my case." Dash gripped his cup.

"I'm certainly not passing an opportunity to help catch my father's killer." Abby pushed away her plate of half-eaten meat and vegetables. "Mr. Welch, you said the operative wouldn't be in Nebraska with me. Is that true?"

"Yes." Welch lifted his cup. "Lassiter will give you the information you require about the students and community, and after that you will not be in contact again until you determine the boy's identity."

Her gaze fixed at the wall for a few seconds. "If you promise to not contact me or come to Wells, Dash, then I suppose I do not require a new operative after all."

"I promise. But I will escort you to the train when you go — don't argue with me, I must report to my superiors that I witnessed you board the train. And you have to stomach me long enough for me to tell you what I know about the boys and their mothers."

"Can you not send a file for me to peruse at my leisure?"

"It's not a ladies' magazine. It's a secret dossier. You'll get an oral report."

"I'll take notes, then."

A thousand times no. "And take them with you? What if the family you live with happens to see them?"

"I'd — hide them in my trunk."

"A place no landlady has ever snooped." Sarcasm dripped like a spring thaw.

Welch smiled. "It's policy, Miss Bracey."

"Oh, well then, of course."

Dash snorted.

The waiter returned, eyebrows lifted halfway to his hairline. "More coffee?"

"No," they all said at once.

Her glaring eyes were cold as polished jasper. "I have thirty minutes to spare you, Dash. Is there a park or . . . somewhere for you to inform me of all I need to know?"

He couldn't think of a one in this area, but he'd find something that offered them a smidgen of privacy in a public place. Best get this over with as quickly as possible. Every question he'd had when he walked in the restaurant — *How are you? Are you happy? Do you ever think of me?* — disintegrated like paper in a fire. A few seconds of heat, then nothing but ash.

"Let's go." He stood and reached to pull out her chair.

She shoved it back before he could assist her.

This would be a long thirty minutes, indeed.

The following twenty-one days passed in a blur of activity for Abby, packing, resigning her post, and creating lesson plans for her students in Nebraska. At last it was time to leave for Wells, thank the Lord — if she did that sort of thing anymore.

Union Station bustled with Christmas Eve crowds, noisy folks coming and going, their loved ones receiving them or bidding them farewell, all of them pushing to get somewhere, to be with someone.

Journeys began and ended with kisses, hugs, the shaking of hands, though, didn't they? From every direction on the platform, affection surrounded Abby. But it didn't touch her. This was the most clinical, awkward goodbye of her existence.

At least it was too loud for her and Dash to bother attempting conversation. They'd been silent since he collected her to escort her to the station. Of course, Dash must have felt the need to say something now that it was time to put her on the train, because his mouth moved and his eyes had a soft-eyed, earnest expression that made him look like the boy she once knew.

She wouldn't be fooled by it. "I cannot hear you," she enunciated, standing on tiptoe to yell in his ear.

He sighed — she could see it rather than hear it — and bent at the waist so his lips were right next to her ear. His breath was hot on her chilled skin, tickling her lobe, reminding her of things she'd worked hard to forget.

A fraction of her wanted to lean into him,

reintroduce her ear to his lips, find warmth in his embrace. That part of her was weak, forgetful, and utterly traitorous.

She screwed her eyes shut and forced herself to stillness, concentrating to hear him. His words might be pertinent to the case, something he'd forgotten to mention when they discussed the situation three weeks ago.

Or maybe, now that it was the final moment of their time together, he would explain where he went six years ago. Maybe he would apologize.

That disloyal part of her wanted his apology desperately.

He bent down again. One breath. Two, hot on her ear and neck.

Tell me why you left me, Dash.

"If you need me," he said, "I will come. You're safe, I promise you, but please . . ."

Please what?

"Do nothing foolish, Abby."

No new facts. No apology. Just a plea that she not ruin the investigation by doing something imprudent. At least he'd asked nicely and said please.

She jerked away. "I won't need you."

"What?" he yelled over the roar of an approaching train.

"You will receive my telegram." She

shouted over the roar. "Merry Christmas."

Something hard and heavy hit her behind the knees and knocked her forward. Dash took her by the elbow, holding her steady. "You all right?" he said in her ear. "That fellow didn't even notice he hit you with his trunk. I have half a mind to inform him."

The man in question was now kissing a bundled-up woman on her plump cheek. "It's Christmas, Dash. People are happy."

But not them.

He released her elbow and bent to her ear yet again. "I'm sorry you'll be on a train, not with loved ones. In church."

It didn't matter. She didn't have loved ones anymore. Or a church. "Goodbye, Dash."

His reciprocated farewell was lost to the conductor's final call. Dash scooped her valise and took her elbow to assist her to the train. The porter took her bag, and then she mounted the steps and found her seat.

She faced forward, toward Nebraska. Toward her future. Toward justice. She didn't look to see if Dash watched her go. She would never see him again.

Even if her elbow still burned from his touch.

CHAPTER 3

Wells, Nebraska
January 5, 1888

The scratch of chalk on the black-painted slate board competed with low murmurings throughout the one-room wooden schoolhouse. Three days into her teaching assignment, Abby had found her students to be both intrigued by and curious about their first female instructor. A few of them had taken that curiosity and used it to test their limits with her.

"My parents." Abby read her chalk words loudly before facing her class of eighteen pupils, eleven boys and seven girls, ages six to fourteen. The biggest boys in the back row, Coy Johnstone and Josiah Topsy, clamped their mouths shut the moment she met their gazes.

The boys might want to test her, but at least they had some respect for her authority. "For our final task of the day, each of you will write on the topic of your parents."

A familiar hand shot up.

"Yes, Willodean?"

"What if I don't write yet?"

Willodean was her lone six-year-old pupil, the oldest child of the Elmore family, who had taken it upon themselves to house the new teacher. Although there was a boarding-house in town, none of its occupants were female, so it was decided by Mayor Carpenter that Abby would be better off residing with a family. She was grateful for the arrangement for many reasons, including the delicious deviled ham sandwich and dried-apple tart Hildie Elmore had packed for Abby's lunch earlier today. However, Abby also appreciated Hildie's knowledge of the local children and their parents.

Hildie had shared a great deal about the families. Dash had been correct, much as it prodded her like a needle poke to admit it. Three boys fit the description of Fletcher Pitch's son: Micah Story, Kyle Queen, and Bud Grooms.

Abby was tasked with determining which lad was the correct one. How better than to simply ask the boys what they knew about their fathers? It wasn't a bad topic as an assignment, either. After all, she was here to educate the children as well as to uncover the identity of Fletcher Pitch's son, raised by Katherine Hoover.

She glanced at those three particular boys before turning to Willodean. "You and I will work at my desk with your slate. The rest of you will use paper. Berthanne, pass out a sheet to each student please. Oneida, Jack, a few sentences about the topic will suffice. Those of you who are between second and fifth grade, two paragraphs will do. Sixth through eighth grade, I'd like a page."

"Aw," Coy groaned.

Another hand shot up. Dark-haired, round-cheeked Kyle's. "I don't got no pa."

"Me neither." The words were soft from blond, slender Micah, the smallest of the three eight-year-old boys, and perhaps the most intelligent.

Bud, a plump wiggle worm, squirmed on his seat. "I got a new step-pa."

Which was precisely why Bud was not her first choice as Fletcher Pitch's son. Not that Pitch's sister-in-law Katherine couldn't have married, but the timing might not work in this particular case. Bud's mother was expecting a baby with her second husband, the town barber. Katherine Hoover would have had to have married immediately after arriving in Wells, an unlikely scenario, but

Abby was not prepared to rule her out quite yet.

"Write what you do know about your father. His name, perhaps? What he did for a living?" She strolled between the columns of plank desks. "Was or is he a farmer or a businessman? What does he look like?"

"And write about our mothers too," Zaida said.

"Of course." Abby may have only been here three days, but she'd already identified the dispositions in her classroom: the studious ones, like Micah Story, Zaida Knapp, and Katie Andersen. The chatty ones, like Josiah Topsy, Coy Johnstone, and Oneida Ford. But they were all good-natured children, and they seemed to have been instructed well by their previous schoolmasters.

Willodean's hand rose again. "Ready, Miss Bracey?"

"Yes." Abby beckoned the little girl to the spindled chair perched beside the teacher's desk. Abby sat in the larger chair at the desk, rubbing her hands together. Here in the corner, she was farthest away from the wood-burning box stove in the center of the schoolroom. After the first day of instruction, she'd used her meager savings to purchase a blue rag rug to place beneath

40

her desk in an effort to stave off the chill, but neither they nor the blue gingham curtains she draped over the windows did anything but add a sense of cheeriness to the space. Ah, well. It was too late in the day to add more fuel to the stove, so she would be patient. "Willodean, what would you like to say about your parents?"

"Pa's name is Bynum Elmore." Willodean pointed to her slate, where she'd already written a large *B.* "He's a farmer."

Abby well knew the fact, since she'd lived with them near on a week now. She spelled out Bynum's name and the word *farmer.* "And your mother?"

"Her name is Hildegard and she's a mama."

Abby spelled those. "Let's practice some other words you might want to include." Abby showed her how to write *corn, oats,* and *cow,* as well as the name of her three-year-old sister, Patty; Patchy Polly, the calico cat; and *baby,* for the little one coming into the family sometime soon, gauging by Hildie Elmore's prominent midsection.

While Willodean practiced with the tip of her tongue caught between her lips, Abby rose to check on the others. Curly-haired Zaida had already finished a page and had started on a second, even though she was ten and not required to write more than two paragraphs. Her parents kept the dry goods store, and oh, she was describing her father's technique for keeping his mustache trimmed and waxed. "Very nice."

Kyle hadn't written a single word yet. "What's so intriguing out the window, Kyle?"

"It's snowing."

So it was, a gentle, picturesque, pretty snow. "Perfect for playing in . . . after school. Please focus on your sentences. You too, Coy. These are due before you go home for the day."

"Aw." It was Coy's favorite refrain. "Can't I take it home to finish it?"

"Coy Johnstone, are you requesting homework for you and the class?"

Beside him, Josiah glared. "No you ain't, Coy. I don't want any."

Coy let out a deep sigh and picked up his pen. "No ma'am, I'll do it now."

She couldn't help glancing at the eight-year-old-boys' work. It would be a miracle if any of them mentioned having a father named Fletcher, but perhaps there would be something helpful. Hmm, not yet. Micah's neat script described his seamstress mother as *pretty, smart,* and *brave.* Bud's large scrawl didn't reveal much of anything yet. Kyle's sentences listed the items his mother baked at the Wells Café, from muffins to pie.

"Miss Bracey." Micah's hand floated above his head, his gaze fixed on the floor.

"Yes?"

He pointed. Redheaded Almos Sweet's green canvas book bag slithered — there was no other word for it. Then went still. She stared at the bag, propped against ten-year-old Almos's skinny shins, willing it to move again.

It did.

"Almos?" She swallowed down the panic squeezing her voice box and making her sound like a toddler. "There's a mouse or . . . something in your book bag. I'm going to take it outside and set it free."

One of the girls shrieked. The scrape of feet on wood planks told her everyone was on his or her feet, but she didn't dare take her focus off that canvas bag for a moment. What if it wasn't a mouse? Mice were far preferable to rats, like the yellow-toothed horrors that kept her up at night in Chicago, scratching their way through her walls. Why, oh, why did God create vermin like that?

Stop it. You're the teacher here. Taking a deep breath, she reached for the bag.

Almos snatched it away. "I'll do it,

Teacher."

"Let me," Coy begged.

"No, boys. Rats — rodents — can bite. Where are my gloves?"

"I wanna watch." Oneida pushed Jack out of the way, so Josiah lifted his little brother up for a better vantage.

"No one move." Abby used her strongest authoritarian voice and hurried to the vestibule at the rear of the schoolhouse, tugging her leather gloves from the pocket of her coat. "Almos, the bag, please."

"No, ma'am." He clutched it to his chest. Almost lovingly.

"Oh Almos, this is your pet, isn't it? Not a wild creature that found its way into your bag?"

He nodded. The sack wiggled against his hold, the ripple too large to be a small rodent. Abby's stomach swooped to her toes and up to her throat in less than a second. Snakes? No, it was winter . . . they hibernated, didn't they? Every zoological fact she possessed fled as her shaking hands dropped the gloves.

Please, God, don't let it be something with fangs.

She hadn't prayed for years, and that's how she started again? Abby picked up her gloves and donned them with more confidence than she felt because the entire classroom watched her. "Almos, what is in that sack?"

The redheaded boy turned pink as a peach blossom. "I don't want to say."

"I reckon it's a cat," Kyle suggested.

"A cat!" Willodean squealed in rapture. "Mine is named Patchy Polly because she's a calico."

A cat. Abby's muscles relaxed in relief. Sweet paws and whiskers and purring throats. But cats did not belong at school, and it was time to put an end to this spectacle. She led Almos to her desk. "You've kept a cat in a sack all day? That's not fair to any creature, Almos."

"I had to." Almos lowered the squirming bag atop her grading papers. "He's injured."

"Then he should be resting at home. Let him out now for a few minutes of fresh air before you take him home."

Although once she said it, she realized not a single child would do any work with a cat loose in the schoolroom. Not to mention, it might be difficult for Almos to catch the long-cooped-up cat to take home once it was out. But it couldn't be helped, for the words had been spoken and Almos had already loosened the knot holding the canvas closed. A black snout poked out of the opening, fur sleek and black as ink.

Cats did not have snouts.

Nor did they have white triangles between their eyes that extended, thick and bright, down their spines in a stripe down their tails.

One of the girls shrieked. Abby hopped back from the skunk investigating her desktop. It delicately sniffed her pencil jar and then hobbled to her teacup, one fore-paw wrapped in neatly tied white muslin.

"Return it to the sack, please, Almos."

"You said to take him out."

"Almos Sweet, do as I say. I didn't know it was a wild animal." It seemed mild now, but it could be rabid. Vicious. Or ready to unleash its odiferous spray.

"Stripey's a good skunk. He don't stink." Almos scooped the skunk into his arms, cradling it like a baby.

"*Doesn't* stink. Yet. But he could well spray me or this class or you."

"His tail ain't twitchin' like he's fixin' on it, but he could, if you scare him."

He was right. The children's noisy exclamations weren't going to keep the skunk disinclined to spray them. She lifted her hand. "Quiet, everyone."

"He's just a young thing. His paw got caught in one of Pa's snares." Now that every eye was fixed on him, Almos lifted his chin as well as his voice. "I'm tendin' him."

"You have a kind heart to care for, er, Stripey, but skunks are not welcome in class."

"Can I pet it?" Vernon Johnstone reached out.

"No, boys, no." Abby waved down Vernon's hand. "Almos is about to put him back in the bag."

"Aw," Coy groaned.

Almos's shoulders slumped, but he obeyed, and when the last bit of inky black fur disappeared into the sack, Almos cinched it closed.

Relief shot through Abby's limbs. "Does your mother know Stripey is here?"

His face pinked again. "She thinks he's in the barn."

Several small hands reached to touch the canvas bag. Abby shooed them away from her desk. "Resume your seats and finish your assignment, class. Almos, are you close to finished?"

"Yes, ma'am."

She hurried to his desk and glanced at his paper. He'd ended his report midsentence, but it was close enough, and the school day was almost over. "You may be excused early to take Stripey home. If you bring Stripey back again, I'll have no choice but to send you home again and inform your parents."

"But he gets hungry, and his paw's hurt."

Her stomach flipped at the thought of what Almos had been feeding the creature all day, outside of her notice. "Other arrangements must be made. Are we understood?"

He stared at his shoes. "Yes, ma'am."

"I'm finished with my assignment, Miss Bracey." Almos's older sister Berthanne raised her hand. "May I go with Almos? Mama wants us to walk together."

At Abby's nod, the two children moved to the vestibule.

"I wish I could go home too," Coy lamented.

"Then do your assignment instead of complaining about it," Zaida said, giving Coy a matter-of-fact look. Zaida had the makings of a future teacher.

Abby grinned and followed the Sweet children to the vestibule, a small area the perfect size to accommodate a coatrack and a stack of split logs. She assisted them with their coats and retrieved the empty tobacco tins they used for lunch pails. "Almos, I meant what I said. I admire your heart for animals, but Stripey stays home from now on."

48

"Yes, ma'am."

She opened the door to let them out, bracing against the cold. She should have braced harder. Dash Lassiter stood on the schoolhouse steps, hand on his hat as if about to remove it.

Her heart gave a powerful thump before coming to a halt in her chest. Dash said he couldn't come to Wells without drawing suspicion, yet here he was at the school, where he'd undoubtedly draw every curious juvenile eye. Back in Chicago, he'd also promised he wouldn't check on her, contact her, or even see her again. A telegram was all there was supposed to be remaining between the two of them. So why had he come?

She had literally just traded one skunk for another.

"Good afternoon, sir." Perhaps if she spoke to him as if they were strangers, he'd take the hint and reciprocate. Already the children would be talking about the stranger visiting the schoolhouse. "How may I help you?"

He glanced behind her. "We need to talk, Abby."

He'd used her Christian name in the hearing of her pupils. There went all hope of pretending they weren't acquainted. "This is not a good time, *sir.*"

"It's important, *ma'am,* else I wouldn't be here."

Oh. Of course. Something had happened regarding the investigation. She softened a fraction, like a handful of snow in a mitten, but at once whispers erupted behind her.

Whatever Dash had to say would be overheard if she didn't go outside with him and shut the door.

But if she did that, every mother in Wells would hear how she went outside with a man during school hours. No matter how innocent an encounter, it could be twisted, questioned. She'd signed a contract promising unimpeachable behavior. If she was perceived to have entertained a man during class time, she would be called upon to explain herself.

Dash had humiliated her six years ago. Regardless of the reason for his visit, she'd be humiliated once again if she spoke to him right now. The matter would have to wait.

"This is not a good time." She widened her eyes to send him a message.

One he clearly didn't understand, because he touched her forearm, right there in front of the entire student body of Wells.

This teacher would now be forced to give

him a lesson he'd not soon forget.

Dash was accustomed to operating in shadows, not on schoolhouse steps in front of a rapt audience of miniature people. Shouldn't that tell Abby how important this was? Hopefully his hand on her arm was making the point clear.

Their touch made another point clear — to him. This was *Abby,* in his life again after all this time. He'd been shocked to see her in Chicago. Then guilt-ridden as he reflected on what his choice to leave had cost them both. He'd shoved his emotions aside, however, to focus on the investigation. Catching Fletcher Pitch was too important.

But touching her now, long-forgotten heat jolted up to his arm socket. He'd loved her, loved the girl he could still see in Abby's brown eyes.

But she was different now too. Six years ago, she was a carefree sprite with fuller cheeks and a ready smile. Maybe she still had a smile for everyone but him, but she was clearly not free of care. Faint pouches beneath her eyes testified to her bearing more burdens now than she once had.

Nor was she adorned in fancy frocks or fripperies like she used to be, the majority of which were pink, her favorite color. Now, her clothing was neat but utilitarian, and not even a simple gold cross on a chain dangled beneath the tiniest of lace collars at her throat. Aside from that scrap of lace, everything she wore was sparrow brown, as if she hoped to go unnoticed.

But he'd notice her no matter what she wore or did or said. He'd noticed her when they were knee high to the carriage horses, and had never been able to tear his gaze away.

Until he left, that is. Hurt her. Maybe the Lord had allowed their paths to cross so he could ask forgiveness for hurting her.

What good would it do now, though? She'd lost her father and mother, her home and friends. He'd be opening old wounds. Nevertheless, fresh guilt kicked him in the gut like a hoof.

"Don't touch me." She twisted so his hand slid off her arm. "You didn't used to be so thickheaded," she whispered.

She might as well have slapped him, the way he recoiled inside. "Sure I did. Couldn't read to save my hide." Literally.

Her eyes clouded. "I didn't mean that."

Didn't she? *Dim-witted Dash.* How could he forget what her father said? What everyone said? That's why he'd left Chicago. Had he stayed, her life would have been even worse than it was now.

Reminding himself of that simple fact made this bit of business easier. He'd come because he had something to say, and he couldn't say it with a dozen or so pairs of little eyes peeping at him. "Come out for a second."

"I cannot."

"But everyone's watching."

"Precisely. And the school day is not finished for another ten minutes."

"You sent home two children already." The gawking girl and the boy with the canvas sack.

"A disciplinary matter. And I really must return to instructing the children. It is not proper for me to leave my class unattended for any reason. Unless you want me to lose my job and any hope for a recommendation in the future."

"Fine." He shoved his hat back on his head. "I'll wait."

"Fine." She shut the door in his face.

He stared at it for a full three seconds before tossing back his head. What else could he do but laugh?

Lord, what am I supposed to do? Aside from not touching her again. His hand on her arm had stirred up emotions he'd banished years ago. No, he needed to focus on the job. Ten minutes, she'd said. Not much time to do anything but get bored, so he did what he always did: look around to glean information.

There wasn't much to learn. The schoolhouse was located just east of town, the site probably chosen to accommodate farming families as well as town children. Snow-blanketed fields abutted the school on either side and across the road, and cottonwoods stood as silent sentries between the properties.

At one of the adjacent farms, a bearded, broad-shouldered man replaced the Virginia rail fence that divided his land from the school with barbed wire, but he wasn't getting much accomplished, the way he watched Dash. Maybe his children attended the school and he didn't like the looks of a stranger loitering on school grounds. Dash had never given the idea a moment's thought before. The only thought he'd entertained today was getting to Abby as fast as possible. But maybe he should have waited until the children were gone for the day so as not to draw interest, as he'd clearly done.

The man was still staring, so Dash held up his hand in greeting and strode toward him. "Afternoon, sir. How's the barbed wire treating you?"

The man dropped his tools and extended his gloved hand over the fence. Faint lines rimmed sharp blue eyes, and a heavy brown beard covered a square jaw. "Afternoon. Yeah, working with wire takes some getting used to."

"You've done a fine job." The wire was taut, the fence line neat. It looked as if the man had years of experience. "Those barbs look downright mean."

"It's worth it to protect what's yours." The man tipped back his hat to better look at Dash.

"Your spring crops? Or animals?"

"Beef. Come spring I'll be building a herd." The man rubbed the back of his neck.

"Best wishes to you, then. I know little of cattle, but this seems like good land for it. I'm more of a horse fellow. I learned at my father's knee and always thought I'd have a breeding ranch on a fine spread like this." Dash hadn't intended to chat, but he had nothing else to do while he waited for the school day to end, and this fellow seemed affable enough. "You have young'uns at the school?"

Blue eyes flashed. "I was about to ask you the same thing."

"I do not have children, no."

"Then what're you doing out here?"

"I need a word with the teacher."

The man glanced at the school with a knowing smile. "I see."

"Not like that, no. So . . ." He changed the subject. "Have you been in Wells long?"

"Handful of months now. And to answer your earlier question, no, no family. Yet. Just me rattling around in there." He indicated the neat farmhouse several yards behind him.

"Well, when you do have a family, you can keep an eye on your young'uns when they're here in school."

A shriek behind Dash drew his attention. A few boys raced from the schoolhouse as if they'd been released from captivity. Wrapped in a rusty-red shawl that on a sunnier day would bring out the mahogany in her hair, Abby stood in the doorway, assisting a little girl with her mittens.

He turned back and tipped the brim of his hat at the man. "School's out, so I'll be on my way."

"Didn't catch your name."

Had Abby called him by name in front of the children? He mentally kicked himself for not having noted it. Well, best assume she had, so he'd have to use his real name now. Usually, he offered an alias when it came to work, not that it mattered all that much. Counterfeiters generally knew the name of the Head of the Secret Service, but not its operatives. "Dashiell Lassiter."

"Burt Crabtree." The rancher nodded and scooped up his tools to resume his task.

Dash crossed the snow-dusted schoolyard, and at once a group of children ran at him, heading to the road. He felt like a large, lone fish swimming into a school of guppies. Ahead, Abby rested a gentle hand atop the girl's cap while her attention fixed on several other pupils. "Bud, you dropped your mitten. Micah, pull your cap down over your ears. Don't forget about the meeting tonight at town hall, everyone. I'd love to meet your parents."

Dash stomped snow from his boot against the first step up to the schoolhouse. "May I come in now, *ma'am?*"

Her head shook in such a way he understood at once: *it's not proper.* Not that he had any intention of coming within ten feet of her ever again, but being a gentleman was cramping his ability to relay vital information. "Then if you could —"

Something thwacked the back of his calf. He spun to see a leather ball roll past, chased by a boy who yelled an apology. When he turned back, a girl with brown braids had inserted herself between him and Abby.

Abby smiled. "Oneida, did you need something?"

"I can't find my ribbon. Mama said if I lost it I don't get new ribbons again, ever."

"Ever, eh?"

"Something like that. I stopped listening, but I need the ribbon."

Abby cast Dash an apologetic look. "If you could wait one more minute."

"How about I walk you home?"

"I do not walk alone. I board with a family, and their six-year-old is my companion to and from school. Besides, I wouldn't wish for anyone to see us and think we were engaged in an assignation of some sort."

She hadn't minded their trysts in the past. He wouldn't fight it, though. "One minute's wait won't hurt."

"All right, Oneida, let's go look for it." She retreated back inside.

Before he had a moment to breathe, someone tapped his elbow, a pale-haired, freckled girl in a yellow cap. "Who are you?" Her voice was high-pitched as a kitten's mew, but something sparking in her blue eyes told him she was as curious as the proverbial cat too.

"I'm Mr. Lassiter. Who are you?" He'd

been trained to throw off inquisitors with questions, and never had he been more grateful for the trick than he was now.

"Willodean Lisa-peth Elmore."

"Nice to meet you, Willodean."

"Why are you here?"

First Burt Crabtree had questions, and now this little wisp of a thing. Well, Dash had expected his appearance in town would draw scrutiny. That's why he and his supervisors decided to use a teacher instead — before things changed and he had to come to Wells himself. "Business."

"Mama says adult biz-ness is none of my biz-ness and she tells me *no eavesdropping.*" She enunciated the last two words, no doubt in imitation of her mother. "But I want to know everything."

Apparently he had something in common with Willodean. "Curiosity isn't a bad thing."

Willodean scooped up snow and patted it in her mittens. "What're you curious about?"

Killers, smugglers, bad money, and, truth be told, her schoolmarm. "The world."

"Me too. Like, where do bugs go when it snows?"

"I don't know the answer to that one, unless they sleep in trees or underground."

She nodded sagely. "Miss Bracey will know. I like her."

"I do too," he said without thinking.

Her eyes took on a suspicious gleam. "Why?"

What did she mean, *why*? The better question was why he'd admitted to liking Abby, a woman who loathed the sight of him. "Just . . . because."

"Mama says *because* isn't an answer."

"Isn't it time you went home, before your mother wonders where you are?"

"I'm gonna play until Miss Bracey's ready to walk home with me. She sleeps in our attic."

"Oh, yes, she mentioned she had an escort home." But an attic? That was a far cry from Abby's elegant dwelling when he knew her back in Chicago.

Willodean hopped in the snow, making crunching sounds with her boots. "Almos brought a skunk to school today and nobody knew until Miss Bracey saw it wiggling in the sack. I reckon it was sleepin' all day, because it's got a hurt leg or maybe because skunks are night critters. I don't rightly know."

The canvas sack he'd seen made sense now. "I imagine Miss Bracey didn't like an animal in school."

She'd been afraid of skunks when they were younger, shrieking when one crossed their path on an evening stroll. Dash had been grateful for the skunk, though, for the creature had driven Abby right into his arms.

With a scrape, the school door opened again, and the girl with the lost ribbon skittered out.

"Ribbon found?" Dash asked.

Abby nodded. "In her coat pocket."

The yard had mostly emptied of children. Two boys threw snowballs at one another, and a few of the girls stared at him — just as Burt Crabtree had — but everyone was at a distance now, and none could overhear anything. Except Willodean, who looked up at them, clearly not going anywhere.

Well, neither was Dash.

Abby patted the child atop her capped head. "Would you please erase the blackboard for me?"

"Yes, ma'am!" Willodean shouted like it was a treat before scurrying into the building.

Abby stared up at Dash. "That gives us about ninety seconds, and this is as much privacy as we are bound to get. What's wrong?"

At last. "You-know-who is coming to Wells."

Pitch. She mouthed the name and then her lips stayed parted in surprise.

"You recall I have certain . . . friends who are not of the best character, who speak to me in confidence about delicate matters in exchange for the Service turning a blind eye to their lesser infractions."

"Informants, you called them."

"Exactly. One such fellow who's worked with him in Kansas City says he has learned his son is here in Wells."

"Are you sure?"

"As sure as I can be. I tracked Katherine Hoover to Wells. He could too. My informant said the moment you-know-who saw the name of the town, Wells, he said he should've known. I don't know why, but it was enough to make him think the boy is here and make plans to come here once he ties up loose ends on his current operation. So on behalf of the Secret Service, I thank you for your sacrifice coming here. I can get you on a train back to Chicago in the morning."

She flinched. "I beg your pardon?"

"Your services are no longer required."

"They certainly are. I haven't found the boy yet."

"It would have been miraculous if you had in only three days."

"B–but I have work to do. Plans."

"It can't be helped. Anywhere that man goes is dangerous, and if he's coming here, it stands to reason you could be in danger. I won't have it."

"You, or the Service?" she muttered.

"Both." Mainly him.

"I do not see why I must leave. He won't suspect a spinster schoolmarm, and I can still identify the boy so you can protect him. Please don't make me go home yet."

"What if he comes to the school, Abby? What do you think could happen?"

She looked away and mumbled something.

"Pardon?"

She sighed. "I have a knife tied to my calf."

A snort escaped him. "Of all the fool things, Abby."

"You don't think I'd use it?"

"I'm pretty sure you'd try, to a frightening result. Abby, he's a mur—"

"I'm not leaving." Her arms folded. "I signed a contract to teach. I gave my word to Mr. Welch I'd help the *cause.* And now that I think on it, *his* coming here might be a good thing. You said it yourself, newcomers stand out in a town like this. You can

63

nab him in an instant."

"In an instant," he echoed, disbelieving.

"This is what we will do. I will continue in my role and I will send you a telegraph the minute a new stranger saunters into town —"

"He won't saunter. He'll slip in, with a false identity and a plausible-sounding reason for being here. Or he might hide outside of town, watching until he figures out who his boy is."

"That could take forever."

"He didn't get where he is without being patient."

"So how will you protect the boy and his mother, then? Visit each widow and say, 'Ma'am, if you used to go by the name *Katherine Hoover*" — she whispered the name — "your brother-in-law is about to come calling.' " Her mouth softened. "Actually, I wonder why you don't do that. This is a matter of life and death. Visit the families who fit the description and tell them the truth. I can provide their names. The mother will help you."

"Or deny it and then run away again, which is why Welch has forbidden me to speak to the families directly. This is the closest we've ever come to apprehending this man, and my superiors want to keep things as quiet as possible. They want the mother positively identified before I confront her, so she cannot lie about who she is."

Abby's eyes were pleading. "If I leave, how can you know who she is?"

"Figuring this mess out is not your job. It's mine." And he had to do it fast.

She shook her head. "There's still time."

"Not much, though. A day, perhaps a week or two since he said something about putting his affairs in order. But it doesn't matter. Welch gave the order. You're to be paid for the term, but your help is no longer requested."

The door opened and Willodean's chalk-smudged face poked through the gap. "I'm finished."

"So are we. Gather your things to go home." The gentleness of her tone for the child contradicted the iron-hard glare cast at Dash.

Pity surged through him. "Finish out the week, if you must."

"I shall finish out the term. I am not leaving Wells."

"Yes, you are." His whisper came out like a hiss.

"I shall send a telegram when I've concluded my investigation, as discussed." She re-entered the schoolhouse. At least she didn't shut the door in his face this time.

Dash stood in the schoolyard, incredulous. No, furious. What was she thinking? She had no idea what could happen here. But there was no use arguing now, with Willodean hopping down the steps and Burt Crabtree no longer even pretending to work as he watched Dash.

There was nothing for it but to go back to town, where he'd left his baggage and intentions to whisk Abby away from here at first light.

Marching the snowy road back to town, he only thought of one thing. Abby's well-being.

It was paramount, more so than apprehending Fletcher Pitch. She would be kept safe.

He'd die if he had to, to keep that promise to her father.

CHAPTER 4

At half past five that evening, Abby perched on the hard stool at the maple bureau in her room and pinned her hair into a tight bun for the meeting at town hall at six. Hopefully the severe style communicated *schoolmarm* to everyone who looked at her, including her hostess, Hildie Elmore, whose disbelieving blue-eyed gaze flashed in the mirror's reflection.

"That feller sounds like a suitor to me, Abby."

"I assure you, he's not. Just an old acquaintance, passing through town."

Naturally, the moment Abby and Willodean came home from school today, Willodean had told Hildie and Bynum *all* about the man who visited Abby at school — and that he'd called her Abby and not Miss Bracey, a veritable felony in her thinking. And he took her arm like he was going to escort her somewhere fancy.

Also naturally, Hildie and Bynum had gaped at Abby.

She'd offered the half truth that she used to know Dashiell Lassiter and he was merely being courteous in coming by. She hoped — almost prayed, before she reminded herself she didn't do that anymore — that her host family would accept her feeble story and leave it at that. Alas, they didn't. After supper, Hildie had followed her upstairs to continue questioning her.

"Willodean said he looks like the prince in her fairy-tale book. Tall and dashing." Hildie grinned from her perch at the foot of Abby's bed, directly behind the bureau.

"He might be tall, but he's no prince." Abby reached for her brown bonnet.

"It ain't any of my business, I know, and I shouldn't tease. But your color's high, and it's clear as well water that this Lassiter was once a beau of yours. Maybe he's here to woo you back."

Abby tugged her bonnet bow too hard, pinching her neck. It ached already anyway from the inside — lies never sat well in her throat. But these lies were spoken to protect the investigation. They were necessary.

Nevertheless, it would be a relief to tell the truth about something.

"You're right. He was my beau once." Her

heart gave an odd thump. "But seeing him today was a complete surprise. I haven't heard from him in six years."

"My, that is a long time." Hildie's eyes grew wide. "But if he's here, maybe he has intentions —"

"I assure you, he said not a word about resuming any sort of friendship with me. Besides, I signed a teaching contract. No beaux."

Hildie shrugged. "Perhaps you'll meet someone else in Wells and choose to stay when your contract is finished."

"Goodness, no." Abby reached for her coat. "About the meeting someone, that is."

"The new postmaster, Isaac Flowers, is Wells's most eligible bachelor, in my opinion. Have you met him?"

"I posted a letter yesterday." The black-haired man behind the counter was around thirty, with dimpled cheeks and a dandy way with a necktie.

"What did you think of him?"

"He was courteous."

Hildie cackled. "He's handsome."

"You're married."

"Not dead. Isaac Flowers has the whitest teeth I've ever seen. But if he isn't to your liking, then the second most eligible fellow in Wells would be Burt Crabtree. Just after

69

harvest, he bought the Gibbon farm, the one by the schoolhouse. Have you seen him yet?"

"Nearly every day. He's replacing his fence."

"I can't say I'd like to see you with him, despite his handsomeness. He's awfully shy and I have never seen him in church. Oh." Hildie grimaced and rubbed her rounded belly. Abby didn't know much about expectant women, but it looked as if Hildie had smuggled a watermelon under her apron. Surely that meant the baby would come soon.

Abby didn't dare ask about something as private as a baby's estimated arrival, however, even though Hildie had insisted they toss formality to the snow outside and use Christian names. *We'll be friends, I am sure of it,"* Hildie had said the day of Abby's arrival.

But even though Hildie couldn't be much more than Abby's twenty-five and was open to friendship, Abby was a spinster who didn't dare ask about delicate things like babies or marriage, no matter how confused she was about how an unborn baby could get hiccups, like this baby had done, or if it really hurt to give birth to it, as she'd heard whispered by others.

She could show compassion, however. "Are you uncomfortable?"

"Always, this close to the birth." Hildie shoved a loose tendril of dark blond hair behind her ear. "It's hard to breathe tonight."

Abby's mouth went dry. "Do you need the doctor? I'll go. Or Bynum can fetch him and I'll stay here with you. I'll put Willodean and Patty to bed." At six and three, the girls were not difficult to tend. She hopped up, ready for action.

"The meeting at town hall is for folks to meet *you,* remember?" Hildie waved her hand in dismissal. "It's not like I can't breathe a'tall. It's just a little strained at the moment. The baby'll move in a minute and I'll feel better."

"Are you sure?"

"Of course. I'll be fine if you and Bynum go into town for a few hours. Besides, I wouldn't dare keep you here when you have a suitor in town. I mean, *former* suitor."

"He won't be at the meeting." He had no reason to be.

Hildie followed her out and down the narrow staircase to the lower floors of the cozy farmhouse. Bynum stood in the narrow foyer by the coat tree, donning his scarf. "Ready to leave, Miss Abby?"

To meet the parents of her pupils? In particular, to get a good look at the widowed mothers of the eight-year-old boys in her class, one of whom was Fletcher Pitch's sister-in-law, Katherine Hoover? "Oh yes, I certainly am."

She wrapped her green scarf about her neck with the determination of a medieval knight donning his helmet. She was a warrior, prepared for battle. Against Pitch, of course.

And maybe against her pattering heart too. She mustn't allow fear to niggle its way into her brain, but with Pitch coming . . . what would she do in the coming days or weeks if she came face-to-face with him?

She brushed her legs together, feeling the hard ridge of her knife tied to her stocking. She was ready for Pitch.

She'd been unprepared to see Dash again, though. But it was not worth another moment's thought. She would never have to see him and his lying, oh-so-handsome face again.

Which was why it was such a shock during her town hall speech to see Dash lurking beside a potted plant in the back corner, silently toasting her with a cup of coffee.

Dash chuckled into his cup. He'd rendered

Abby speechless. In nearly twenty years of knowing her, this was a first.

She flushed pink as a berry, which was *not* a first for him. Dash had brought her to a blush on plenteous previous occasions. But she'd be purple with rage later, when she learned why he was here, not hiding as he ought to be, in full view of half of Wells.

"Miss Bracey?" The mustached general store owner, a fellow named Knapp, if Dash recalled, raised his hand. "You were saying about the primers?"

The color in her cheeks faded a shade. "Yes, pardon me. The primers are fine in content but worse for the wear. I recommend that the school board consider replacing them in the near future, as finances permit. Otherwise, all is excellence — especially your children. It has only been three days, but I find them to be bright, kind, and curious."

Curious about his visit, perhaps? Dash hid a smile as he took another sip of the bitter coffee.

"One last thing before I conclude." Abby stepped from behind the polished podium at the front of the hall. She made a fetching sight against the vibrant yellow paint, which softly reflected the lamps' glow and emphasized the tinge of red in her hair. "The stove in the schoolhouse has a flat top, which I've used to warm my teakettle. I thought we might put it to another use as well, if the children brought ingredients for a warm snack one day a week — anything simple that can simmer all morning, like hot apple cider, mush, or stewed fruit. Culinary skills are useful for both boys and girls."

Abby then folded her hands over her stomach, looking every inch the prim schoolmarm as she stood at the front of the attendees. "And now, if it's well with you, Mayor Carpenter, I thought I might address any questions from the floor."

"Excellent notion, Miss Bracey." A distinguished, well-dressed gentleman with a balding pate and thin lips rose — the mayor himself, apparently. "Perhaps I might start with a statement rather than a question. Mrs. Carpenter and I appreciate your interest in our children and in our community, first by suggesting this meeting, and second by proposing ways to meet with each family privately to discuss our children's progress. I shall be honored to host you at our home for supper next week."

"Thank you, Mayor."

"And now, questions." The mayor gestured to the gathered crowd with a flourish.

A woman wearing a floppy bonnet raised

her hand. "My Florence has a beautiful singing voice. Will she have an opportunity to sing at school?"

Memories of school programs rushed into Dash's brain. They were far more fun than book learning had been.

"Yes, Mrs. Johnstone. I thought we might have a choir for our end-of-year program. Florence is a lovely girl, and I cannot wait to hear her sing. In fact, I would love for all the students to find ways to use their talents this term, whether they are musical, artistic, or in another area."

"Miss Bracey?" A woman with plump cheeks waved.

"Yes? I'm sorry, I don't know your name."

"Sara Queen, Kyle's mother."

Abby's face changed. Perhaps this woman was one of the candidates for Katherine Hoover. Dash committed Mrs. Queen's face to memory as Abby continued speaking. "Pleased to meet you, ma'am."

"I like the idea of the children practicing cookery. I work at the Wells Café, and I'd be happy to donate supplies for your use."

"How kind, thank you."

Abby turned to address another raised hand. "Yes, sir?"

A lean, wiry-built man in his middle years stood, bracing his hands on the chair back in front of him. Older than the other parents, he nevertheless emanated strong interest in the proceedings. "I ain't a parent, but I got something to say. These youngsters are a bunch of hooligans, makin' so much noise they scare my horses."

Abby's eyes narrowed. "I'm sorry to hear that. Do you live on one of the farms adjoining the school?"

"Nah, he lives in town," a man announced.

"So your objection isn't to noise made at recess." Abby's head tilted. "I'm not sure I can control their behavior outside of school, but I'll remind the children about showing good manners and keeping their voices down in public."

The man scratched his salt-and-pepper beard. "They ain't gonna listen to no citified gal. I say instead of gettin' new primers, the school board looks for a qualified teacher. A man."

Dash's stomach soured.

The mayor rose again. "Now, Mr. Yates, that's not appropriate."

Yates rolled his eyes. "Your offspring need discipline, and she's talkin' manners and singin' and hot apple cider. Sounds uppity to me."

"Sounds like you could use a course in manners too," a redheaded woman announced with a scowl.

Yates shook a finger at her. "Don't get smart with me, Mrs. Ford."

She stood. "I don't need to *get* smart, Maynard Yates. I've *been* smarter than you since I was born, just like every woman here, you ol' coot."

Abby gaped at the pair, who were nearly toe-to-toe. A few folks clapped, some laughed, and one man hooted. The mayor, however, covered his eyes with his hands. "Ladies and gentlemen, please."

"Y'all are fools." Yates waved his hand in dismissal.

"I beg your ever-lovin' pardon?" Mrs. Ford enunciated.

Dash set down his cup and stepped farther into the hall, fixing his gaze on Yates's hands to ensure he didn't do something reckless, like reach for a weapon. The man's fingers flexed, but unless he was a quick draw, Dash would have ample time to disarm him should he draw a pistol from his coat pocket.

Abby held up her hands, signaling for quiet. "If I may? I appreciate your opinion, Mr., er, Yates, is it? But I am certified, with four years of teaching experience. I assure you I am instructing the children in mathematics, history, geography, and other subjects beyond warming food on a stove. In addition, I intend to honor my contract for the term. If the school board wishes to find a male for the position after that time, I understand. But I have no intention of leaving my position early."

Her gaze met Dash's. She wanted him to hear that last bit and hear it good.

"Why do you keep talking about cookery? You cain't cook, so you want to practice with the young'uns?" Mr. Yates snorted.

Someone gasped. Abby's head dipped. "I beg your pardon?"

"I'm sayin' you don't have the skills required to get a husband, so you had to become a teacher."

Dash couldn't keep his mouth shut any longer. "That's enough."

"I ain't done speakin' my piece," Yates said.

"Yes, you are." A light-haired fellow with the build of an ox rose and extended his arms to escort Yates out. Dash tensed, ready to assist.

Yates offered a humorless chuckle and held up his hands. "I'm goin'. Hope that little girl lives up to her big words."

Enough was enough. "Didn't your mother ever teach you not to talk about a respectable lady that way?" Dash gripped Yates's elbow and none-too-gently guided him into the red-walled lobby.

Yates made no further protest as Dash nudged him out into the night. It was cold, but Dash couldn't feel it, angry as he was. He had some not-too-redeemed words he'd like to lay on Maynard Yates. *Talking that way about Abby — any woman — Lord, it just riles me up.*

"I'm sorry, Miss Abby," the thick-built man was saying when he returned to the hall.

"It's all right." She was a fine actress, the way she smiled.

"How distressing that he came intoxicated like that." A woman in a wide yellow bonnet that matched the walls frowned.

"You and your little boy are new here, so you haven't learned yet. He's just mean," someone else said.

"Hates women." Mrs. Ford was her name, wasn't it? "Poor wife o' his was probably happy to go to the grave to escape the likes of him."

"Not now, Ginny." Her husband patted her arm.

Something ticked in Dash's brain. The woman in the yellow bonnet was new here, and had a son? Perhaps she was another of Abby's candidates to be Katherine Hoover. He memorized her features. Jotting notes would be obvious and, well, he didn't jot notes. Ever.

Abby held up her hands to regain attention. "If there aren't any other questions, I'll close the evening by restating how much I'd enjoy sharing coffee or a meal with each family to get to know you. In the back of the room, I've left a schedule and a pencil, if you'd like to pick a date and time."

The oxlike man moved to stand beside Abby but faced the crowd. "On the same table is an urn of coffee and a plate of Mrs. Dean's delicious oatmeal cookies. Help yourself. Would you care for a cup, Miss Abby? Extra milk, like usual?"

Dash's muscles tensed again. The brawny fellow was mighty familiar with her, using her Christian name and knowing how she liked her coffee. Had she found an admirer already?

"Thank you, Bynum, yes." Abby smiled, and then she was swallowed up in folks eager to converse.

So Abby was comfortable enough with this Bynum to call him by his first name too. Well, she'd best remember she wasn't here for romance. She was here on behalf of the Secret Service. Besides, she'd signed a teaching contract, and those always had clauses that women couldn't court, didn't they? She'd said as much at the school-house. Abby might need a reminder that she had a job and this Bynum fellow wasn't part of it.

Stop it. Let her be happy. That was what he'd wanted six years ago. *Right, Lord? I left so she'd ultimately be happier?*

He rubbed his temple. *Cure me of this jealousy, if You have a mind to. I don't like how I am right now, feeling things like this.*

Puffing out a long breath, Dash picked up his coffee, scanning for the woman in the yellow bonnet. Ah, there she was, chatting with another woman across the room. What would happen if he strolled up to her and called her Katherine?

If she wasn't Katherine Hoover, she'd think him an idiot. And if she was . . . she'd deny it and be gone by first light. Welch would have his head. *God, would You reveal Katherine and the boy before Pitch arrives? We don't want anyone hurt —*

A calloused hand thrust in front of Dash. The burly man who knew how Abby liked her coffee. "Good evening."

Dash's stomach churned with acid, and not from the coffee. "Hello."

The man's grip was tight as a vise. "Thanks for stepping in with Maynard Yates. Despite his manner, he's all talk. Not nice talk, but talk is all it is."

"My pleasure." Literally. The man was horrid to Abby and womankind.

"Sorry, where are my manners? I'm Bynum Elmore."

Elmore. As in Willodean? So this man wasn't knowledgeable about Abby because he had designs on her. He was Willodean's father, Abby's host. Sweet relief shot down to Dash's fingers. "Dashiell Lassiter."

"Lassiter, eh?" Bynum rocked on his boot heels. "I think I know who you are."

Keen to learn how Abby had explained his presence to her host family, he feigned mild interest. "Oh?"

"You're the old beau passing through town. Railroad business?"

"Not quite. How'd you know who I am?"

"Because you're a stranger and you're mighty protective of our schoolmarm, escorting Yates outside. And you haven't taken your eyes off her since you walked in."

Of course he hadn't. Protecting innocents was part of his job — not officially, of course. The Secret Service paid Dash to identify and ensure the arrests of those who created and traded in counterfeit currency: boodle carriers, dealers, and shovers. But on occasion, he'd had to fight his way out of a tangle. He was fully prepared to do what was necessary to keep his asset safe.

Abby was more than an asset to the Secret Service, though. She was . . . well, best not to think overmuch on it.

His distraction must have shown more than he'd like, because Bynum patted his shoulder. "I don't mean to overstep, but you'll be all right, so long as you don't do anything to hurt Miss Abby. We're all fond of her already."

"I don't want her hurt, trust me." That was why he was here.

Bynum seemed about to speak, but the storekeeper Knapp tapped him on the shoulder to inquire about an order, allowing Dash to slip away from what would probably be an interrogation into his intentions. Mingling around the room, he met a few folks curious about who he was and why he'd come to the meeting, but a few vague words put them off well enough. Meanwhile he kept an eye on Abby, who mingled among the parents.

When the crowd had thinned and he'd finished his second cup of coffee — he'd be up all night, but he'd needed something to do with his hands — Abby marched over, hands clenched, her smile for any onlookers as phony as a wooden nickel. "What are you doing here?"

"Meeting folks, same as you."

"You know what I mean. You're drawing an awful lot of attention for someone who says he has no intention of doing so. Maybe you don't care since you're leaving in the morning. Which begs the question, why aren't you in your hotel room, packing to go on your merry way?"

"I'm not staying at the hotel. I'm bunking in the spare room above the post office, boarding with a fellow named Isaac Flowers. Know him?"

"The postmaster with the good teeth, of course I know him."

"You've noticed his teeth?"

"It's kind of him to put you up for the night, I suppose." She ignored his question about Isaac's snow-white grin.

"Oh no, I've signed a monthly lease."

Was that a sputter from her pretty lips? "Monthly?"

"I need a place to lay my head, since I found a job this afternoon."

Her eyes narrowed. "You don't need a job. You already have one."

He glanced around on the pretense of finding somewhere to place his coffee mug, but thankfully, no one stood within earshot. It wasn't easy to hear, anyway, over the scraping and clattering of the few remaining menfolk stacking chairs. "I had to explain my presence here somehow, didn't I?"

"No. You could just go."

"Not happening, as long as you're here." Her eye roll made him grin. This was more fun than he'd had in a long while. "Besides, it'll be good to be with horses again."

"You're working at the livery?"

"Actually, I'm the new hostler at Wells Inn."

"I didn't think they had a hostler."

"They didn't until today. Widow Miller runs the place with her two boys, who can't be around horses for some reason, so they've been using the livery for their guests' needs. They weren't happy with the service, though." He shrugged. "Good for the investigation, eh? I'm hoping any strangers passing through Wells will check into the hotel, and I'll be right there to tend their horses."

He could tell she understood he meant Pitch, but didn't like his plan. "This is ridiculous."

"My job?"

"That you're still here. Not the employment part." For the first time, her eyes softened. "You planned to breed fine carriage horses when you grew up, remember?"

He remembered a lot of plans he'd harbored in his youth that didn't come to pass. "I do. But the job doesn't matter, Abby. If you aren't leaving, I'm not either."

She huffed. "I don't need you."

He scanned their surroundings once more. No one close enough to hear their lowered voices. "Actually, I think we need each other. To catch our villain, I mean. I'll watch for him at the inn and in town, and you continue to glean information from your students and their parents." He thrust out his hand. "Looks like we'll be neighbors as well as partners."

"Pah!" She ignored his hand and spun away in a rustle of brown skirt.

Dash burst into laughter, but not hard enough to make his eye water. He was still grinning when he returned to his cozy room above the post office.

Despite having to associate with a rougher sort of individual, and sometimes getting into scrapes, not a single operative had been killed while on duty. *May it ever be that way, Lord.* But it wouldn't surprise Dash if someone murdered him on this assignment. Not Fletcher Pitch, dangerous as he was. Oh no. It would be a miracle if Abby didn't kill him. Even if it was just with her glaring eyes.

He'd take it, just to be around her again.

CHAPTER 5

As it had for most of the night, Abby's stomach clenched tighter than a knotted ball of twine when she made her way down to breakfast the next morning. The sun hadn't yet risen and the window was coated in frost, but two lamps illuminated the tidy kitchen decorated with blue chintz curtains and a blue-and-pink rag rug. Hildie poured her a cup of fragrant coffee. "This'll get you going. Drink up."

Abby flashed a smile at her busy host and took the cup. The warmth felt good on her fingers after washing up in the frigid water in her bedroom.

While Abby added cream to her coffee, Hildie set a steaming platter of ham on the table beside a tureen. Abby took her seat across from a sleepy-looking Bynum, and after grace, while Hildie chatted, she dutifully finished a bowl of cornmeal mush laced with molasses.

87

"It's bleak now, but just wait until you see Wells in the spring, Abby. It's the most beautiful place on earth." Hildie's brows pulled low. "You didn't touch the ham. Would you rather have more mush? Bynum, pass the molasses."

A gallon of molasses wouldn't increase Abby's poor appetite. "I'm not hungry this morning, that's all."

How could she be hungry when anxiety cinched her stomach closed tighter than a sugar sack? Two things kept her awake half the night, and one, of course, was the news that Fletcher Pitch was coming. His search for his son leading him to the doorstep of her schoolhouse should scare the corn mush out of her, but instead, she felt something equally as potent but far different. Eagerness.

This must be how Patchy Polly felt last evening when she cornered a mouse in the parlor. Knowing it was only a matter of time. She would see Pitch brought to justice.

The other, less invigorating thing on her mind was Dash putting down roots — however shallow — in Wells. He'd be here until Fletcher Pitch was identified, and Abby could only hope it was fast, because she could not tolerate running into him around town, thank you very much. His hostler duties would keep him occupied part of the day, of course, but Wells Inn was not that large.

To avoid him, she'd have to keep close to the school and the Elmore house. No need to go to town. Especially not the post office, now that Dash was renting a room above it. She didn't require postage, anyway. She'd posted one letter to a friend she'd made during her teacher training, but beyond that, she had no one left with whom to exchange letters.

But she'd have to go into town at some point, to shop. Oh, and to go to church every Sunday. It was one thing to ignore the Almighty in her heart and mind, and another for the world to know she behaved like an unbeliever. Not that she wasn't certain of God's existence, but she didn't like how He did things. How He ignored things. How He allowed the innocent to struggle and flounder.

Back in Chicago, she and Mother hadn't participated in Father's crimes, but they'd suffered as a result of them. They'd lost their home, reputations, and friends. Then again, perhaps it was a gift to lose certain so-called friends. The upstanding, God-fearing folks from church had turned up their noses at the Bracey females once the news about Father was printed in the papers.

Abby hadn't been the one who'd peddled in counterfeit currency. She hadn't lied to her family. She hadn't done anything, but overnight she'd become a pariah. Clearly, appearance was more important in society than substance.

She'd gone to the Lord in prayer, but it didn't seem like He'd heard a word she said to Him back then. She fell into melancholy, which was something Mother had no patience for in the days before Father's death. Mother used to go on about the fighting spirit flowing in their veins, inherited from their ancestors who sailed on the *Mayflower,* but once Father died, she seemed to have forgotten the boldness and faith of the women in the family who'd gone before. Abby had tried to remind Mother. She'd opened the old Bible, not just to read scripture, but to show Mother the family genealogy printed on the first few pages, going all the way back to the *Mayflower.* Mother had just cried.

It didn't seem like she stopped crying until she succumbed to pneumonia a year ago. Abby blamed Fletcher Pitch for robbing Mother of her will to live, but she also blamed God. Why did He ignore her pleas during her direst time? How could He allow her and Mother to suffer the consequences of her father's actions?

That was when she decided that if He could ignore her, surely He wouldn't mind or notice if she left Him alone for a while . . . or always, seeing as He hadn't wooed her back the way she'd once heard the preacher say God did with His people. There had been no tenderness in her spirit, no word from another human being, no parting of the heavens. No, God was no more interested in wooing her than Dash had been.

Nevertheless, she had to present the image of a churchgoing woman in order to be accepted by the community. Again, appearance over substance — she'd learned that lesson. Sitting through church was part of this job.

Further interaction with Dash, however, wasn't supposed to be. He'd promised.

She should have known he'd break this promise too.

"You're a little pale, Miss Abby." Bynum's words recalled her to the present. "Are you feeling well?"

"Forgive me. I'm preoccupied this morning."

"I hope Maynard Yates isn't the source of your distraction." Hildie refilled her milk glass. "Bynum said he was poorly behaved last night."

"It wasn't the warmest welcome I've ever received."

"No one likes him," Willodean said.

"That's not true." Hildie sighed. "But he is a difficult man."

"A crank and a coot," Bynum added.

"A coot!" Patty echoed.

Hildie shot Bynum an exasperated look before returning her gaze to Abby. "Well, I'm glad you aren't letting Maynard upset you. And that you're not taking ill."

Willodean, who had been chasing Patchy Polly beneath the table minutes ago, pushed her half-eaten bowl of mush back. "I'm not feelin' good, though. I'm too sick to eat."

Patty, who did everything Willodean did, nudged her empty bowl toward her mother. "Me too."

Hildie's brow arched. "And this has nothing to do with you not liking mush, Willodean?"

"No." But Willodean's lips twitched.

"You ate all of yours, Patty," Bynum noted.

"More, pwease." The little girl's head tipped to the side. "Wif more m'wasses."

Abby chuckled at Patty's hasty reversal, but Hildie adopted a feigned air of resignation as she ladled a small scoop of mush into Patty's bowl. "I'm glad you're healthy enough to attend the mayor's birthday party Saturday night, Patty. Poor Willodean will have to stay home and miss the cake, since she's sick."

"There's cake?" Willodean's eyes widened.

"Oh, of course. Mrs. Queen is baking it."

Kyle's mother, one of Abby's candidates for Katherine Hoover. Abby looked forward to interacting with her at the party on Saturday, but for Willodean's benefit, she made an exaggerated *mmm.* "I love a good cake."

Willodean straightened. "I think I feel better now. I'll try to eat more mush, Mama."

"Good." From her seat, Hildie gathered Bynum and Abby's used utensils and plates.

Abby rose to assist with clearing the table. "Let me help."

"Not part of your contract." Hildie stood and instantly winced.

"Is it your breathing again?" Abby whispered, not wanting to alarm the girls.

Hildie shook her head. "Just a kick, is all."

Bynum rose and rested a work-rough hand on the side of his wife's extended midsection. "Little one, you need to stop giving your mama such a hard time."

Hildie looked up at Bynum. "He's stopped

already. He listens to his pa."

"Or *she,* another pretty girl like you."

They exchanged a look so tender, Abby had to turn away. Not that they made her uncomfortable — on the contrary, they modeled a healthy marriage for their children. It wasn't even that Abby was a boarder, neither part of the family nor a real friend. It was more that she wondered if she would ever have love in her life again. The romantic kind, but also the family kind. A wave of loss for her parents washed up from her stomach, dampening her eyes.

She'd done an admirable job of blinking them back when Hildie patted her shoulder. "I'm packing lunches now. Tongue sandwich today."

"Oh, I forgot to mention. Last night I asked parents to schedule time with me so we can get to know one another. Most of the parents invited me to supper in their homes, but Micah's mother, Mrs. Story, offered to bring me lunch today. She said she has an hour off from her work and enjoys taking walks at that time, so she asked to meet me at the school." Abby's stomach fluttered anew at the knowledge she'd be able to speak with one of the women who could be Katherine Hoover. Would Mrs. Story let anything slip to indicate Micah was really Fletcher Pitch's son?

"That will be fun," Bynum said before pointing to Willodean to keep eating.

Perhaps this would be a good time to glean more information about Mrs. Story and Micah from her hosts. "I understand Mrs. Story is a seamstress?"

"An excellent one." Hildie sighed. "I envy the items in the shop window."

"What do you know about her?" My, that sounded too obvious. "That is, Micah is a lovely boy."

Willodean watched a congealed clump of mush slip from her spoon back into the bowl. "Smartest boy in class."

"Quiet too," Hildie added. "He and Geraldine, his mama, have been in Wells since, oh, right before school started."

The timing was right for Geraldine Story to be Katherine Hoover, as Dash had said, but Kyle Queen and his mother Sara had also come into town at about the same time. Fortunately, Mrs. Queen had invited Abby to supper in a few days. Perhaps these meals would help Abby determine which pair might be the best candidates to be Katherine Hoover and the Pitch boy.

Hildie chuckled. "Abby? You listening?"

"Sorry, I was woolgathering again."

"Woolgathering and not hungry," Hildie

said. "I suspect this has to do with Dashiell Lassiter coming all this way to woo you back."

With an exaggerated head shake, Bynum stepped backward. "Gonna turn out the cows now. Want me to see to the chickens for you, Hildie?"

"I'll do it," Abby announced. Anything to escape Hildie's teasing about Dash. Besides, Hildie was rubbing her back, clearly in pain, and should stay inside where it was warm.

"I should say no, but my back thanks you." Hildie turned to the sink.

Abby donned her outerwear, gathered the bucket of feed from the mudroom, and stepped outside. Her heavy layers of clothing weren't enough to protect her from the stark cold that bit her face. She doubled her pace to the coop.

"Colder this morning." Bynum led two fawn Jersey cows and their calves into the paddock closest to the barn, his speech creating thick vapor in the frigid air.

"But not too cold for them?" She tipped her head at the cows.

"For a short time. They need exercise."

Abby knew nothing about the care of cattle, but they seemed happy enough to be outside for a change of scenery. The two mothers lumbered along, pink udders peeking from beneath their buff-brown bellies, while their calves pranced ahead in the snow, adding white socks to their buff legs to match the little blazes of white on their foreheads. Their jaunty steps seemed a sign of bovine satisfaction.

Where she was deficient in her knowledge of cows, however, she knew something about feeding chickens. As a child, she'd helped the servants with that particular task in the animal pens hidden by screens of evergreen trees behind the house. That was how she'd met Dash, the groom's son. She was eight, and when he realized what she was doing, he'd eyed her with skepticism.

"You've never fed a chicken before?"

"I've fed a cat. And a dog."

"I get to feed horses." His narrow chest puffed with pride. *"I'm going to own a bunch of them someday. Horses are better friends than people sometimes."*

"I think I'm a better friend than a horse."

"We'll see about that."

Abby shoved the memory from her brain, banishing it into the cold. Every childhood memory, even the happy ones, brought pain, because of the direction her life had taken.

Besides, she'd have to hurry so she could get to school on time. She let herself into the little whitewashed chicken coop near the barn.

A dozen or so Cochin hens clucked and cackled at seeing her, craning their necks and gathering close to her skirt. "Good morning, ladies, how do you fare?"

A plump, buff-colored hen shoved a silver-laced sister aside.

"There's enough breakfast for all." Abby poured the prescribed amount of grain and kitchen scraps out for them. While they pecked and scratched, she took advantage of the empty roosts to search for eggs. One small speckled egg revealed itself among the straw, and she tucked it into her coat pocket. "Farewell, ladies. Stay warm today."

She would do well to do the same, so she arrived at school with Willodean a few minutes early to light the stove. Once it got going and the other students arrived, the schoolhouse warmed up enough that Abby's toes no longer ached. At least Almos had left Stripey the skunk at home, and the children attended to their lessons, although Coy chatted through sums and Kyle had the fidgets.

At last, lunchtime arrived, and Abby released the students to play in the yard. She polished her desk with a rag to accommodate a picnic with Micah's soon-to-arrive mother, Geraldine Story. Was she Katherine Hoover? Perhaps Abby would get the answers she sought.

When the door opened, she looked up with a welcoming smile.

For a second, seeing that once-familiar smile on Abby's lips made Dash's gut flop like a fish — caught with no hope of going back to the life he knew, but he didn't care. That smile hooked him every time.

The nervous thrill only lasted a moment, however. It died when Abby's smile transformed into a bitter scowl that reduced him to the poor stable boy he once was, although to be fair, he looked the part, since he'd come from the inn. Dressed in mud-smeared trousers and a patched coat flecked with horsehair, he'd clearly been at work with horses all morning. Out of courtesy for Abby, however, he'd switched from his manure-caked boots to clean ones.

She didn't seem to notice his shoes, though. Her glare hadn't left his face. "What are you doing here?"

"Trying to catch you alone." He rooted a few yards away from the teacher so every little witness to his visit could report he'd kept his distance. He'd learned his lesson last time about putting her in a compromising situation.

She hopped to her feet. "You've found Fletcher Pitch already! He checked into the inn?"

"Sorry, no new guests at the inn."

She threw her hands up. "Dashiell, you'll be the ruin of me."

She'd already ruined him, where his heart was concerned, anyway. Hearing her call him by his full name didn't help, because six years ago, she'd used it as an endearment.

Leaving her was the hardest thing he'd ever done, and this . . . this chaos with Pitch had reopened all his old wounds. Self-inflicted, but wounds all the same. Even though things could never return to the way they were, he still cared for her, and he couldn't help but believe God brought them together again for a reason. Maybe so Dash could apologize.

But this moment wasn't the time. "Sorry the news isn't what either of us wanted, but — is that all the firewood you have?"

"You came to ask me about our fuel supply?"

"No, but look at it." The stack of split logs piled in the vestibule wasn't even half as high as the wall. "That won't last you long."

"Wood is a precious commodity here. I'm

sure someone plans to replenish it soon."

"I hope so. Spring's a ways off, and you'll burn through that long before then."

"I'll bring it up with Bynum. So, you dropped by because . . . ?"

"We need to square a few things away before Pitch's arrival, starting with calling him something other than his name for the sake of discretion. Let's refer to him as 'our friend' when we speak about him." Even though Fletcher Pitch was nothing of the sort.

"That shouldn't be too often. I don't think there's a need for us to speak unless something pertinent arises."

She was bound and determined not to resume any sort of relationship with him, wasn't she? He couldn't help but tease her. "Can I say 'howdy' if I pass you on the street?"

"You've never said *howdy* in your life."

"Sometimes I do, depending on who I'm greeting. But for you, I'll say 'how do you do.' "

"Are we finished here?"

"Not yet." He leaned his shoulder against the doorjamb. "You may not want to talk to me often, but I'll need to seek you out every few days. It's standard procedure. Daily reports are required by my superiors."

"Daily?" Her eyes widened.

He nodded. "Let's compare notes Saturday. Unless you determine Mrs. Story to be Katherine Hoover today, of course."

"Wouldn't that be wonderful?"

"Don't confront her without me, though. Drop by the inn or the post office to inform me. Whatever you do, don't send a note to me explaining things."

Her jaw hardened. "I wouldn't do that."

"Good, because I still can't read. Witless as a stone."

"Don't say that —"

"Anyway." He forced a smile. "Folks won't be surprised to see us converse, since it's evident we already know one another."

Her eyes rolled. "And *how* we know one another. Hildie thinks you're here to woo me back."

Excellent. "Whatever helps explain my presence here is fine with me."

"I don't care for it."

"I'd be astonished if you did."

"But . . ." She sighed. "I suppose you are right."

The hair at his nape lifted — not from the shock of her saying he was correct about something. Nor from the cold. Someone was coming.

He turned. A woman in a green-blue cloak

and a wide bonnet with a basket over her arm turned off the road to the schoolhouse path, staring at him. Ah, yes. Last night she'd worn a yellow bonnet with geegaws sewn on it and suggested Maynard Yates was inebriated. She was a woman with spirit — and possibly Katherine Hoover.

Abby brushed past him. "Micah's mother, Geraldine Story. We're having lunch."

Mrs. Story paused on the path to greet a blond boy — her son, a small lad he'd remembered seeing last time he visited the school. When she'd sent her son off to play, Dash doffed his hat. "Hello, ma'am."

"Hello." She was a pretty woman not much past thirty, with curious light eyes, a dimpled chin, and fair curls peeking from beneath the brim of her stylish bonnet. "Miss Bracey, is lunch still convenient?"

"Absolutely." Abby welcomed the woman inside. "Mr. Lassiter was just leaving."

Not quite yet. "Mrs. Story, I saw you at the meeting last night. Did I hear you're new to Wells too?"

"Our relocation here was somewhat recent, yes." Did the question make her nervous? Hard to tell when she looked down to brush snow from her skirt and he couldn't see her eyes.

"I've hardly been here two days, but it

seems like a warm community," he said.

"Except for a certain individual, whose behavior was most distressing. Suggesting you don't know your way around a kitchen! I'm sure you're a fine cook, Miss Bracey."

"Thank you, ma'am. I was taught to cook by an admirer of Italianate cooking, which has been popular in Chicago for ten years or more. What dishes are popular where — where did you say you are from, Mrs. Story?"

Brava, Abby. She'd turned the conversation just so, sounding conversational when it was clear to Dash she was investigating.

"New York, originally. Would you like the basket on your desk?"

"Yes, I thought we could use it as a makeshift table. Please, sit here." She withdrew two mugs from a deep desk drawer. "Nebraska is a long way from New York."

"I had no trade when I found myself alone with a young child to care for, but I'd always enjoyed sewing. Becoming a seamstress allowed me the ability to work and care for Micah at the same time. Several months ago, a friend invited us to join her in a nearby town, but when we arrived, I learned she'd passed away."

"Oh, how terrible," Dash said as Abby

made a sympathetic noise.

Mrs. Story unpacked the basket, laying out two white plates, starched napkins, forks, a bowl, and something wrapped in an embroidered dish towel. "These things happen. In the meantime Micah and I were halfway across the continent and required a new home. I learned the dress shop here needed help, so we thought, why not?"

Mrs. Story's eye twitched. Twice. In Dash's experience, most folks revealed their falsehoods by displaying some sort of involuntary, physical response. Was this hers? Was she lying to them?

"A new adventure," Abby said.

"As both of you have done, it seems." Mrs. Story glanced at Dash.

"Mr. Lassiter left Chicago six years ago for his adventure. Ah, sounds like the water is warm for our tea." Abby strode to the stove, turning her back on Dash and waving one hand behind her in a discreet shooing signal.

Hint taken, even though the steaming, fragrant tea she poured from the kettle into the mugs made his mouth water for something warm to drink. "Enjoy your lunch, ladies."

Mrs. Story looked up with a catlike smile. "You'll be at the mayor's birthday party on

Saturday, won't you?"

"Birthday party?"

"At town hall. Everyone is invited." She snuck a glance at Abby.

Social gatherings like this were excellent opportunities to talk to townsfolk. This would also be an excellent opportunity for Dash to speak to Abby about the status of the investigation.

And to try to make her blush again. "I wouldn't miss it for anything."

When he tugged the schoolhouse door shut, he was whistling.

CHAPTER 6

"I'm sorry about that," Abby said, gesturing toward the door as Mrs. Story speared a vinegar-soaked potato. "Mr. Lassiter is —"

"Smitten with you." Mrs. Story popped the potato into her mouth.

"Nonsense. He stopped by to . . . assess the firewood supply." It wasn't a complete lie.

"I thought the parents provided firewood."

"I'm not sure who is in charge of restocking our fuel, but we will need more soon. So, Mrs. Story, thank you for coming. I appreciate you giving up your hour off."

"I don't mind at all. I'm allotted a good amount of time to eat and conduct my errands, and some days I simply walk for exercise, since Micah and I live above the dress shop. The owner, Mrs. Leary, rents the extra room to us. It's been quite a blessing."

If this woman was really Katherine Hoover, she hadn't experienced much in the way of blessing during her life. Abby swallowed down the ache in her throat. "Speaking of blessings, Micah is a wonderful boy."

"He is, isn't he? Shy, but a lot goes on between his ears." She beamed the smile of a loving mother, joyous and proud.

Geraldine Story didn't resemble Micah, but that didn't mean much. Abby hadn't taken after her mother either. From the shape of her head to the tint of red in her hair, she was the image of her criminal father.

Don't think about that now. Abby bit into her sandwich — ham with English mustard. Delicious. Once she'd washed it down with a sip of tea, she sat back. "As I'm certain you are aware, Micah is an excellent writer and reader. He keeps up with children in the fifth and sixth grades. His last school must have been exceptional. Was it a rigorous program?"

"Oh no, he's just a curious child. Even when he was too young to attend school, he'd ask me about letters and numbers while I sewed. More fun to him than playing with his toys."

This conversation wasn't yielding as much as she'd hoped. She finished her sandwich while Mrs. Story continued to describe

Micah learning to talk and walk. Adorable, but not enlightening as far as Fletcher Pitch was concerned. At a natural break, Abby patted her lips with her napkin. "Yesterday I asked the children to write about their parents. Micah said the kindest things about you."

Mrs. Story lifted her shoulders in a gesture of delight. "He's such a sweet boy."

"I mention it because Micah didn't mention his father other than he'd passed on, and . . ." She broke off. It was possible Micah didn't write about his father because the man was a murderous counterfeiter. It was also possible he didn't mention him because memories of him brought pain. But Abby was duty-bound to investigate. "I apologize if I upset Micah, or you, by bringing up his loss."

Mrs. Story drained her tea. "Oh, not at all. Micah doesn't even remember his father. He's been gone a long time."

"I imagine you do what you can to keep his memory alive."

"Actually, we don't talk about him, ever. It's far better that way."

"I apologize for pressing." Actually, Abby wanted to press more, but how could she without seeming like a callous busybody? There had to be a way to find out if Mrs.

109

Story avoided talk of Micah's father because he was Fletcher Pitch, or because he was a normal, law-abiding man whom she'd loved so much that saying his name was like an ice pick to her freezing heart.

How well Abby could relate to that. She hadn't wanted to say Dash's name ever again after he left. Father agreed, and Dash's name never passed her family's lips again.

"More potatoes?" Mrs. Story offered the last spoonful.

"Yes, please. They're wonderful." The tang was a perfect complement to the ham. "Is it a family recipe?"

"From my mother."

"Do your sisters make it too?"

Mrs. Story set out two gingersnaps. "No, I have no sister. I wish I did."

"Me too. I was an only child."

She bit into the crispy cookie. Mmm. Just the right amount of spice, and the perfect conclusion to a simple but tasty meal. If only their conversation had been as satisfying.

Abby helped pack and clean up from their lunch before calling the students back inside. After bidding Micah farewell, Mrs. Story left, and Micah was at Abby's hip with an expectant expression.

She smiled down at him. "Your mother and I had a lovely lunch, Micah."

"Ham sandwich?"

She nodded. "You too?"

"Yes. And a cookie."

"Me too. We talked about how bright you are."

He looked away, pleased but clearly embarrassed. Such a sweet boy.

Kyle appeared at her other hip. "You're coming to supper tomorrow at the restaurant."

"I am. And I will tell your mother how good you are at your sums."

Kyle's grin revealed the first tips of erupting eyeteeth.

"All right, everyone, take your seats for geography." She picked up her wooden pointing stick and strode to stand beside a map of the United States. She may not be a competent investigator when it came to hunting for Fletcher Pitch's boy, but she was a decent teacher.

Nevertheless, her lack of progress plagued her through the rest of the lesson and into the afternoon. If she still prayed, she'd be on her knees asking God for help. Insight. Wisdom. Something, if only His listening ear.

When she sat down to grade math pages,

her midsection ached. Staring at her desk, she realized it had nothing to do with Mrs. Story's lunch. It was a yearning type of ache, a loneliness. After all this time, she was starting to miss talking to God.

Or maybe she always had, but was just now admitting it.

"Fine pair of grays you have, sir." Dash had been instructed by the inn's owner, the widowed Mrs. Miller, not to talk overmuch to guests, but a compliment here or there on the quality of a customer's horseflesh — especially when the horses were as expensive as these — would be tolerable. How could he ignore these animals? Anyone with eyes could see how fine these beauties were, high-steppers with identically hued coats, hitched to a fine carriage.

"I imagine you don't often see horses like these hereabouts." The horses' owner, a full-bellied man with yellow teeth, grinned. A quick glance inside the snow-speckled coach informed Dash the gentleman traveled alone, and that the upholstery within the carriage was as fine as the horses. And the man's fur-trimmed coat.

Was he Fletcher Pitch, come to find his son? Thanks to his counterfeiting endeavors, Pitch was undoubtedly affluent. Why wouldn't he flaunt his ill-gained fortune?

It had been a full day since Dash had seen Abby. It was best that he leave her be for a while, although he was curious if her talk with Geraldine Story yielded any results. He'd also have to tell her about this guest at the inn. He might not be Pitch, but Dash intended to keep close watch.

One of the horses shook its head, bringing Dash's attention back to his role here at the inn. "I'll have them ready for you when you leave. Tomorrow morning?"

"No, I'll be here a few days at least. You know how business can be."

"I reckon so, sir." Dash dipped his head again as the man entered the inn and Mrs. Miller's two sons, Frank and Sy, unloaded the man's trunk. Dash saw to the horses with haste, but care, talking to them as he saw to their needs. As soon as they were stabled, brushed, fed, and watered, he ambled to the servant's door at the back of the inn to do a little scouting on the new guest.

As he hoped, Frank and Sy sat in the green-papered dining room, a place their mother had invited Dash to use when he had no pressing tasks. He helped himself to coffee from the enamel pot on the sideboard and joined the brothers, young men around twenty years of age. "That new guest's got one fancy rig. Good horses too."

Sy whistled. "I'll say. Wish I could get closer to 'em, but it'd about kill me."

"Both of us, from hay fever," Frank explained. "Hay makes us sneeze and choke up, and we turn red anywhere our skin touches horsehair. Which is why we hired you."

"Sounds awful." Dash took a pull of the strong brew. "Take my word for it, though, the horses are magnificent. Has that guest come through before?"

"Nah." Frank brushed his greasy bangs from his forehead. "Must be in town because of the railroad."

"That's my guess." Sy stuck his long legs out to warm his feet before the crackling fire. "I heard him check in. Name's Unger. Sounds like a railroad man's name, don't it?"

Frank laughed, and Dash had to smile. How easy it was to present a false name. Nevertheless, he'd inform his superiors of Mr. Unger's arrival. Sooner rather than later. In fact, his daily report had been overdue . . . for three days now.

He should see to it at once. "I didn't realize it's past lunchtime."

"Go on and take your meal break. We'll

keep an eye on things here." Sy gestured with a wave. "But before you go, I need to ask. Is it true about you and the pretty schoolmarm?"

Dash drained his coffee. "Is what true?"

"That you're here for her?"

"Why, you got designs on her?"

"Maybe."

Frank pounded his brother on the back. "Looks like Lassiter don't like that idea too much."

How did it show? Dash had spent the past few years working for the Secret Service, schooling himself to hide his reactions. He willed himself to look disinterested. "I don't have a claim on her, if that's what you're asking."

Sy flicked his hair out of his eyes again. "So I can ask her to dance at the mayor's birthday party."

"You can, I suppose. Whether or not you should?" Dash shrugged and ducked out the door, chased by the brothers' laughter. Maybe they were just teasing him, or maybe Sy really did like the look of Abby. Who wouldn't? She was beautiful.

He had no right, but the thought of her dancing with another fellow made his hands clench.

Tightening his old blue scarf around his

neck against the cold, he hurried to the post office. He waved at Isaac, who stood behind the counter helping a woman in a large hat — Mrs. Story. Dash took the back stairs two at a time and passed Isaac's bedroom, its door, as ever, shut. Isaac was a good landlord, but he had some strict rules about his privacy. Dash couldn't blame him, as he had his own secrets. Blowing on his cold fingers, he took a seat at the small desk at the north-facing window.

Paper. Pen. Ink. He placed them just so on the desktop. Adjusted the paper. Looked out the window at the gray sky. Dipped the pen into the inkwell. Five times.

The task couldn't be avoided any longer.

God, may my words be legible and clear. Help them to make sense to my superiors. Carefully, slowly, he penned the first character, the *D* in *Dear.* Then the next letters, one by one, until he finished *Dear Sir,* and after that, a full sentence.

It looked entirely wrong.

He'd been told the Treasury folks in Washington wouldn't care about his spelling. They could figure out what he was saying. His job wasn't a scribe, after all. He was an operative. Action and results trumped penmanship skill.

Nevertheless, these reports were part of

his duty.

Dash swallowed what was left of his pride and jotted a sentence about the new hotel guest, Mr. Unger, making mention of his appearance, vehicle, and horses, but noting he had not made any payment to the hotel as yet in genuine or artificial currency. Thus far, he was the only newcomer to Wells who could be Fletcher Pitch, although he was more flagrant about his wealth than Dash imagined. Maybe Pitch didn't care anymore.

Dash started a new paragraph, noting that he had not encountered any counterfeited currency here, nor heard talk of it.

There. That should be enough to satisfy his superiors.

He blotted the mess of the letter and stuffed it into a pre-addressed vellum envelope — his Kansas City superior had shown Dash a great kindness by addressing a stack of envelopes for him. If Dash addressed them himself, who knew if his reports would ever get to Washington. They'd be so misspelled, they could end up in West Virginia. Or a dustbin.

Dash hurried downstairs and turned the corner to the post office. Mrs. Story, still here? Isaac leaning against the counter frame in a casual, interested pose? Clearly they weren't discussing philatelic matters.

Isaac's gaze jerked up to meet Dash's, his grin melting into a guilty expression. "Didn't hear you, Dashiell."

Obviously. Dash bit back a smile.

Mrs. Story put one gloved hand to her rosy lips. "Pardon me. I was just leaving."

"Don't mind me. Here, Isaac." Dash reached past her to drop the letter and two cents on the counter.

Regaining his professional composure, Isaac affixed a brown stamp to Dash's letter. "Washington, DC, eh? Government stuff," he teased.

"A letter to family." It was Dash's automatic response, and it was true. His Treasury friends were the only family he had left. He waved on his way out. "Good day to you folks."

Isaac and Geraldine Story! Interesting. Romance blossomed even in the depth of winter. Folks always talked about love in springtime, but Dash's affection for Abby was born the winter he was fifteen. By summertime his love had grown into a sapling with strong roots. His blood transformed into gooey, sentimental sap, and what was even worse, he didn't care.

"That's love, boy," his pa had said, catching Dash whistling while mucking the stalls.

Pa had been happy about it too, as if there

hadn't been a single impediment to a stable boy forming a tender attachment to the boss's daughter. Why hadn't Pa warned him that loving Abby would lead to nothing but heartache?

He'd tried to make it work out, of course. Tried harder than she ever knew. But eventually, he'd realized he had to leave Chicago to allow her the opportunity to have the life she deserved but couldn't have with him. Along the way, he'd even convinced himself he'd fallen out of love with her.

He just might have been wrong about that.

"Lassiter!" Sy jogged toward him.

"Something wrong?"

"Not with the guests' horses, but Burt Crabtree brought in a gelding. Might be frostbit or something. He said you told him you know something about horses."

"I know some. Enough to know frostbite's pretty rare in horses." God had designed equine feet and legs to endure standing in deep snow, and their manes, tails, and thick eyelashes to protect against cold temperatures. However, frostbite could happen, especially in a horse that was older or already sick. "There's no veterinarian in town?"

Sy winced. "The closest thing we've got is Maynard Yates at the livery, but you've met him, haven't you? Somethin's always stuck in his craw. I can't blame Crabtree for bringing a horse to you instead in the hopes you know a bit about husbandry, 'cause you ain't gonna yell at him the way Yates would."

"I'll do what I can." He parted ways with Sy and entered the stable, where Burt Crabtree patted a bay quarter horse on the neck.

He sighed in relief. "Hope you don't mind me bringing Jasper here."

"Not at all, but like I reminded Sy, I'm no veterinarian."

"You're more of one than I am. Jasper got out and it took me all day to find him. I think his feet got too cold, because it looks like he's favoring one side over the other."

"Let me see here. How do you do, Jasper?" Dash stood in the animal's line of vision and patted him with soft strokes. Then he glanced at Burt. "Eyes look good. Nose is a little wet, as you can see. Let's check the rest of him."

Dash led Jasper closer to the better light of the west window and fastened him in cross ties. Jasper didn't protest Dash's examination of his ears, and to Dash's relief the skin was flexible, with good color. No frostbite there. With gentle strokes, Dash felt for heat, swellings, wounds, and tenderness all over Jasper's body, taking his time before he examined the legs. Front legs seemed fine. He squatted to get a better view of the hind legs — ah, there was the source of concern, a liquidy bubble on the left hock. "Looks like a capped hock."

Burt bent down. "Where?"

"This bursa here. The lump." Smaller than a baseball but plenty big to cause discomfort.

"What does that mean?" Burt's voice held an edge of panic. "Do I have to put him down?"

Dash rose from his squat. "No need for talk like that. You said Jasper's not walking well?"

"Just a little hitch that I noticed."

"Hmm." Dash checked Jasper's feet. "Maybe talk to the smithy about these shoes. Looks like he could use an adjustment."

"I can do that. But the burs— what did you call it?"

"Bursa. A sac of fluid. It's often a result of trauma of some sort, or repeated kicking against a stall door or wall. Does he do that?"

"I–I've never seen it. Why would he do that? He trying to get out?"

"Could be bored." Dash brushed a few

horse hairs from his hands. "You can leave it be, or treat it by draining it, putting some salve on it, and bandaging."

"Can you do it now and keep an eye on him overnight? I'll pay."

"Like I keep saying, I'm no veterinarian. And there's always risk of infection."

"I want you to do it, though. How much?" Burt withdrew a leather wallet from his coat pocket and thumbed through numerous bills. "This is for the Millers for boarding him."

Five dollars. Genuine, by the color and feel of it. "I'll offer it to the Millers, but they'll say it's too much."

"And here's another for you, for your trouble."

Dash whistled. "No, that's generous of you, but I'm just doing my job."

"So am I. I hate to see an innocent animal suffer. Makes my blood boil. And I told you I protect my own, right?"

"But —"

"I need to get back to the ranch. School will be out soon and I don't want any of the children playing around the unfinished fence and getting hurt. I'll be back for Jasper in the morning."

It was clear there was no stopping Burt. "Until morning, then."

Burt didn't shut the door all the way, but the cool air trickling in the crack carried in fresher smells. Dash would leave it for now. "Well, Jasper, the last time I helped drain a bursa was at my pa's knee. I think I remember how to do it well enough, though."

Jasper blinked his dark, heavily lashed eyes.

"How'd you get this bursa, eh? Seems like Burt feeds you well but doesn't know much about horses." Cattle ranching — any ranching — was probably a second career for Burt. Tending Jasper himself would have saved Burt ten dollars.

Ah well. Dash was happy to do it, and he needed to stay at the inn anyway to watch Unger's movements, although he envied Burt going past the schoolhouse right about now. He still had a thousand questions for Abby. Did her lunch with Mrs. Story yield anything interesting? Did she like Nebraska? Had she ever thought of him over the past six years, and did she care for him, even a smidge —

Jasper nudged Dash's shoulder. "All right, fellow, let's take care of you."

Dash might not really be a hostler, but he couldn't walk away from an animal in need any more than he could fall all the way out of love with Abby Bracey. No matter how hard he tried.

CHAPTER 7

Abby spent a busy evening in Hildie's kitchen, baking treats and then staying up late to clean the stove, table, and floor. It was the least she could do, after using the space.

After school the following day, she went home with Willodean, washed her face, and packed the cinnamon-scented fruits of her labor in a tin. She had an early supper planned with Kyle and his mother, Sara Queen, at Wells Café, but first she had a stop to make. "Girls, I left some cookies for you after your supper." She pointed to the plate of treats.

Willodean and Patty jumped up and down. "Can't we have one now?"

"Not until after supper." Hildie held out an unlit lantern to Abby, her brow etched in concern. "Are you certain you don't wish Bynum to come fetch you afterwards? It'll be dark when you walk home."

"It might be dark, but it won't be late." Besides, her knife was strapped to her stocking, and she wouldn't hesitate to use it. She glanced at the walnut carriage clock ticking away on the mantel. "Thanks, though. I'm later than I planned. Goodbye, everyone."

Their farewells followed her out the door. As she walked past the house, she waved at the girls watching her from the parlor window, but she didn't linger. She was late, and her strides were long and quick, but they might not be fast enough.

Cutting through the churchyard would shave valuable minutes. Abby stepped over a fallen portion of the rail fence and entered the cemetery, all white and gray stone protruding from a fresh dusting of snow. She wove through headstones, gauging the quickest path —

Her foot slid, yanking her legs into a split. Clutching her cookies, she grasped the nearest headstone and held on as she regained her footing. At least nothing hurt. Abby brushed snow off her cloak, which was smeared with the snow that had covered the headstone.

The name on the stone caught her eye.

MAGGIE YATES. 1843–1885

Yates. Was this Maynard's wife? No *Loving wife,* or *At home in heaven.* Just the date.

Beside it was another stone.

EUGENE YATES 1863

That was the year of Abby's birth too. This Eugene must have been an infant. Maynard had lost a child?

Perhaps these were other relatives who'd lived in Wells. Ah, here, another Yates. Another Eugene, to be precise. His stone offered a pinch more detail, though.

LOVED BY ALL. 1838–1863.

He'd died young. How sad.

Goodness, what was she doing, lollygagging like this? She'd be late. Determined not to slip again, she picked through the cemetery, resuming a more normal gait when she reached the road at the front of the church.

As she passed Knapps' store, however, two boys at the checkerboard table on the other side of the large display window waved at her. Chester Knapp and Micah Story. She paused to wave, and they hurried out of the store to meet her, grinning.

"Miss Bracey!"

"Hello, boys. Nice to see you both." Despite being in a hurry.

"Chester invited me to play draughts," Micah said.

"I won one and he won one." Chester wrapped his thin arms around his chest. In their haste, the boys hadn't donned a stitch of outerwear. The temperature fell with the winter sun's early descent, and although the workday wasn't yet finished for the businesses lining Main Street, it would be dark soon.

"Perhaps you should go back inside where it's warm."

"We won't be long. Whatcha doin'?" Chester glanced at the tin in her hands.

"I'm on my way to visit Kyle and his mother at the café."

"Are those cookies?"

"They are." She pried the lid off to show the boys her cinnamon molasses cookies. Chester licked his lips. "They sure smell good."

"Would you lads be so kind as to taste one for me? I want to be sure they turned out well."

"Sure." Chester selected a large one on top and bit off half of it. Micah followed suit but only took a nibble. Chester swallowed and nodded. "Yup. I'd say these are mighty fine."

"I don't like cinna-minna-mon but these are good, I guess." Micah gave his nipped cookie to Chester.

"Thank you for your honest opinion, lads. I'd best be on my way."

"We should escort you wherever you're going, ma'am. Mama says it's part of being a gentleman." Micah shivered, but bore a resolute expression, so she didn't argue.

"Let's make haste, then, before you catch cold."

Chester peered up at her. "Say, Miss Bracey, some of us were hoping . . . can Almos bring Stripey back to school?"

"*May* he," Micah corrected. "And she'll never say yes."

"Micah is correct on both counts, Chester. I'm sorry, but Stripey is a wild animal. In the classroom, the least he would do is cause a distraction. At most? I shudder to think what a skunk could do."

Chester twisted an arm behind his back and mimicked a tail lifting to spray. "I wanna see him do that."

"I do not." Abby stopped at the livery door. "But he could also bite, scratch, or make a terrible mess."

"Almos says he's a good skunk, though."

"Even good skunks have accidents or

misbehave from time to time. I'd rather neither occurred in our classroom."

Micah glanced at the sign above her head. "Why are you stopping here?"

"We've arrived at our destination. The cookies are for Mr. Yates."

Micah's light eyes grew wide. "Oh."

"Are you sure you want to do that, Miss Bracey? Mama tells me not to talk to him," Chester whispered.

"My mama said the same thing," Micah said. "Some folks can't be helped."

"Thank you for your concern, boys. Go on and warm up now. See you tomorrow at the mayor's party?"

"Yes, ma'am." Micah turned around.

"Yep. Bye, Miss Bracey." Chester skipped backward toward the store.

A wave of affection surged in Abby's chest. She'd already grown fond of her students. If anything good had come out of her father's betrayal, it was teaching. She was still smiling when she slipped inside the livery's sliding door. At once she was met by the odors of stables everywhere, horse-flesh and manure and wood, smells that always reminded her of Dash. She felt her smile falter as she skirted a wagon. "Hello?"

Mr. Yates appeared from a horse stall across the building. "Unless you want to rent something, I'm closed."

She held out the tin. "I won't stay. I just wanted you to know I can cook."

His glower twisted into a confused expression. "What're you talking about?"

"Wednesday night you asked if I became a teacher because I couldn't cook. Well, judge for yourself."

A stabled horse nickered in what Abby imagined was approval.

That made his forehead wrinkles deepen. "You came to town with night fallin' for this? To give me cookies?"

Mr. Yates was not a likable man. She'd baked for him in part to salvage her pride, at which he'd taken a broad swipe the other evening. Not the best reason, perhaps, but she also hoped it might sweeten him up a pinch. She'd also probably baked for him because he was of an age with her father. If her father were still alive, that is.

And now that she'd seen those headstones, especially the one for the little Eugene who'd be her age had he lived, well . . . she couldn't help but feel Mr. Yates must be grieving. Lonely.

She set the tin down on his desk. "Not just to give you cookies. I'm going to the restaurant after I drop by the inn."

His scowl returned full force. "Thieves

and robbers at that inn."

"What do you mean?"

"They stole my business, didn't they? I stabled their guests' horses until they hired your tall fella as a hostler." He squinted at her. "Now I see. You and he are in cahoots. These cookies got somethin' in 'em they shouldn't, don't they? You're tryin' to give me a stomachache."

"I assure you these are perfectly good cookies."

He swiped the tin to the ground anyway. It landed with a clatter. "The rats can have 'em."

"Mr. Yates, really. I baked those for you last night out of fresh ingredients." Whatever compassion she'd felt for him a minute ago dissipated. She started to bend down to gather the tin of what was now crumbles before stopping herself. Her father may have been full of his own importance, but that didn't mean he'd been wrong to teach her to preserve her dignity.

She stood tall. "The rats will feast tonight, then. Good day."

The horses were silent, as was Mr. Yates, when she exited the livery and crossed the street. This was the part of her visit to town she dreaded most — stopping by the inn. It was adjacent to the café, however, and she owed Dash a report.

Still, she didn't wish to do it. Her steps slowed as she passed it to reach the drive to the stable. White, and three stories high, the structure was well kept and inviting. Windows framed from within by jade-green curtains — damask, if she was not mistaken — spilled golden lamplight onto the darkening street. The steps and long porch had been cleared of snow. In structure, the inn did not resemble the house she'd grown up in, and yet it reminded her of her home all the same.

Cozy winter evenings in the parlor with her parents, a fire blazing in the hearth. Cups of cocoa to warm the hands and the tummy. The cold world outside couldn't penetrate those happy evenings . . . until, of course, it did. Father died and Abby's world hadn't been sweet since.

"Abby?"

Dash stood on the wide drive, bundled against the cold in a rich-brown leather jacket and a bright blue scarf that had seen too many winters. For a moment — just one, traitorous moment — she wished she could curl into his arms the way she once did, absorbing his strength and comfort and warmth. To cast off her burdens for a while.

Dash could never be that for her again.

Why did she still want him to, deep down in the hidden places of her heart?

She forced a smile. "Good afternoon."

"Are you looking for me?"

"Yes, before I meet Mrs. Queen and Kyle for supper. Do you have information for me? Is *he* here yet?"

He glanced behind him, but no one was there to overhear. "A single male guest checked into the inn. Name of Unger. Rich as the proverbial Croesus, by the looks of his rig and horseflesh, but that doesn't mean he's our friend. Best I can tell, he's only been to the café and the lawyer's one street over. If he's been to the school to spy for a little boy, it's a surprise to me."

"No one's visited the school since you dropped in." Her lips pressed together. "Could he be our friend, though? Maybe hoping to recognize Katherine Hoover?"

"Our friend and Katherine never met, remember? So he has no idea what she looks like. However, she has that tintype of him and her sister. She might be able to identify him, depending on how much he's changed in ten years." His eyes glinted gold in the light of the setting sun. "You look the same, though."

"Stop it, Dash."

"What? You do."

This wasn't about how she'd changed, and oh, how she'd changed. This was about boundaries he was perilously close to trespassing. "I can still read your face like a newspaper headline. If you intend to reminisce rather than limit our interactions to work, I cannot do this."

He stared at her for a moment. Then he held up a hand in apology.

Good. But her breath hitched when she inhaled.

"So how was your lunch with Mrs. Story?"

"The only crumb she spilled was that Micah's father has been gone a long time. And her exact words were 'We don't talk about him, ever. It's far better that way.' Maybe she doesn't speak of him because he's a criminal and she had to abscond with little Micah to protect him. But maybe it's because it's too painful for her to talk of someone she lost."

"I like to talk about my parents. It keeps their memories alive."

"Your parents weren't murdered. Or criminals."

"I'm sorry, Abby. I'm saying everything wrong today." He glanced around again, but no one was close enough to hear them. "I know you don't want to talk about personal matters, but I pray the hurt will go away for

135

you someday."

"I think it will always hurt, Dash." Not just her father's history, but what Dash did too. Would he ever understand that?

"Your father made some bad choices, but he put a stop to working with our friend. He knew God too, from what I recall. I think there's hope. Hope is the one thing that kept me sane when my folks passed, that and knowing they're safe and whole in God's presence."

How contrary to Abby's experience. The one thing keeping her sane was focusing on the knowledge that Fletcher Pitch would get his comeuppance someday. Hopefully with her help.

"There's that verse in the New Testament, 'ye sorrow not, as others who have no hope.' Or something close to that. Is that Colossians?"

She adjusted her gloves. Hmm, the thumb had a small hole. "Maybe."

"No, it's First Thessalonians, I reckon. Or is it Second?"

"I'm not sure." She tipped her head toward the restaurant. "I don't wish to be late for supper."

"Sure, but will you look up that verse for me and tell me later? I'd like to know where it is."

Look it up for yourself. The words were on her tongue, but they were cruel, considering his hardships with reading. "I'll try to find time."

"Maybe tonight when you're at your evening devotions."

She stepped away. "I don't do them anymore."

"Morning prayers, then." He followed after.

She spun to face him. "Dash, I — didn't bring a Bible with me from Chicago. If I find time I can borrow Hildie's, but it would be faster if you asked the pastor. Surely he'll know."

He blinked. "Why didn't you bring your Bible?"

"My trunk was full."

"Too full for a Bible? Abby, what happened to your faith?"

She couldn't bear the disappointment in his eyes. "I'm late, Dash — oh, pardon me."

The postmaster, Isaac Flowers, blocked the entrance to the café. "My apologies, Miss Bracey."

"None necessary." Isaac Flowers was her hero, saving her from Dash's judgmental gaze. "Good evening, gentlemen."

A twist, and she sashayed around Mr. Flowers and into the restaurant. The aromas of yeast rolls and onions made her stomach rumble. And there was little Kyle, waiting for her by a table in the back.

Was he young master Pitch? Abby intended to find out.

Isaac scanned Dash from hat to boot, shaking his head. "Your pursuit of the schoolmarm isn't going well, from the looks of it."

Ah, yes. The gossip. "You heard about that, did you?"

"A few ladies were nattering in the post office, and your names happened to come up. Don't get angry, Dashiell. Folks enjoy a good romance."

"I'm not angry, nor would I call my relationship with Abigail Bracey a romance."

"You came a long way to find her here, didn't you?" Isaac wiggled his brows. "That takes bravery. I envy you, pursuing a woman with such confidence. I'm not good at that sort of thing."

Isaac and his good teeth? "I doubt that."

"Oh, it's true. Talking to women is hard, unless I'm selling them postage stamps."

"Is that what you were doing with Geraldine Story when I barged in?"

Isaac grimaced. "It's not like that. Her little boy collects postage. Pastes them into a book."

"Seemed like you were conversing well enough, and not about postage collecting either."

"I'm not sure why we're discussing Mrs. Story instead of you and the schoolmarm."

"Because there's nothing to discuss."

"Sure there is. What did you do to deserve her wrath?"

"I'm not in the mood."

Isaac mock-punched Dash's shoulder. "You need some cheering. I was just on my way to the café for supper. Allow me to treat you." Isaac dined out frequently. Clearly being postmaster paid well. Better than being an operative, anyway.

"Nah, thanks. Abby's in there. I don't want to upset her."

"We'll sit across the room. Come on, you've got to eat." Isaac tugged Dash's arm. "You can give her that sad-eyed look over your soup. My mother's vexation with me used to dissolve when I did that. Forgave me anything."

"Mothers tend to be forgiving."

"Aren't all women like that?" Isaac opened the café door for them.

"You're not serious, are you?"

Isaac nodded.

Oh, did he have a lot to learn.

■ ■ ■ ■

Abby's chair in the café's far corner gave her an excellent vantage of the restaurant, so she couldn't miss Dash's entrance with Isaac Flowers. She gritted her teeth. When would that man leave her be?

"Something wrong with your pork chop?" Mrs. Queen frowned.

"Oh no, it's delicious. So tender."

Mrs. Queen's full cheeks rounded as she smiled in obvious relief. "Thank you, Miss Bracey. I didn't do the pork, though — I do the sweet things. But I did the fried apples."

"I'd love the recipe, if you'd be inclined to share." Abby determined to focus only on her dining companions, Mrs. Queen and Kyle, not on Dash.

"I'm happy to."

The café was not like the Chicago restaurants she'd visited with her parents, not with its family-style fare and homey decor, from the lace curtains to the plain sconces on the walls. Abby enjoyed the pleasant atmosphere and tasty, ample portions far better than any restaurant her parents had favored. The fried apples in particular were hard to eat with the dainty sense of decorum Mother had taught her.

"I appreciate you meeting with me so I can get to know you both better. I love having Kyle in my class."

Kyle wiggled on his chair, clearly pleased.

Abby took the opportunity to discuss Kyle's strengths, which he also seemed to enjoy. It was important for him to know he was a special young man, as each child was special. But after a few minutes, Abby shifted topics, the better to discern whether or not these two were Fletcher Pitch's family. "Kyle did an excellent job with an assignment I gave the class the other day. He wrote about you, ma'am, and mentioned he was born in Pennsylvania. What brought you to Nebraska a few months ago?"

Mrs. Queen chucked Kyle's chin. "The job. An uncle of mine works for the railroad and passed through Wells. He dined here at the café and learned they needed a baker, so he telegraphed me. Kyle and I came right away."

"From Pennsylvania?"

"No, Saint Louis. We've moved around a fair bit."

Interesting. Katherine Hoover would have moved around a fair bit too. "You baked for a restaurant in Missouri, then?"

Kyle sat up. "What's for dessert?"

"Crumb cake," Mrs. Story answered.

Abby wanted an answer to the question. "You've worked in restaurants before, I take it."

"Not quite. I baked at home and sold to restaurants to supplement the savings I had when Kyle's father passed. Kyle was a tiny thing then, and you know how it is, money runs out — this must be boring you to distraction, Miss Bracey. Ready for crumb cake?"

"Yes, please, but I'm not bored." And so far, all she'd learned was the Queens moved frequently and Kyle's father was not around past the boy's infancy. Circumstantial clues. She required more. Perhaps she could inquire into Mrs. Queen's relatives —

"Kyle, fetch us some of that cake, dear boy?"

"Yes, Mama." Kyle was off his rump before the word *cake.*

"Walk, don't run."

Abby chuckled. "He's a lively boy."

"He's my whole world. Which is why . . . well, Miss Bracey, I wanted a moment alone with you. Kyle says your beau has been to the school. I'm not sure that's appropriate in front of the children."

Oh dear. "I assure you, Mrs. Queen, nothing untoward has happened, and I have instructed Mr. Lassiter not to come to the school anymore. Besides, he is not my beau."

"Then why is he staring at you?"

"What?"

"All supper long, with eyes like a basset hound." Mrs. Queen widened her eyes, looked up, and turned her lips down in imitation. "Like you hurt his feelings. It's a little sweet, you know."

Whatever it was, it wasn't *sweet.* "I'm afraid to look."

"Believe me, I wouldn't mind a handsome fella looking at me like that. You should be grateful."

Thankful for whatever antics he was pulling right now? Ha.

"Much as I don't approve of a schoolmarm having a beau, you should forgive him and put him out of his misery," Mrs. Queen added.

"If he's in misery, I am not the cause." She said it as lightly as she could, but she had no intention of forgiving him. Forgiving meant ignoring what he'd done to her, acting as if it had never happened. How could she do that, after he left her without a word?

Kyle returned, balancing three plates of crumb-topped yellow cake.

Grateful for the diversion, Abby smiled.

"This looks delicious."

"It is," Kyle assured her, crumbs already coating his lips. He must have sampled some in the kitchen.

But Abby forgot to pay attention to the taste, knowing Dash was watching her with sorrowful eyes.

CHAPTER 8

Forgive, forget, forgive, forget.

The words formed a rhythmic refrain in Abby's head, in time to the beat played by the group of fiddles and banjos Saturday evening at Mayor Carpenter's birthday party. Strange to be mulling such a painful concept as forgiveness while she danced to an upbeat, festive reel, but the subject had been niggling at her since last night's supper with Mrs. Queen.

She might not be able to forgive or forget what Dash had done, leaving her without a word, but she could choose to respond differently. With less anger.

Who could be angry tonight, anyway? Town hall's yolk-yellow walls were draped in banners wishing the mayor a happy birthday, and streamers hung from the central brass chandelier. Additional kerosene lamps had been brought in to illuminate the space, and the chairs that had been set up for her meeting with parents the past Wednesday ringed the room, offering seating while leaving the room's center clear for dancing. Abby had been inundated with partners from the moment she arrived, and every one of those partners, for reel and quadrille alike, had been her students.

Most of her pupils were here, although she hadn't yet spied Kyle or Micah. She glanced for them again and, oh, Bud's hands reached for hers. It was their turn to sashay down the center of the reel.

The eight-year-old's hands were slick with sweat as they skipped to the end of the rows; hers might be damp too. She hadn't been this warm all winter, but exercise and the press of so many bodies heated the room with greater efficiency than any stove. Her nape and back felt sticky, but it also felt quite good to be warm for a change.

At the song's final notes, Abby curtsied. "Thank you, kind sir."

"Yes, ma'am. Now I gotta dance with my grandmammies."

"Your grandmothers? They're here?"

He nodded. "Mama's mama and Papa's mama. My real papa, not my step-pa. They came for a visit."

Interesting. Bud Grooms was one of the three candidates to be Fletcher Pitch's son,

146

but she'd not ranked him high on her list because of the timing of his mother's remarriage and pregnancy. Now that Abby knew Bud's grandmothers were here, however, it seemed almost impossible that he was Fletcher Pitch's son. Katherine Hoover had no family, certainly not a mother and mother-in-law. Who, now that Abby had gotten a good look, strongly resembled Bud.

She crossed Bud's mother off the list etched in her brain. "I hope to meet them later."

"Traveling dance!" someone hollered as Bud sauntered off.

Coy Johnstone appeared at her elbow and cleared his throat. "May I have the honor, Miss Bracey?"

"My, you asked so nicely. Of course. You'll have to teach me, though. I've never done a traveling dance."

"Me neither, but you change your partner when they say so."

"So we won't be partners for long?"

"I reckon not."

She didn't recognize the song at all, but it was a two-step. She and Coy moved to the beat, although no dancing master would endorse their form. Abby didn't care in the slightest. It meant the world that her students liked her well enough to want to spend time with her — even Coy, whom she often reprimanded for chattering.

"So, ma'am, I was talking to Almos about Stripey."

Ah, so Coy had asked her to dance with an ulterior motive. "Oh?"

"Are you sure you won't let 'im back in the class?"

"Almos or Stripey?" she teased.

"Stripey." His lips twitched. "I was thinking we could study skunks' habits and such. He'd be a good object lesson."

"You've thought this through, haven't you?"

"Yes, ma'am. Please say you'll think on it."

"I shall, but I doubt I shall change my mind. There's no telling what a skunk loose in the classroom would do."

"Change partners," the fiddler hollered over the song.

"To whom?" Abby asked the air as Coy released her hand and dashed to claim his new partner. Then someone came to her rescue: the bearded fellow whose property abutted the schoolyard. He tipped his head as if to ask permission. She nodded. "Hello, neighbor."

"Good evening, Miss Bracey." His touch was light, respectful.

"You know my name, but I don't know yours."

"Burt Crabtree."

She'd never seen him this close-up before. His beard was thick and rather scruffy, but he presented an otherwise neat appearance. In fact, his coat fit him so perfectly it appeared professionally tailored. No wonder Hildie thought him the town's second most eligible bachelor.

But Hildie was correct about his shyness. He didn't look at her, nor did he speak, and the awkwardness was palpable. Abby cleared her throat. "How is your fence coming along, Mr. Crabtree?"

"Well. And your class?" Ouch! He stepped on her foot. "Sorry. I'm not much of a dancer."

" 'Twas nothing." Her students had been clomping on her feet all evening. Good thing she'd worn her heaviest boots. "And the class is well indeed."

"The young'uns are fun to watch, running around while I'm working. So full of life."

"That they are — oh." There went his boot again, square on her toes. "I'm fine."

"I doubt it, but looks like we're about to get new partners anyhow. I think I'll go home after this dance."

"You should stay. The mayor hasn't even cut his birthday cake yet."

"I'm not much for parties. Hope your next partner is a much better dancer than I am."

The fiddler held his bow aloft. "Time to travel!"

Mr. Crabtree ducked out of her hold, and her hand was claimed by the postmaster. Hildie would smirk at seeing her dance with her choice for town's most eligible bachelor, the finest-dressed man in attendance, with his blue silk tie and a suit so well-fitting her father would have asked for the name of his tailor.

"Miss Bracey. Having fun?"

"I am, Mr. Flowers. You?"

"Sure." He didn't sound convincing. His gaze flitted to the vestibule door. Was he watching for someone in particular?

"It's wonderful to see so many people celebrating the mayor."

"Agreed." His gaze caught on a passing figure. She twisted her head to look. Maynard Yates shuffled the perimeter of the room, lips fixed in a scowl. "I don't know why he even attends events. His disdain for the townsfolk is mutual. You think he'd learn."

That sounded familiar. Three years ago in Chicago, after Father's criminal activities were exposed, their well-meaning pastor invited them to attend a hymn sing in the church fellowship hall one Sunday evening. Mother felt too unwell to attend, so Abby went alone with a sense of anticipation for the first time since Mr. Welch and the Secret Service entered their lives.

Is this chair taken? Pardon me, how about this one? No? This one, then?

It had taken her a full minute to realize none of the empty seats were open — to her.

As she left, tears streaming down her cheeks, the gathered flock started the hymn sing. Sweet harmonies of "Amazing Grace" followed her out into the street.

Did any of them understand the irony of it? Clearly not, for none acknowledged knowing her when they passed in public. When Abby told the pastor why she hadn't stayed at the sing, he declared it shameful, but there was nothing to be done about it.

Tonight might not be a hymn sing, and this might not be church, but folks avoided looking at Maynard Yates the way her former fellow parishioners had pretended not to see her on the streets of Chicago. A few people even turned their backs. When he approached the punch bowl, the woman filling cups bustled away before he arrived.

Abby's chest ached. With pity, or kinship?

In her experience, she felt she'd done nothing wrong; her father had been the guilty party. Mr. Yates, however, was rude, insulting her at the meeting on Wednesday, and then tossing her tin of cookies to the livery floor. He bore a responsibility for how others treated him that Abby had not, back in Chicago.

Nevertheless, she knew exactly how he must feel, unwelcome among his community.

"Switch, folks!" The fiddler waved the entire violin this time.

Mr. Flowers passed her off to another partner — Mr. Ford, her students Robert and Oneida's father — and they discussed his children until the song ended. She thanked Mr. Ford and then slipped toward the punch bowl, where Mr. Yates lurked, arms folded and shoulders hunched.

"You look thirsty." She ladled a cup and handed it to him.

He shrugged as if to deny it but took the cup from her hand. "At least I know the punch isn't poisoned."

"Neither were the cookies I made for you."

"I figgered. No dead rats in the livery."

Abby burst into laughter. "You have quite a wit, Mr. Yates."

"I didn't try to be humorous-like." He sipped. "Why don't you go back to hoppin' all over that dance floor?"

"Was that an invitation to dance, Mr. Yates?"

His eyes bugged. Both knew that, as a lady, she couldn't ask a gentleman to dance. Both also knew he couldn't say no if an invitation had been perceived to have been issued.

With a grunt, he set down his cup by the punch bowl. "You're a shrewd one, missy."

"Maybe it's a good thing I'm a teacher, then."

She felt the weight of everyone's stares as she made her way to the dance floor beside a scowling Maynard Yates. The strains of a Bavarian folk dance began — oh dear, it had been some time since she'd danced the five-step schottische. Probably even longer since Mr. Yates had. He was adept, though. Two side steps to the left and right, a turn in four steps. They didn't speak for concentrating on the figures.

When the song ended, she dipped in a curtsy, but he was gone when her knees straightened. Oh well. Now he couldn't say he didn't dance tonight.

Hildie and Geraldine Story rushed to her — when had Geraldine and Micah arrived?

Must have been when she was focused on her dance with Mr. Yates.

"What was that about?" Hildie's eyes were wide.

"*He* asked *you* to dance?" Mrs. Story looked impressed.

"I tricked him into it." Abby waved her hands over her flushed cheeks.

The baby must have kicked, because Hildie rubbed her stomach. "Why would you do that?"

How could Abby answer honestly? *Because good Christian folk ignore him? Because I've been ignored too?*

"My words burst out before I gave it much thought."

"I doubt that. You're kind, and too modest to say it," Mrs. Story answered.

"No —"

"See, she's too modest to admit she's modest." Hildie grinned, then gasped. "Don't turn around, Abby, but your beau is here."

Dash had arrived? She spun around, scanning the crowd. "He's not my beau."

"So you keep saying." Mrs. Story snickered.

There he was. Damp hair slicked back from his broad forehead, clean-shaven, looking much like he did when he came calling

154

in Chicago. Mercy, she'd tried to forget all those things that used to make her heart sputter but now ached to the bottom of her being.

Forgive, forget, forgive, forget.

She couldn't. But she'd decided to be less angry about it, hadn't she? Tonight was a good time to start. She decided to smile at him.

There, that wasn't so hard, was it?

Dash gulped. With her hair curled like that, cheeks flushed, eyes bright, *smiling,* Abby looked seventeen again. Eager to see him. Eager for the life they were going to start.

Of course, everything had changed since then. He deserved her loathing. She didn't look like she hated him right now, though, smiling like that. Was there someone behind him she smiled at instead? He turned around. Nope.

Isaac Flowers stopped square in front of Dash. "Took you long enough to get here."

"I had something to do at the inn." Spy on that guest, Unger. He'd asked for his bed to be moved away from the window, and Dash had been delighted to volunteer. It gave him a chance to peek at anything Unger might have left lying around: correspondence, currency. Alas, the bills had been legitimate and the correspondence had been difficult to read, but he could make out enough words like *engine* and *railroad* to know it had nothing to do with counterfeiting. Unless it was an excellent code, of course.

But it didn't seem like Unger was Fletcher Pitch.

Then Dash had stopped for a word with the sheriff, showing him the Secret Service commission book he'd hidden in his coat pocket. It was a matter of professional courtesy. Sheriff Grayson, a compact-built fellow with graying temples, hadn't seen any counterfeit bills himself, or newcomers who could be Pitch, but he'd inform Dash if he did. And he'd keep Dash's real job to himself.

"You aren't the only latecomer." Isaac adjusted his tie. "Geraldine Story and her boy recently arrived as well."

"Oh?" He wiggled his brows. "Perhaps you can share a dance with Mrs. Story. To discuss postage, of course."

"I just might. And you can dance with your schoolmarm and ask her why she danced with a particular fellow."

"Sy Miller?" He had to ask.

Isaac gave him an odd look. "No. Maynard Yates."

"She didn't. Really?"

"Yes. And she didn't appear to mind it."

Hmm. "Where's Yates now?"

"He left. So did a few other folks, like Burt Crabtree. Neither are the most sociable of fellows."

"Burt seems nice enough."

"I s'pose. Haven't had many dealings with him. He doesn't talk much."

On the small stage at the front of the room, a lanky fiddler stood and lifted his bow. "Time for the handkerchief dance."

Dash hadn't heard of it. "I sure hope he doesn't mean used handkerchiefs."

"Come on. This'll be good." Isaac grabbed his arm.

Dash hadn't danced in years, not since a to-do at Abby's house. He'd felt out of place and miserable. "No thanks."

"Trust me." Isaac led him to a gathering group with two other men he recognized but hadn't met yet. Inside the men, four women clustered: Mrs. Story, a gal who couldn't be long out of the schoolroom, another who hadn't seen the inside of a schoolroom in decades, and Abby.

"What is this handkerchief dance?" Abby avoided looking at him.

"Wave your hankie like this." The gray-haired lady in their midst wiggled hers in the air. "The fellas move around us in a circle. When the shout comes, throw your hankie, and whichever fella catches it is your dance partner."

Dash didn't need much in the way of book smarts to figure Abby would throw her handkerchief at any of the men in the group except for him. He wouldn't lunge for it. He didn't feel like riling her up, and besides, he fancied a dance with the grandma here. She was probably a fount of information about folks in town.

The music started. A girl shrieked. Everyone was smiling with excitement. The grandma nudged Abby. "Get out your hankie!"

Grudgingly, Abby withdrew a square from her sleeve.

The women walked in a small clockwise circle while the men moved around them, counterclockwise. The grandma waved her checkered handkerchief with enthusiasm. The youngest lady waggled a plain linen square. Isaac locked his gaze on Mrs. Story, whose hankie had pink ribbony things dangling off the corners. Who could blow their nose in that fancy thing?

"Now," the fiddler called.

Dash was right in front of the young girl, but she tossed her handkerchief behind her, out of his reach. No worries, the grandma's handkerchief floated over his head.

One of the other fellows snatched it, glancing at Dash with a grin. Dash ran for the girl's handkerchief, but oof — Isaac shoved Dash directly beneath Abby's hankie, a simple thing with a pink *A* stitched into the corner.

What could he do, let it fall?

He caught it an inch from the ground. "Sorry. Looks like you're stuck with me."

She held up her hand for his, almost as if she didn't mind. "You didn't have much of a choice in the matter either."

"Well, I am supposed to be your beau, come back to woo you."

"Quite right. At least this gives us an opportunity to speak a little. About our friend, of course."

"Of course."

Her hands weren't as soft as he remembered, but their touch still sent a jolt up his arms. She fit within the hold of his arms too well, and it was impossible not to recollect when there was no hostility between them, only hope and love.

She wasn't hostile right now, however. "What have you been doing today? Besides tending horses, I mean."

He guided her to the far side of the hall,

where the dancing couples were spaced farther apart and no one sat in the chairs against the wall. No one should overhear them here. "Talking to folks, but not learning much. Buying things too, to see if I receive counterfeit change."

"Have you?"

He nodded. "Change for when I paid my rent."

Her eyes widened. "From your landlord? Isaac Flowers?"

"Of the good teeth? Yep." He glanced around for eavesdroppers. "And the dollar was made by our friend too."

Her lips parted. "My stars, that's — that's horrible. So *he's* here? We missed him come to town?"

Pitch? "Just because his bills are here doesn't mean he is, Abby. A large fraction of bills in circulation are counterfeit. It's not incomprehensible that one of our friend's bills made it to Nebraska, even if he himself is not here yet. Money travels. Folks spend it at one store, it's given to another as change, and they take it on a journey and spend it in another state."

Her features didn't relax. "But don't you think the timing is interesting? *He's* coming, and his money appears around the same time? Seems like more than coincidence to me."

"Our friend has been making money for a long while, but I see your point."

"Good, because Isaac's suit is pretty expensive. Father wore well-tailored suits like that, and they were dear in price. He has money, and I don't believe it came from the post office. What if Isaac is working with our friend as — what did you call it? A shoveler?"

"Shover." He didn't like the idea of Isaac earning ill-gotten funds, not a whit. Isaac was becoming a friend. Sure, he kept his door shut all day and night, and as Abby had noted, he had more money than one would expect for a postmaster. But he'd passed *one* bad bill, to Dash's knowledge — and a small denomination at that. No, Isaac couldn't be involved in disseminating counterfeit money for Pitch. He tried to offer Abby a reassuring smile. "One bill does not a crooked man make. Nevertheless, I will keep my eyes open, all right?"

She gave Isaac a sideways glance. "Just be careful. You live with the man."

"I am a paragon of discretion."

"Says the fellow who drew a ridiculous amount of attention to himself when he arrived in town. Coming to school like that?"

"I was in a bit of a hurry that day, you

161

may recall."

She bit her lip, a sure sign she had a question but was afraid to ask. He jiggled her arm once. "What?"

"How can you tell when money is . . . bad?"

"Lots of ways."

"Don't you have to, well, *read* what's on the dollar bill to judge if it's phony?"

He shook his head. "Most of the time it's easy to tell the difference. The ink isn't quite the right shade, or something else is off. Our friend's work is convincing, though. I can only tell by the feel of the paper. I can show you sometime."

"It might be helpful. For future reference, of course."

"Of course." The faint scent of lavender swirled around them as he pulled her closer to avoid knocking into another couple. "That Unger fellow who checked into the inn seems to be a railroad man. He hasn't been to the schoolhouse, has he?"

"No. No one has visited the school."

Good. "So our friend isn't in town yet, even if his currency is. That gives us more time with your half of the investigation. Any news?"

"I'm sure Bud Grooms is not the boy we're seeking. His grandmothers are in town." She tipped her chin toward a short expectant woman flanked by two elder ladies, one of whom shared the same build.

Not to mention, Katherine Hoover had no family. "Very well, Bud is not our lad."

A shriek drew their attention. Geraldine Story giggled on Isaac's extended arm, her skirts swirling around her ankles.

Abby chuckled. "He didn't twirl me once."

"You danced with Isaac?"

"I danced with a lot of people tonight."

"Even Maynard Yates, I hear. He's a tough one."

"He's . . . crusty," she amended.

"*Crusty* suggests he's got a soft interior." Like a good loaf of bread.

"I think he does. Soft and sad."

That was almost as surprising as Abby's willingness to dance with Dash, be touched by him, even though he'd been all but forced to catch her handkerchief. "He doesn't seem sad to me. He seems ornery."

"He was ornery when he threw my cookies to the floor."

"What cookies?"

"It doesn't matter." She managed a light shrug as she danced.

He tipped his head back, the better to look at her. "Do you have a fever? Touch of the ague?"

"If I'm hot, it's because I've been dancing."

"That's not it. It's that you're rather . . . relaxed."

"I — I'm not angry tonight, Dash."

"At me?"

She sighed. "At the world. But mostly you."

"I'll take it." He released one of her hands and nudged her into a spin. Her spring-green skirt whooshed around her boots.

She gasped. Oh no, was she back to being angry with him? He pulled her back, bracing for her wrath.

She stared at him. "What was that for?"

"You said Isaac didn't spin you. Thought you might feel left out."

She laughed, and oh, it was glorious. "How thoughtful of you."

He did it again, whirling her out and whipping her back into his arms.

"Dash Lassiter, you're having too much fun making me light-headed."

"I am." He tugged closer, enough that he could feel the warmth escaping her, breathe in the subtle lavender scent she dabbed behind her ears. "Having fun, that is."

She shifted back. "Dash —"

"I know, I know. We have rules." Confounded rules, but they were in place for good reason. He'd hurt her in Chicago, and working with him now refreshed all those unhappy memories.

Despite the music playing, he stopped and let go of her. "Sorry I overstepped."

Her features hardened. "What are you doing?"

"I crossed a boundary you constructed, Abby."

"Dancing? We had to dance, and it was a good opportunity for us to talk about the investigation."

"And we've done that. No need to bother you any further. Enjoy your evening."

She glanced around. "But Dash —"

"I'm afraid you've confounded me, Abby." She always had, hadn't she?

"You can't just quit a dance and leave your partner on the dance floor. For the sake of propriety and . . . don't you care how it makes me appear to everyone? Or . . . or how I might feel about it?"

What was she talking about? "Do you want to keep dancing?"

"No, Dash, at this moment, I do not want to dance. What I want is to be the one to leave you this time."

And with that, she marched off the dance floor, leaving him standing like a fool in the middle of twirling couples.

CHAPTER 9

Abby snaked through the gathered crowd and hurried outside into the cold. Her nose stung and started to run as a precursor to tears, and she would not cry in town hall. If she had her druthers, she wouldn't cry at all over Dash Lassiter. Never again.

Breathe. In, out. In, out. The deep drafts of frigid air smarted down her windpipe, but her pulse decelerated and her tears stayed put behind her eyes, so it was worth the pain. At least no one else was on the street to see her pacing under the lampposts. She focused on the sounds around her, the gentle hiss of the lights, music and chatter escaping the hall, a horse's nicker down the street. Her own footsteps crunching the thin layer of snow on the boardwalk. A few more minutes of quiet, and she could regain her composure.

The creak and thud of the wooden hall door opening and shutting behind her knotted her stomach. Sure enough, Dash stood outside the hall, looking up and down the street. She slipped farther away from the lamplight.

"Abby?" So much for her attempt to hide. He strode straight toward her. "Come back inside and tell me what's wrong."

"Not yet."

"It's cold out here, though. You don't have a coat."

"Neither do you. I'll come in when I'm ready."

He didn't take the hint, coming to stand before her. He shoved his hands in his pants pockets and looked up. "Pretty clear. I see stars. It'll get colder before dawn."

He was talking about weather? Like a normal person did on a normal evening when he hadn't done anything wrong?

A frantic force surged within her, begging for release in some unladylike manner. Like kicking something. Wrenching the icicles off the hall porch and throwing them like spears into the street. Being a lady, expected to pretend all was well, was severely frustrating. And she was tired of pretending.

"You have no idea why I'm upset, do you?"

"I'm pretty sure I shouldn't have stopped dancing, and you're worried about what folks thought. But who cares what people think? What if I had a rock in my shoe? Can't a man stop dancing for that?"

"You are impossible, Dash."

He brightened. "Just blame me, if anyone asks. Since they all think I'm here to woo you, tell them you're not ready to forgive me."

Forgive, forget. Forgive, forget. She shuddered.

"See, you are cold. Come inside."

"I'm not cold."

"You're shaking."

"From fury, and I am not going back in there yet."

His brow furrowed like a plowed field. "Clearly, I don't understand. I had no idea it was so wrong for me to halt midsong like that, but I'll never do it to you again."

"That's right, because that's the last time you'll dance with me."

"I hadn't planned on dancing with you *tonight.*" His voice grew more frustrated. "We were shoved into it by that stupid handkerchief, if you recall."

"Believe me, I know you'd never *choose* me as a partner."

"I'm trying to respect your rules. I just didn't know stopping a dance went against them too."

"The boundary between us is my rule, yes, but I did not invent etiquette, Dashiell. Halting a dance is not *my* rule. It's everyone's."

"I must've missed that particular lesson about dancing decorum when I was mucking out your father's stable." He was upset now too, his tone chock-full of sarcasm. "Shouldn't surprise you that I lack manners, though. Folks like me don't know which fork goes with the fish."

Everything tinged crimson. "Don't behave as if this is a matter of class distinctions. It's a matter of common courtesy. You don't walk away from a dance, because it makes the person you left look like a fool. An utter, rejected, stupid fool."

"I didn't leave. I stopped dancing, but I didn't leave. You did."

"Not just tonight." The words erupted from her innermost being. "Six years ago. You left."

His angry expression fell. "Oh. That."

She waited, but he didn't speak again, just gulped so hard his Adam's apple jerked against his stark white collar.

He might not have anything else to say, but six years' worth of swallowed-down words battled to escape her throat. "You disappeared, abandoning me on a day that

169

caused me the maximum amount of distress and fear and shame."

His eyes went soft, damp. "You're right. I'm sorry, Abby. I've wanted to apologize to you since I first saw you again, but you didn't want to talk about it, remember? We set guidelines in place — boundaries, you just called it." He glanced around, ensuring they were alone. "Business only, right?"

True. "I'd like to alter our guidelines. For now." She braced herself to hear the truth at long last.

"All right, then." He scanned their environs and beckoned her to the bench in front of the general store. It was darker here, quieter, but visibility was better. No alleys or anything for anyone to overhear. She adjusted her crinoline and perched on the edge of the bench. Cold seeped through her dress, but she wouldn't be here long.

Dash shrugged out of his coat and offered it to her. She lifted a hand to refuse but he shook his head, so she took it and wrapped its warm weight around her shoulders. She breathed in the long-forgotten smell of his clothing as he sat beside her.

He stared straight ahead. "Leaving like that on the day we planned to tell your parents our intention to become betrothed, well, it must've sliced you to the bone. I'm sorry I left like that, without a word."

"Thank you. For being sorry."

"I am. I was then too, but believe me, it's better that I went away."

She waited ten seconds. "Why?"

He rubbed the bridge of his nose. "I don't know if it's the best time to do this."

"Six years ago would have been the best time for it."

He didn't respond, so she twisted toward him, a physical reminder she was here and she was owed an explanation. "Why did you leave like that, Dash?"

"I can't tell you what you want to hear."

"Say something, then." Anything. He'd dragged her to this quiet spot and offered his coat as if they'd be here for a while, but he said nothing more. No crumb of insight. No reason for him shirking away from the common courtesy he'd owed her as his practically betrothed.

Deep breathing didn't ease the bitterness churning in her gut. She barked out a humorless laugh. "Perhaps you're right, Dash. I'm thankful you revealed your true self before I married you."

"Dim-witted Dash, my true self, all right."

"Stop it. You're diverting the conversation, and I resent your intimation that I would ever have judged you on your reading and writing. Dim-witted Dash, indeed." Her hands shook with rage. "What you are is Deceitful Dash. Deceitful and viperous, mendacious, cruel —"

"I think you'd better keep *dim-witted* on that list of yours, because I don't know what 'mendacious' means."

"Look it up in the dictionary."

They both knew he would struggle mightily to do that.

He snuffed like a horse. "That's low, Abby. But I deserve it and worse, leaving without saying goodbye."

"You shouldn't have left at all." The last two words hung heavy in the thin, cold air.

It took him a long time to meet her gaze. "Well, like I said, I thought it best."

She waited again for an explanation, a story, a sign of regret. Nothing came.

And probably never would.

It was time to toss this — whatever it was between them — to the dustbin. She removed his warm coat from her shoulders and dropped it in his lap. "Once upon a time I knew you well, Dash, and we shared everything. Dreams, aspirations, struggles. Yet you couldn't tell me the truth when you stopped loving me. I never took you for a coward, but I guess behind that badge you're hiding somewhere, that's what you

172

are. A coward."

The words tasted victorious, sugar sweet, for a moment. Then her tongue recoiled at the bitterness filling her mouth.

She'd launched the words as weapons, well chosen in their intent to wound as deeply as possible. Only now that it was done did she recognize them as cruel, crueler than she ever imagined she could be. Words like that could never be taken back.

But what was worse, she wasn't sure she wanted to. Especially when his eyes narrowed. "And you, Abigail Bracey, have become an unforgiving, hardened, vengeful soul."

She snorted. "Vengeful? You mean because I want to bring Pitch to his knees?"

"Quiet, Abby." He swiveled to look around.

The street was empty. "No one can hear me, so answer my question. We're both working to catch him. Why am I vengeful and you're not?"

"I'm trying to bring him to justice. Is that what you want, or do you want him to suffer? To take God's work into your own hands and repay Pitch for what he did to your father?"

"How can you ask that? You and I are doing the same thing."

"Are we? I'm trying to serve the law, and through it, God and His people. Doesn't sound like God plays much of a role in your life anymore, though." He sounded so pious.

"Because God stopped intervening."

"The way you want Him to, maybe. But who are you to determine how He should act?"

Oh! She sputtered a moment before finding her tongue. "You don't know what you're talking about, Dash. You don't know me at all."

"I did once, when you lacked the strength to take me as I was. But you're right, I don't know you anymore. I don't like who you've become. I guess I did us both a favor, leaving Chicago when I did."

Abby rooted to the bench, watching Dash stride off on his long legs, leaving her once again. She shook, but no longer from rage. From spent emotion, yes, but also cold. She felt it now.

Once he was gone, she bustled back inside town hall.

Hildie stood inside the vestibule door, one hand on the small of her back. Relief flickered across her features. "There you are.

It's about time to cut the cake." She reached for Abby's arm and gasped at the contact. "You're like ice. How long were you outside?"

"Not long."

"Long enough to turn your fingernails blue. Where's Mr. Lassiter?"

"I don't know."

"Oh dear. You argued."

"Let's sample that cake, shall we? Kyle's mother has a way with desserts."

Hildie sighed. "I never could say no to anything sweet."

Abby could only nibble the mayor's birthday cake, but half of her students crowded the table for second helpings. Hardly a morsel was left, and Kyle's mother received plenty of attention and praise. Once their plates were empty, folks began to disperse into the cold night, including Abby and the Elmores. Abby nestled beneath a heavy, rough-textured blanket with Willodean and Patty in the back of the wagon. Both girls were asleep almost at once, so the adults didn't speak, so as not to wake them.

The moment they were in the house, however, Bynum carried both girls to bed in his strong arms and Hildie beckoned Abby into the kitchen. "Would you like a cup of tea before bed? It'll warm your bones."

"Thanks, but tea past supper keeps me awake."

"We don't have to drink anything. I thought you might want to talk about what happened with Mr. Lassiter." She smiled. "I'm a good listener."

That may be, but Abby would be a fool to confide in Hildie about anything. After losing her friends in Chicago, she'd closed herself off to deep relationships. She'd made new acquaintances in teacher training, but they were shallow, and Abby withheld any information about her father, sure if they knew they'd reject her just as her Chicago friends had.

Much as Abby liked Hildie and Bynum and their children, she'd created a similar boundary with them, not telling them much about herself. She'd had to, because she was lying to them for the sake of the investigation. When they learned why Abby had really come to Wells, they'd reject her, and it would hurt. No, it was better to keep a sturdy fence between them and stick to lighter topics of conversation.

"Thanks, Hildie, but you should probably get some rest."

Hildie waved a hand. "I'm wide awake.

The baby's doing the five-step schottische."

"Funny baby. I'm exhausted, though."

"Oh." Hildie shrugged. "Maybe tomorrow then, if you want to talk."

"Thank you, but I probably won't." Maybe now Hildie wouldn't pester her further.

Hildie busied herself with straightening her cuff. "I see."

"Good night, Hildie."

Abby went upstairs, donned her flannel nightdress, and climbed between the cold sheets, curling into a ball to warm her toes. An icicle lodged inside of her, though, poking at her. Maybe Hildie had been hurt by Abby's refusal to talk. But Abby had a right to privacy, didn't she? Then again, maybe Dash was right that she was a hardened soul. But if so, whose fault was that?

She smacked her fist into her pillow.

He'd also said she lacked the strength to accept him as he was. How dare he say something so flat-out wrong? They'd had differences, sure. His father worked for hers. Her father wanted her to marry someone wealthier, with better connections. Ironic, considering how well connected he was with the likes of Fletcher Pitch.

But she never cared that Dash was a groom's son. She supported him, encouraged him, fought for him. Loved him more than her own life. When Father had offered Dash a job in the bank, she'd told Dash not to take it. He didn't need to abandon his dream of breeding horses. She wanted to marry him even if it meant living simply next to a stable until his business flourished and they could afford a house.

But Dash had accepted Father's job offer, to save up money, he'd said. She'd worried about the arrangement. Dash had always worked with his hands. Horses kept him sane, whereas numbers and letters drove him halfway mad. Abby buoyed him in the effort, regardless.

And then after a few weeks, he disappeared from the bank. And her life.

Since he'd reentered her life, she'd imagined what it would be like to confront him about it. In her visions, she'd been controlled, no longer the victim of his abrupt departure. In reality, her anger spewed out, and now that it was spent, she felt hollow, boneless, like everything that had been holding her upright was gone.

But he needed to know what his decision had done to her, didn't he?

She shouldn't have said some of the things she said, but he shouldn't have blamed her for not accepting him — a lie if ever he told one. And calling her names?

You are unforgiving, though. You refuse to even entertain the notion. And seeing Fletcher Pitch brought low has been on your mind every day for four years.

Abby rolled over in a huff.

The night was long and cold, and thankfully, everyone was too tired from the party to linger in the frosty churchyard the next morning after Sunday services — even Dash, who left quickly. All four Elmores napped in the afternoon, but Abby used the quiet to plan the coming week's lessons, including a sketching project where the children would draw their own faces and write a paragraph about whom they looked like in their family. She must remember to procure some twine from which to hang the finished products to brighten the room.

Artistic expression was not her only reason for assigning the task, of course. Maybe either Kyle or Micah had been told he looked like his father, and she would at last have a tidbit of information about Fletcher Pitch's looks — hair color or build or something.

The sooner they figured out how to apprehend Pitch, the sooner Dash would leave Wells. It couldn't come soon enough for Abby.

■ ■ ■ ■

For the next few days, Abby focused on her classroom duties as well as assisting around the house. She tended Willodean and Patty, fed the chickens, dried dishes, and anything else Hildie would allow. She also ran into the post office to buy postage she didn't need, paying with her "emergency" five-dollar bill in order to receive change from the charming but now suspect Isaac, who'd passed on Pitch's counterfeit currency. Knowingly or unknowingly?

Isaac had made a quip about how Abby would have done better to break her large bill at the general store first, but hopefully he didn't suspect her motives. With the skill of a seasoned actress, she'd grinned, thanked him, and gone home, laying out the four dollar bills in change, and stared at them. Felt the paper's thickness, texture, weight. And couldn't tell if one of them was counterfeit.

She had little else to do in the evenings, quiet as Bynum and Hildie had become lately. Hildie didn't ask about Dash again. In fact, she didn't ask much of anything, or invite conversation. At first Abby assumed the baby was taking all of Hildie's strength, but Wednesday evening after Abby donned her brown coat to walk into town for supper at Mayor Carpenter's, Hildie didn't look up from setting the table when Abby said goodbye.

This wasn't about Abby rejecting Hildie's offer to talk, was it? Guilt needled her abdomen, but it couldn't be helped. Abby had to protect herself, and that meant guarding her privacy.

Nevertheless, she offered a truce in the form of a smile. "I won't be late."

Bynum appeared in the kitchen, dressed in his hat, scarf, and coat. "Team's hitched. Ready, Miss Abby?"

He'd hitched the team? "Oh, no, Bynum, I'm walking. No need for you to drive me. You'll be late for supper."

Willodean was in the parlor chanting, "Elk stew, elk stew." It was close to ready, judging by the smell, rich with onion and herbs.

Hildie shifted to lay out spoons. "Can't exactly let you walk to town and back in these temperatures, now can we?"

"If the temperatures drop any more, I'll stay in town, unless the mayor offers to drive me back."

Bynum shook his head. "We're the ones being paid to care for you, Miss Abby. It's our responsibility. I should've driven you

181

into town for your supper last week. Wasn't right of me to let you walk."

"It's my choice. I didn't want to inconvenience you, but I see now that I have. I should have asked you before scheduling these private meetings with parents. I'm sorry." She turned, but Hildie had slipped out of the room, silent as a cat.

She called out a goodbye before stepping outside with Bynum.

Once on their way, she cleared her throat. "I truly didn't mean for you to have to hitch the horses and drive me out, and then return for me later."

"I won't come back. I'll wait. Nurse a cup of coffee at the café."

That was even worse. "You'll miss supper."

"Hildie will keep a bowl warm for me."

"I feel awful. I truly didn't think this would affect you. I don't mind the walk. Besides, your farm is close to town. It hardly takes any time at all."

"Like I said, it's our job, Miss Abby."

Until the past few days, Abby hadn't felt like a job to the Elmores. She'd felt almost like one of them, part of an extended family. But everything changed when she'd turned down Hildie's offer of tea and sympathy.

Abby's heart was heavy when Bynum dropped her off at the Carpenters'. He glanced at the two-story house. "I'll come back in an hour. Don't rush, though. I can wait for you out here."

"I insist you do not, Bynum. I can't have you and the horses sitting outside in the cold. The café is less than a block away. I shall collect you."

"You sure?"

"Yes." She hopped from the wagon unassisted, her bustle waggling from the effort.

She fixed a smile as he drove away.

At fourteen, Bartholomew Carpenter was one of her older students, but he was the baby of the family, according to his responses to her assignments. In her attempts to learn more about Kyle's and Micah's fathers, she'd gleaned copious amounts of trivia about her students' parents, but never the answers she truly sought, which would lead her to identifying Fletcher Pitch.

Tonight, however, held no ulterior motives, nothing beyond getting to know the Carpenters better. She should set aside her anxious thoughts about Pitch and, yes, Dash too and attempt to enjoy herself. She mounted the porch steps and rapped on the door.

After an evening of genteel conversation

about Bartholomew's skill at geography and a filling feast of chicken and dumplings, Abby finished the last bit of her custard tart. "This has been wonderful. Thank you for having me."

"Thank you for meeting with families." The mayor leaned back in his chair. "I love to see the folks of Wells learning more about one another."

"Speaking of such, I must inquire about your recent dealings with a certain someone." Mrs. Carpenter, a full-figured woman whose dark hair was pulled back into a tight bun, folded her hands beneath her chin.

Oh no. Not more questions about Dash. Abby set down her fork.

"Maynard Yates." Mrs. Carpenter's voice was rich with curiosity.

Not Dash? Abby released a pent-up breath.

Mrs. Carpenter leaned forward. "We heard you tricked him into dancing with you and wondered how you accomplished such a thing."

"And why you'd want to," Bartholomew muttered.

"Bartholomew," his mother scolded.

Because I saw myself in him. She couldn't say that, though. "He and I didn't get off on the best footing. I thought to try again."

"He isn't on good footing with anyone," the mayor said with a sigh.

And no one ever said why. Abby bit her lip. She didn't approve of gossip, seeing as she'd been the subject of it on numerous occasions, but perhaps a bit of explanation might help her understand. "May I ask, seeing as you're the mayor and know a great deal about everyone, well, I noticed three headstones for folks named Yates when I walked through the churchyard. Are they his people?"

"His brother, wife, and son." Mrs. Carpenter lifted the delicate blue coffeepot. Wedgwood, if Abby wasn't mistaken. "More?"

"Thank you, no."

"Amazing you could read the stones. He's never tended them that I could tell. They're covered in snow all winter and hidden by weeds in summer." The mayor tutted. "Upkeep is important for town pride."

"How sad that he lost his family."

"It wasn't all at once." Mrs. Carpenter sipped her coffee. "His younger brother, Eugene, died first, from fever, wasn't it, dear? Or he drank bad water. I can't remember, as I was a schoolgirl then. But it was sudden, and Eugene was supposed to marry Maggie. Date was set and everything. Then he died, and she up and married Maynard.

It caused a little talk."

The mayor cleared his throat.

"What? It's not gossip. It's true." She turned back to Abby. "They married, but their baby died within days, and they never had another, more's the pity. Or maybe not, because about that time, Maynard got mean. To Maggie, to her friends, to anyone who said a nice word about Eugene. Then to everyone."

"Why?" Bartholomew leaned forward, elbows on the table.

The mayor cleared his throat again, far louder.

"Well." Mrs. Carpenter's cheeks pinked. "I suppose that's all the facts I have on the subject."

"I must be going, anyway. Bynum is waiting for me at the café." Abby rose.

"Well, isn't that lovely of him?" Mrs. Carpenter led Abby to the foyer and handed Abby her outer garments. The males in the family followed her out.

"Thank you again for the delicious supper. See you in the morning, Bartholomew."

Bartholomew snapped his fingers. "I almost forgot to tell you. Mama said I could bring a jug of apple cider tomorrow to heat on the stove, like you suggested at the meeting."

186

"Wonderful, thank you."

"Have you a large pot?" Mrs. Carpenter lifted a finger. "If not, I can send one with you tonight."

"No, we'll be fine, thank you. That reminds me of one last matter I've neglected to ask, though, Mayor Carpenter. Our wood supply at school is getting low."

He smacked his forehead. "I meant to inquire about it, but the matter slipped my mind. Tomorrow I shall ask a few of the men to replenish it. Have you enough to finish the week?"

"Oh yes." That business seen to, she thanked them again. "Good night."

Bundled to her ears, she marched out into the night for the short walk to meet Bynum at the café. Only Main Street boasted streetlights, but sufficient light from kerosene lamps spilled from house windows to illumine her steps. Few people were out and about, but the hour wasn't late, nor was she afraid of the dark.

As she walked, she considered tomorrow's lessons. Mathematics, of course. Preparation for Friday's spelling test. The art project, and oh, she mustn't forget twine. And she must carve out time for the pot of apple cider. It would be a treat but also serve as some of the children's first lesson in cooking. Perhaps the experience of warming a sweet beverage would even encourage some of her pupils to pursue more difficult tasks at home.

She turned onto Main Street. The inn was just ahead, and beyond that, the café. Both were lit from within and without. A man strolled the inn's drive to the road, whistling. Dash.

What was the name of the tune? Something decades old and lilting, like a folk dance. She hadn't heard it in six years, but the melody caught her up short. Memories she'd buried unearthed, like cicadas pushing up from beneath the ground, loud and insistent, impossible to ignore. *Dash whistling for the horses. Dash smiling at her. Dash's eyes going soft before he kissed her.*

His head turned toward her. The whistle stopped midchorus.

They stood like that for the span of several breaths. And then he turned away, walking in the opposite direction.

But what if she'd come here tonight to report something about their investigation against Pitch? Didn't he care about that?

Maybe he was still too upset with her. She'd called him a coward and a liar, and told him to turn to a dictionary when the last time he'd tried in her presence, he

188

became so flustered he couldn't find the *m*'s and ended up in the *w*'s. School was a tortuous experience for him. What had become of her, that she could fling that at him like that?

He was right about her. She was horrible.

She stood on the dark, quiet street a full minute, holding her aching chest.

"Miss Bracey?" A female voice called from the inn's porch.

Mrs. Story, Micah's mother, toddled down the steps toward her.

"Hello, ma'am."

"Seems we're both silly enough to be out on a cold evening. I had a delivery for the hotel — late, I know, but a curtain tore this morning and they paid double to have it repaired today. Oh my, you look upset. Is something wrong?"

Everything was wrong. "It's nothing."

"Clearly not. Can't I be of help? I don't mean to pry, but you look so sad —"

Abby stepped away from Mrs. Story's outstretched arm. "I'd like to be alone, please."

"Of course." Her arm lowered, as did her gaze.

Abby marched past, arms folded over her chest, feeling worse than she had a minute ago. Needing another moment to compose herself, she passed by the café. Bynum could wait a bit longer.

Tears fell thick and hot, warming her cold cheeks. She swiped at them, but her kid gloves did little to absorb the wetness streaming down her face. Breathing deeply didn't stop the flow this time. She walked as she blotted her eyes, blind to obstacles.

"Hey."

She recognized the voice even if she couldn't focus through her tears. "Mr. Yates. I'm sorry, I didn't see you there."

"You ain't the first to pretend that, despite the fact that I'm standing in front of my own livery." His tone was colder than the bitter gust of wind swirling around her skirt.

She couldn't help it. She choked out another sob.

"Hey, you weren't joshin'. What's with the waterworks, missy?"

Her lips parted. Would anyone in town believe Maynard Yates was inquiring into her well-being? A watery chuckle escaped her lips. There was indeed something soft in him after all, but he'd get the same answer she gave Mrs. Story. "It's nothing."

He made a disbelieving noise. "Didn't take you for a liar."

If he only knew she'd lied to everyone about why she and Dash were in Wells.

She'd lied to herself about the sort of person she was too. "Very well, it isn't nothing, but it's nothing that can be helped."

"Must be that hostler fella. Did he do somethin' untoward?"

"No, that's not it. It's the past catching up to me, is all. I keep hoping I'll escape it altogether someday."

"It's been twenty-five years, but someday never came for me."

That prospect was bleaker than the muddy snow clumping on the sides of the street. Twenty-five years? That was when his baby died, from what she recalled of the headstone. A long, long time.

According to Mrs. Carpenter, he hadn't started out as a cantankerous curmudgeon, but he'd changed somewhere along the way.

So had she, just as Dash said.

After Father's death, she'd stopped praying. Stopped reading her Bible. Stopped wanting God as part of her daily life.

Stopped wanting *anyone* in her life who could know her well enough to hurt her. That was why she hadn't wanted to talk to Hildie or Geraldine. Abby had hurt them both. She hadn't meant to, but she had to protect herself from future pain.

Is that what Mr. Yates had done once upon a time? Tried to protect himself? Perhaps the wall he'd built to shield his heart had also done too good a job of keeping people away. All the while, bitterness planted into his heart and spread its roots like tentacles, squeezing out any joy in his life.

She'd tended the plant of bitterness too. Nourished it with years of resentment. Hatred.

A heavy fatigue fell over Abby. *Hate* was a word she never used regarding her own emotions — no one did. Hate was wrong, everyone knew that. But in truth, when she turned her back on God, she'd allowed hate inside her heart. She hated Dash — and Fletcher Pitch, and maybe even Father for what he'd done to her and Mother.

That hatred — that bitterness, thirst for vengeance, dissatisfaction — hadn't brought her one iota of good. Not a moment of sleep, not an instant of peace. Loathing had left her empty, aching, unfulfilled.

She looked at Mr. Yates. Really looked, at the dark, deep pouches beneath his eyes, the set of his downcast mouth, the tight angles of his crossed arms. Was this her future, if she allowed her hatred and bitterness to erode her inside for ten, twelve, twenty-five years, as he had done? Meanness could become her involuntary response, just as it had Mr. Yates's. Oh yes, she could see her future in the weary curves of his shoulders.

What about her eternal future? She hadn't given much thought to what would happen were she to die unprepared, and oh, she was unprepared. Did hate and bitterness follow a person to the grave and beyond?

She didn't want that. Not for eternity, not for another second.

Her hands clutched together over her aching chest. What could she do to help Mr. Yates? To help herself?

Nothing. You can do nothing but accept Him. No works can save you.

The once-familiar, silent voice echoed in her head and her heart. She didn't ignore it this time, but she wasn't sure what to do about it. She couldn't weed hate out of her heart like a dandelion. How did one stop hating?

The Good Book says to love your neighbor and your enemy alike.

But it's hard, she prayed consciously for the first time in years. *I can't just forget what Dash did, leaving me like that. Embarrassed. Empty. Alone.*

Still, the echo of the voice remained in her head. *Love.* And love meant forgiveness.

She licked her lips. "Have you ever tried to forgive, Mr. Yates?"

"You sound like the church."

"I'm just asking, because I don't want to forgive Dash. That would be like . . . excusing him for what he did."

"Now, that don't sound like the church."

"Nope." Her laugh was shaky.

"I ain't got a mind to forgive either. What she did was wrong and don't deserve mercy."

She. A woman who'd hurt him bone-deep, the way Dash had hurt Abby. "Your wife?"

He answered by spitting in the snow.

So that was what had happened twenty-five years ago. His baby had died and his wife had somehow caused him additional pain. The specifics didn't matter, because for the first time, Abby was not alone in her grief over being hurt by the one she loved. It didn't take away the ache but soothed its edges, like a balm. There was indeed a comfort in sharing one's heart with another. "Do you want to talk about it?"

His posture stiffened. "No, I do not. You'd probably take her side."

"Because I'm female?"

"Because everyone took her side, and they don't even know the truth."

"I might not."

He scowled. "I ain't tellin' you, nosy

194

woman. I told one person, the pastor, and it did me no good. He said to forgive and love my wife, but she didn't love me."

Without knowing what the departed Mrs. Yates did or whether or not she loved her husband, Abby couldn't offer any words of comfort. All she could do was reach out and pat his arm.

He flinched like no one had touched him in a long time.

Years of being untouched and untouchable. No, Abby didn't want to be like this someday. But she didn't want to be hurt by others again either.

It wasn't a voice in her head this time, but an awareness of facts she hadn't considered. *Others* had hurt her. Not God. She had expected them to treat her with kindness because they were Christians, but they had failed her. Was it because they were hypocrites, like she'd always believed, or because they were imperfect people?

Abby wasn't perfect. Far from it. Mother had talked about their ancestor who sailed the *Mayflower,* as if it meant their family had more to be proud of than others. But what if the legacy of her ancestors who sailed on the *Mayflower* was faith? They came to America to worship God, didn't they?

How had things become so twisted?

Abby had done her fair share of twisting, acting as if God had abandoned her. But she'd left Him, not the other way around.

It was real to her now: He was still close at hand, waiting. Forgiving, because it wasn't as much about what she had done as what He had done for her. Wanting her to forgive and live in freedom. She knew it as certainly as she knew her name.

Forgiveness wasn't quite the issue right now, though. Forgiveness was a fruit of the tree, not its root. The root was her obedience — or disobedience, in this case. She had to return to God as the first step to changing into a new person.

And there was only one way she could see to achieve that. In His strength, with His help.

I'm sorry I turned my back on You, but here I am. A long way from You, still as sore and aching inside as ever, but I want things to change. I want to be friends with You again.

Something like hope warmed beneath her rib cage. She turned back to the man she never thought she'd call a friend, but he was the one she'd been given to share her heart with tonight. "When I get back home, I'm going to open the Bible, Mr. Yates. I can't guarantee I'll be able to forgive anyone right away, but I'm going to ask God to help me."

"And that hostler fella? You gonna have a talk with him about it?"

The idea didn't sound palatable, but at the same time, it sounded right. "I . . . think I have to."

He grimaced. "Don't think I'm goin' to talk to my Maggie."

How could he? Dash was alive, but Maggie was dead, so —

"I haven't been to her grave once. Never."

"Oh, I see." He meant he'd speak to her headstone. Tell her in person, as it were. "Even if you can't speak to her the way you could when she was alive, you could consider speaking to God about it. Perhaps if you and I pray, we might both have a sense of peace."

"You're a pushy gal."

"I'm a teacher. I'm accustomed to issuing instructions."

"And you make a decent molasses cookie, I s'pose."

"You ate one?"

"The ones I could clean off." He cleared his throat. "Sorry for shovin' 'em to the ground."

She grinned. "I forgive you."

"Don't get ideas that I felt guilty and

that's why I ate 'em. They just made a faster supper than beans. Appreciate if you didn't tell anyone that. Or . . . anything else we've discussed."

"Of course . . . I'm grateful for your confidence as well. I've needed someone to whom I could speak my mind."

He harrumphed.

"I'd better go. Bynum Elmore is waiting for me at the café."

"Sure." He sounded irritated she was ending their conversation, but irritated was a far cry from feisty. "G'night, missy."

She paused before she entered the café. "Are you going to look at a Bible tonight?"

"Maybe. But don't get no ideas about me goin' to church on Sunday."

"I think *maybe* is a good place for both of us to start, Mr. Yates." Maybe was far better than *never.*

CHAPTER 10

Snow dusted them on the drive home, but Abby's burning heart flooded her with warmth. After asking Bynum about his time in the café, she twisted on the bench to better look at him. "I apologize for you having to drive me into town and back tonight —"

"We've already talked about this, Miss Abby."

"I know, but with Hildie so close to delivering, it won't do for you to be hauling me hither and yon. I will arrange for my upcoming appointments to take place on weekends or during lunch hour. You and Hildie and the girls have been so kind to me. The last thing I'd ever want to do is inconvenience you."

"Thank you, but we'll manage things."

"I'd much prefer to stay home evenings with you. Not to be a bother, of course, but to be of help when the baby comes."

His brows lifted in surprise. "I know

Hildie will appreciate the assistance. And the companionship."

"I intend to be a better friend to her." Even though the closer she grew to Hildie, the more she'd miss her once Pitch was caught and Abby left Wells.

Abby repeated her intentions to Hildie once she returned home. Hildie fussed with her cuffs, something she must do to avoid making eye contact. "That's right kind of you."

She didn't trust Abby yet. Maybe she was still hurt, but in time hopefully Abby could prove to Hildie that she cared. In the meantime, she could pray about it. But first she needed a Bible. Surely they wouldn't mind if she borrowed the one in the parlor.

It felt heavy and cool in her hands as she carried it to her room. Once she opened it, the thin, delicate pages rustled at her touch. Where to start? There was something about grace in Ephesians; she remembered that. Saved by grace through faith and not works.

There it was, in chapter two. *"For by grace are ye saved through faith; and that not of yourselves: it is the gift of God: not of works, lest any man should boast."*

She ended up reading the entire epistle, and might have read more had her bedside candle not sputtered. It was cold, though, and her fingers were like icicles. She snuggled deep under the covers.

Lord, we're talking again. I suppose You may have been trying to talk to me for the past few years, but I've not been a good listener. I ask for Your forgiveness, and I ask You to help me forgive. I don't precisely want to, but I know it's important, for both me and Dash. Fletcher Pitch is another matter entirely. I'm not sure I can forgive him, ever.

Did God mind her frankness? Abby shrugged. He knew her mind. She might as well be honest with Him.

Will You also help me with Mr. Yates? How may I prod him toward peace? I'm so glad he ate my cookies, Lord.

She fell asleep thinking about him brushing dirt from them.

The next morning, she dressed quickly and hurried downstairs to assist Hildie. The kitchen was empty, but breakfast bubbled on the stove — mush by the sweet, corny smell of it. Hildie's voice carried from the girls' room. They must be dressing and Bynum must be outside doing chores. Abby grabbed her outerwear and the pail of food for the chickens before stepping onto the back porch.

Drip, drip, plink. The icicles above the back porch trickled drops onto the stairs. Her boots squelched the watery snow along the path to the henhouse. My, things had warmed up, hadn't they? The sky was gray and a light southern wind nipped her cheeks and nose, almost as if spring was on its way.

Bynum exited the barn, leading out the cows. "Morning."

"Good morning. Is spring upon us?"

He laughed. "We'll be up to our knees in mud, just you wait."

Mud sounded wonderful, if it meant sunshine too.

No eggs awaited her in the henhouse. Ah, well. The chickens might be inspired to lay a dozen today.

This gift of a milder day was like a symbol of the new start she'd begun last night. Abby knew she had a long journey ahead of her, of learning, repentance, and hopefully forgiveness. She'd taken her first steps, however. Like the icicles above the porch, she was thawing.

Later, she'd have to seek out Dash. He may not like her anymore, but she couldn't allow their harsh words to stand between them.

She'd also look for Mr. Yates and see how he fared. Perhaps he'd considered looking at a Bible last night too.

When she returned to the kitchen, Hildie

peered out the window. "My word, are those icicles melting?"

"They sure are. We'd best watch our heads today when walking beneath them."

Willodean allowed mush to fall off her spoon in clumps. "If they're melting, then it's too warm for me to wear a coat to school."

"It's not that warm," Abby cautioned. "Maybe a few degrees above freezing."

"Freezing means *coat*," Hildie said.

"We have a treat today." Abby hoped to distract Willodean from the oh-so-terrible prospect of wearing a coat. "Bartholomew is bringing apple cider for us to heat on the stove."

"I wish it was cocoa." Willodean tugged at the neck of her red sweater.

"Can I have cocoa?" Patty tilted her head to the side.

"Maybe we'll make some tonight." Hildie smiled at Abby for the first time in days. Perhaps her wounded heart was healing a little after their talk last night. "Abby, don't forget to take the big cook pot with you for the cider. I put it by the front door for you. Now then, I was going to bake today, but since it's not freezing, I think I'll launder sheets instead. We'll be getting out the tub, Patty."

Patty clapped. "Can I give dowwy a bath?"

"Yes, when I'm finished with the sheets, you may bathe your doll."

Abby glanced at Hildie's protruding midsection. "Are you sure, Hildie? All that wringing and stretching's sure to fatigue you. I can do it after school."

"They'll need all day to dry. Besides, the fresh air will do me good."

Nevertheless, Abby stripped the sheets from everyone's beds before she and Willodean left for school. Hildie kissed Willodean's cheeks. "Wear that coat, you hear? And if you find mud puddles, don't splash, please. Your shoes are so new and nice, I'd hate to have to scrub them already."

"Yes, Mama." Willodean rolled her eyes and hugged Bynum and Patty goodbye.

Abby took up the cook pot and her lunch pail. "Thanks for these. See you this afternoon."

"Have a good day," Bynum said. Hildie and Patty waved.

How could it not be a good day? The sky might not be blue, and if she wasn't mistaken, a few snowflakes drifted onto Willodean's shoulders, but they melted on contact. No matter the weather, though, Abby had a new heart this morning.

Lord, I'll start the day with prayer. Thank

You for each of my students. Please reveal their needs to me today and show me how to help them be all that You would have them be. I also ask for Your protection from Fletcher Pitch. Where is he, Lord? Protect Dash too. I'm so sorry I said those awful things to him, Lord . . .

Her prayer might be rambling, but she was pretty certain God didn't mind. Mother had always said the conversation between friends was more important than the content. She'd meant that Abby could be silly with her friends, but the notion held some wisdom. It was good that folks talked, whether they were friends, or creature and Creator.

Maybe Mother's tidbits came down through the family from her *Mayflower* ancestor.

"Say, Willodean, do you remember learning about the *Mayflower* from your last schoolmaster?"

"We didn't learn about flowers, but I want to."

Abby grinned. "It's not a flower; it's a ship. A special one. I think we should talk about it in class." Eighth graders Coy, Josiah, Bartholomew, and Berthanne would be tested on American history before graduation, anyway, and she must be certain they were prepared.

Willodean sighed. "Can we learn about flowers too?"

"We *may*. What's your favorite kind?"

"Daisies."

"I like those too."

It was hard not to think of flowers and spring today, with the temperature rising. It was such a lovely change that it was difficult to concentrate on anything once they arrived at school, especially once the aroma of apple cider filled the schoolhouse. At last Abby excused the children for noon recess. "When you come back in, we can enjoy our cider."

Fortunately she'd had the foresight to request the children bring a tin mug to school. She downed her sardine sandwich quickly — it had never been one of her favorites — and used her remaining lunch break to pin twine along the north and south walls, above the windows, from which to display the children's artwork. She hung the self-portraits they'd made — neither Micah nor Kyle said they resembled their deceased fathers, unfortunately — but there was still ample room on the twine for more artwork. After cider, she'd give her pupils some colored paper scraps to make flowers, and she would pin them to the twine too. The classroom would look like a garden, even though it was winter.

She picked up a stub of limestone chalk and wrote on the board beneath today's date of January 12. *Create a flower and enjoy cider.* A delightful way to end the day.

She mixed glue paste and went outside. "Come inside now." Abby waved at Burt Crabtree, who was working on his fence in his shirtsleeves. He too must be enjoying the unusual weather today.

Once inside, Abby moved to the stove. "Gather your cups, and I'll ladle cider for you. Youngest to oldest, please. Yes, Willodean, that means you're first. Get in line, thank you." She scooped a steaming mugful for Willodean, then served Oneida and Jack. "While we drink, let's do another art project. Glue pieces of scrap paper together to make flowers to decorate our wall."

Coy's groan was not unexpected. "I don't like flowers."

"You may make a tumbleweed if you prefer, Coy."

He shrugged. "All right."

She'd make a flower too. She settled at her desk and took a sip of the warm, sweet cider. "Delicious. Bartholomew, please thank your mother for me."

"You're most welcome, ma'am." Bartholomew's legs shifted after he spoke, drawing

Abby's gaze to the ground. Almos was seated in front of Bartholomew, his canvas sack at his feet. Nothing moved beneath the fabric this time, but it definitely bulged in a skunk-like shape.

"Almos?"

"Yes, ma'am?"

She glanced at the sack at his feet. Instantly, his shoulders wilted into a guilt-stricken frame.

"You brought Stripey back to school? Oh Almos."

He scooped up the sack, cradling it like a baby. "I had to. He misses me."

"That may be, but we cannot bring animals to school." Stripey wriggled. "I shall have to speak to your parents, but I expect you to tell them why you're home early today."

"Now? You're sending me home early?"

She glanced at her timepiece. "It's not that early, but yes. I warned you what would happen if Stripey returned to school."

Coy snickered. "Maybe if I get a skunk I can get sent home early too."

"You and I would work out an arrangement for Saturday school."

His jaw dropped in horror.

Almos loosened the sack. "Can he tell everyone goodbye?"

"*May* he, and oh dear, you've already pulled him out." Abby's stomach flopped. The creature nestled in Almos's arms, blinking against the light, ears rotating. Almos lifted one little paw in a wave. She had to admit, Stripey was rather endearing.

The classroom erupted in coos, shrieks, and exclamations of rapture. But if Stripey were frightened or intimidated? Her classroom would reek for weeks. She nudged a few small pairs of shoulders back. "Return to your seats and finish your flowers. Almos, we'll see you tomorrow."

Almos gently lowered Stripey into the sack. "What about my flower?"

"You can finish tomorrow after the spelling test."

Almos's sister Berthanne, of course, had finished her red-and-pink blossom. The circular petals reminded Abby of a peony. "Yours will be the first I pin to the twine, Berthanne. You may be excused with Almos. I know your ma prefers you to walk together."

"Yes, ma'am."

Abby escorted them into the vestibule but didn't involve herself with their coat buttons as she usually did. She didn't dare move her gaze from Stripey in his sack, and besides, it wasn't that cold out. After waving goodbye, she fastened Berthanne's peony to the twine, first of their spring garden. It was spring in her heart too.

Lord, thanks to You we have this wonderful day in the midst of winter. After school I'll go to the inn to speak to Dash. Please give me words to say so he'll see how sorry I am.

She was humming when she sat down to finish her own flower, a vibrant yellow daisy. She didn't realize until she got to the chorus that it was that melody Dash used to whistle.

Dash whistled as he left the inn for his lunch respite. His growling stomach was louder than the tune, but little wonder, since it was what, two o'clock? Hours since he'd had his breakfast of corn cakes and bacon. Lunch was late today, thanks to that guest Unger's request that Dash clean and polish his carriage before he checked out.

Unger clearly wasn't Fletcher Pitch. No one in Wells was, to the best of Dash's knowledge. So where was Pitch? Dash's informant in Kansas City was certain Pitch was en route to Wells to get his son. He'd said the name of the town and said he should've guessed his boy was here, once he saw the name on a map. Whatever that meant.

So where was he? Waylaid, or was he biding his time, hiding on an outlying farm somewhere?

Dash didn't know anything for sure when it came to Pitch — or much of anything else, either, except he and Isaac were out of coffee, which was why he headed to the general store before he grabbed a bite to eat.

He also knew his scarf was much heavier than the day required. What odd weather. Yesterday he'd slipped on the shell of ice coating the walk, and today his footsteps punched through.

One other fact he knew: he was miserable.

He'd brought his misery on himself, though. He'd allowed his temper to get the better of him when he told Abby he didn't like who she'd become.

It wasn't even true. Well, he didn't like some of her choices, like leaving her Bible behind, but that didn't mean he didn't care for her. He always had and always would, and he shouldn't have said such things. Especially that she didn't accept him for who he was back then.

She had accepted him, to the best of her ability. She probably didn't understand the ways she didn't accept him, but her father had been right. She wouldn't have been happy, had he stayed in Chicago. He believed it to his core.

He'd been hurt at her calling him viperous and deceitful and that other word he couldn't even remember now, but he understood why she lashed out. He'd embarrassed her when he stopped the dance, but he assumed she'd take him to task for twirling her around like he had. What a foolish thing that had been, but she'd been so sweet, laughing like she had years ago.

He'd have to apologize, and do it right this time. Tell her the truth, or at least a version that wouldn't cause undue pain. Not that he wanted to have that discussion right this minute. Seeing her last night had sliced through him with greater efficiency than a skinning knife. But maybe in a day or two . . .

He'd worry about it in a day or two.

Lord, I said things I shouldn't have. But oh, this is harder than I want it to be.

Dash had asked Jesus to be his Lord when he was ten or thereabouts, before his mother died but after he'd met Abby. Seventeen years ago? A long time in some ways. He still had plenty of questions, and lacked confidence in his faith. He sought the approval of others more than he ought to. He didn't love the Lord more than himself, if he was honest. He wanted to, but did he really?

Maybe for five minutes. Then he put himself first again — he had things to prove, after all. To his father. To Abby's father. To Abby — or the shadow of her, anyway. Each time he achieved something, a thought burned in his brain, quick as lightning. *If only they could see me now.*

He'd spent the past six years working to be a man worthy of Abby in her father's eyes, even though Mr. Bracey would never have been pleased by Dash's job for the Secret Service. But Dash was starting to come to the understanding that he should be striving to be his best self, not to impress Abby's father or to prove something to the world.

He should be striving for the Lord and let the Lord sort it all out.

Thanks for the reminder, Lord. Now please help me to live it.

The bell over the door of the general store chimed at his entrance. Mr. Knapp, the proprietor, looked up from helping his sole customer, a gray-haired woman Dash recognized from the handkerchief dance at the mayor's birthday party.

"Hello." His shoes made damp thumps on the floor as he approached the counter.

The woman gave Dash a sly smile. "Hello, again. You tried to catch my handkerchief at the party."

"I did."

"I'd have let you, if I hadn't been instructed otherwise." Mercy, did her lashes flutter? "Won't you introduce us, Mr. Knapp?"

He stroked his neat mustache. "Mrs. Leary, meet Mr. Lassiter, the new hostler at the inn."

"How do you do?" She offered her hand.

After the exchange of pleasantries, Mrs. Leary tutted. "So you're the one who came to Wells for our new schoolmarm."

He forced a laugh. "Alas, schoolteachers must remain unwed."

"Perhaps that's why I never taught school." She cackled. "I'm a seamstress."

"You must employ Mrs. Story." At her arched brow, he grinned. "I live with Isaac Flowers."

"Ah, yes. They're becoming friends, aren't they? Mrs. Story isn't just my employee, you see. She and little Micah live in my spare rooms."

Mr. Knapp cleared his throat. "Speaking of your work, Mrs. Leary, did you care to finish selecting the notions for your order?"

She sighed and returned to the catalog on

the counter between them. "These and these."

"I shall put in for them. Anything else?"

"Not today. I must see to a few more errands and return to work. Nice to meet you, Mr. Lassiter."

He tipped his hat. "And you, Mrs. Leary."

Once he'd received his coffee from Mr. Knapp, Dash paid with a twenty-dollar bill, a far larger denomination than was necessary, but it ensured he'd receive several smaller bills in change in his never-ending quest to locate counterfeit currency. Since no one was in the store, he took his time, feeling the bills.

Mr. Knapp leaned over. "I didn't count right?"

"No, you did." Dash placed the bills in his wallet, two of which varied from the others in thickness. They were Pitch's. So, Pitch wasn't here but more of his bogus currency was. Coincidence, or had someone brought them here intentionally? "You ever have a problem with counterfeit money here in Wells, Knapp?"

"Once. Customer left a dollar on the counter and Oneida spilled her lemonade on it. I'd told her not to drink it in the store, but good thing she did, because it made the ink run."

Dash had seen that approach to counterfeiting a few times. The process was painstaking for the counterfeiter, requiring long hours copying a genuine bill. As long as the bill didn't get wet, it could pass muster. Pitch's work, however, didn't suffer the same weakness. His inks were of the highest quality.

Knapp shrugged. "I'm sure it was left by someone passing through. Wells isn't that type of town."

"I hope that's always the case." Tin of coffee in hand, Dash nodded farewell and ventured into the street. He nodded at Mrs. Leary, who'd paused several feet away to fiddle with her gloves, and started toward home and his plate of bacon.

The air was still, heavy, with that strange silence that happened in the summer when the bugs and frogs ceased their chirps and croaks for no discernable reason. Like something was about to occur. Odd. His next breath was tinged with cold and the peculiar smell of air before a lightning strike.

A roar thundered behind Dash, so loud and intense that his first thought was a train derailed. *But the train hasn't come to Wells yet.* The noise wasn't just in his ears, though. It was in his body, vibrating. He turned to look for the source of the clamor.

Dear God. The northwest sky was alive with a rolling black cloud, tumbling over itself toward town. Heart filling his throat, Dash rushed toward Mrs. Leary. He hadn't taken two steps when a violent blast of frigid wind hit them, knocking him sideways and stealing his hat. Mrs. Leary bent forward. No, she *was bent,* forced from behind, her head shoved almost to her knees. She pulled herself upright and it looked like she cried out, but any noise was carried away by a second gust, more powerful than the last. Far colder too.

Pain like a thousand needles pricked his face, hands, ears, the part of his neck not covered by his scarf. Shattered glass?

Ice crystals. Dash knew it the moment he saw what looked like flour caking Mrs. Leary's shoulders and hair.

He grabbed her arm, but she tugged away. "No!" Could she hear his shout? "We must get to safety!"

Her mouth worked, but he couldn't make out her words. But then he understood. Her bonnet had gone the way of his hat and she wanted it back.

The snow and wind seemed to be coming at them sideways, and the sting was unbearable. They couldn't retrieve hats or anything else, not now. But she pulled from his grasp, her gaze on the ground.

There was nothing for it. He scooped her into his arms.

The storm followed them inside the general store and sent papers flying in swirls of cold. Someone shut the door behind them — Mr. Knapp, speaking, but Dash still couldn't hear. His ears buzzed.

Dash lowered Mrs. Leary into a chair near the stove and then dropped to the ground at her feet. He was vaguely aware of Mr. Knapp covering his shoulders with a blanket.

"What's happened?" Mrs. Leary's tremulous voice was the first bit of conversation he comprehended.

Mr. Knapp went to the window. "Never seen a storm come on that fast."

Dash cleared his head with a shake. What time was it? Close to two, wasn't it?

If it was after two, then school was out for the day.

Abby.

Dash shoved the blanket from his shoulders and ran for the door.

CHAPTER 11

At first, Abby thought one of the children scraped a desk across the rough floor. Then she realized the noise was far too loud and persistent, like a trackless train sped toward the schoolhouse. The children rushed to the north windows.

A wall of dark cloud seemed to touch the ground. Before she could react, wind slapped the schoolhouse, shaking the door and windows and smacking them with hail — no, it was snow, loud as bullets but fine as powder, sneaking beneath the panes. And with it came cold.

In Chicago, she'd seen her share of wind and snowstorms, but there had been hints, warnings. A minute ago, she'd fancied spring. She'd never seen anything like this. *Lord, show me what to do. Keep the children here or send them home?*

She had little fuel left. No blankets. No food but for a little cider in the pot and half a kettle of water. She spun from the window.

"Children, don your coats and mittens, quickly. Coy, move away from the window. We haven't much time if you're to get home before the worst hits."

She could scarcely hear the children's excited chatter over the howling gusts of wind. Her hands fumbled with fastening buttons and searching for matching mittens. When the coat rack was empty, she grabbed her own coat and hat and surveyed her students.

Josiah, Vernon, and Robert wore denim jackets, little defense against the cold, but better protection than Oneida's linsey-woolsey dress or Florence's calico frock. "Have you no coats, girls?"

"Didn't need one this morning." Florence's voice was high with fear.

"You can have my sweater," Willodean offered.

"It's too small for me." Florence looked desolate.

The children offered solutions while Abby's mind raced. Aside from the two girls without coats, several hadn't brought mittens, hats, or scarves with them. She had a spare shawl in a desk drawer, since her workspace was so far from the stove. One girl could wrap in that, but the other?

Abby shrugged out of her coat and handed it to Florence. Oneida was much smaller, so Abby rushed to collect the shawl for her, offering her bonnet as well.

Then she opened the door and lost her breath. In those few minutes it had taken to put on outerwear, the storm had worsened. Though she faced south, away from the wind, snow as coarse as sand blew into her eyes and nose. The wind pushed her sideways.

She slammed the door shut.

"No going home," she yelled over the wind. "We'll stay here tonight."

Thank God for showing her what to do before she sent the children out in this.

Except . . . she had sent children home. Two. Berthanne and Almos . . .

Her stomach revolted. One hand went to her mouth. *Lord, please, don't let them be lost. Guide them to safety, oh please.*

Over a dozen pairs of eyes looked at her. She mustn't retch, mustn't frighten them any more than they already were. Except for Coy and Josiah, perhaps, for they were in the far corner of the vestibule dancing a jig about spending the night in school. Their antics were enough to settle her stomach so that she didn't require the slop bucket.

Yet.

"Let's return to our seats." She beckoned them within the schoolroom.

Zaida fingered her top button. "Shall we take off our coats?"

"I don't think so." It would get colder in here, but at least they had enough firewood to last the night. She gestured at Coy and Josiah. "Carry the logs inside for us, please."

"This'll be fun." Coy was grinning when he dropped an armful of logs in front of the box stove.

"I don't think so." Nellie huddled wide-eyed at her desk.

"Why don't we pray?" If there was ever a time for her to start praying in public again, it was now. "Lord, we know You are here with us, as You were with Jesus and the disciples on the storming Sea of Galilee, as You were with Jonah in the dark belly of the whale, as You've been with us our whole lives, snow or sun, good times and bad. We ask for Your protection, and we ask this with gratitude that You've provided us shelter. Thank You." Not wanting to frighten the children, she silently added a fervent prayer for Berthanne and Almos. "Amen."

A chorus of amens surrounded her.

"Now, I'll put more logs on the fire. You can work on your flowers or read or play quietly."

Quiet was too much to ask, with the wind lashing the school. Abby wasn't sure which was worse, the noise or the cold seeping in the cracks in the walls and under the door and windows like oil up a wick, saturating everything it touched.

Smack! The door had flung open, admitting a blast of cold, roaring wind. Abby rushed to shove it closed, but the latch wouldn't hold any longer. Pressing against the door with her back, she met the gaze of the curious, frightened students who followed after her. "Bring a desk."

Bartholomew and Josiah scrambled away and returned, carrying one of the plank desks. Coy carried another by himself. They shoved both desks against the door, barring it shut.

"Thank you, boys."

"What if we use up the fuel, ma'am?" Bartholomew whispered in her ear.

"We'll burn desks if necessary."

"Miss Bracey, what if my mama worries?" Micah's already large eyes were round and wide.

"I hope your mamas trust that you are safe here at the schoolhouse."

Kyle went still as stone, a first for him. "What if we're not safe?"

"We might be hungry by the time the

storm ends, but we shall persevere, snug around the stove." Although *snug* was too generous a word.

Willodean rubbed her eyes. "I want to go home."

A few of the younger children started to cry. Meanwhile the wind whipped up with such vigor that Abby wanted to wrap her arms around her head to block the noise.

But she couldn't. She had to be strong, brave for these little ones. "Come, let's push the desks away from the stove and all gather around it. I shall put the kettle on and we may all have a sip of tea."

"Mama says I can't have tea until I'm older," Willodean said.

"She won't mind today." Abby smiled. "While it heats, I'll read a story."

Mark, the Match Boy had enough of a plot to hold their interest. Adjusting her bustle behind her, she perched on the ground among her students and began the Horatio Alger story. The frigid floor stung her legs and feet, and the little box stove was not a match for the storm. Tonight would be uncomfortable, but they would survive.

She was thinking in terms of survival? Her stomach flopped again. *Do not retch. Oh, you mustn't let the children know how afraid you are.*

Had last night taught her nothing? She'd spent years talking to herself. It was time to talk to God.

Lord, we need Your strength and wisdom. Your peace.

"Miss Bracey, I'm scared," a small voice said.

She hadn't realized she'd stopped reading. "I am too, Micah. But courage isn't the absence of fear. It's striving despite it. We must all take courage today."

Micah nodded. Kyle dashed a tear from his cheek. Willodean stared at her boots.

"Think of the story we will tell our families later. Let's finish the story about Mark the match boy and —"

The scream of splitting wood had her on her feet. Impossible, but a section of vestibule ceiling was gone. Tattered tar paper whipped like a shredded sail, and snow swirled into the hole.

No matter how many desks they burned after the wood was gone, they would freeze to death before dawn.

Abby ordered the children into a line based on age, older, younger, older, younger, dispersing the stronger among the weaker. She went first, Willodean next. Coy volunteered to bring up the rear. Those without gloves pulled stockings over their hands, and she'd helped those without hats to pull their shirts or coats up about their ears.

Then, after scrawling their destination on the blackboard in case anyone came to the school looking for them, she'd taken the coil of twine she'd brought for the art projects and wrapped it around each child's waist, knotting it over and over. Pity they had nothing thicker, but thank God they had something to tether them together.

Lord, have mercy on us. Imbue this twine with the strength of iron and guide us straight on to Burt Crabtree's. Amen.

"If the person in front of you or behind you falls, help them to stand. We leave no one behind," she shouted, hoping they could hear her over the wind.

Since she'd given her coat to Florence and her shawl to Oneida, she wrapped her scarf about her head and tucked it into the neck of her blouse, leaving a small hole over her face for her eyes.

Ready, then.

She shoved away the desks in front of the door and stepped out. The vestibule had been frigid as an icehouse, but now that she was outside, the air smacked her face like a slap. There was no choice, however, but to step out into the blizzard. Into . . . a nothingness of white.

Where was the well? The cottonwoods, or the fence between the school and Mr. Crabtree's? All she could see was whipping snow, which grated like sand in her eyes. Keeping them open was agony. *Oh Lord, I'm blind. I'll get us lost.*

Her lungs ached, and she couldn't catch enough air to fill them. They were cold, yes, but panic also clawed at her chest.

Remain calm and think.

How far was Burt Crabtree's house? A hundred yards, as the crow flew? A map formed in her mind, simple but clear. Burt Crabtree's front door was due east of the schoolhouse and then a few paces north. She had the schoolhouse as a guide for now. Once the schoolhouse stopped, if she continued straight, she could find the well, and beyond it, the fence he'd been repairing. At the fence, she'd bear left, to the north, which was into the wind, but the fence would guide her for several paces before she and the children would have to climb over it and cross his yard. If she walked straight . . .

Easier said than done. The wind pushed from behind, knocking Willodean into her.

She turned around to set Willodean on her feet and then pressed her palm against the schoolhouse, starting their march east. At the end of the school, she took as deep a breath as she could manage. She must walk straight, eyes closed, to the well. Extending her hands ahead of her, she focused on her steps. *Straight line, straight line.* One after another.

Her foot thumped against something. The edge of the well's brick wall. *Thank You, Lord.* She gripped it for three steps until she had to let go in pursuit of Burt Crabtree's fence. She'd forgotten until this moment that it was barbed wire. It would hurt to touch and crawl over. The children would be cut or scraped.

Better that than frozen.

Her arm swept the air before her like a sideways pendulum, grasping for the fence. Step after step. The snow felt like fire, not ice, burning her beneath her clothes, and her heart raced from exertion and fear.

Something tugged her leg. Willodean? No, more like a bramble caught her skirt. *The fence. Thank You, Lord.* She focused on the imaginary map in her head. Now that she'd found the fence, she must walk, oh, twenty paces north before she'd be parallel with Burt Crabtree's porch. A pace was taken at full stride, however, and her windblown steps were shorter, labored and staggered.

Double the number, then. Forty steps. She counted as she traced the sharp fence with her hand as she struggled on. Later, she'd probably find wounds on her fingers, but she couldn't feel pain now. At thirty paces, the fence disappeared —

She groped. Opened her eyes and instantly regretted the pain, but she made out the dark, narrow shape of a Virginia rail fence. Burt Crabtree must not have replaced this section of his fencing with barbed wire yet. She'd cry an alleluia, had she sufficient breath, but she shouted it in her heart. This would be so much easier to climb over than barbed wire.

Maintaining contact with the wood, she stumbled forward, counting an additional ten steps before she stopped and hitched up her dress to climb over. She slid on landing but gripped the fence and leaned against it to assist Willodean over, then Florence. After that, she couldn't help anyone else. She had to move to make room for the others to get across. Squinting into the snow and wind, she plotted a step due east.

Now that she'd stopped, though, it was difficult to start again. Every muscle from her abdomen down ached, but at least she had sensation somewhere. She'd lost it in her hands and feet. Soon it would be over, if she and the children kept on —

Her ankle gave way, sending her tumbling forward. There must be a dip here, a small valley in the otherwise-flat field that had filled with snow. How far did it extend? Going through it would slow them down and make them wetter, colder. Going around it, she could lose her bearings.

Lord, show me where to go.

She scrambled to her feet. The fastest way out was through.

"It's deeper here," she yelled behind her. "Take care and tell the others."

Willodean tugged the twine. "They're saying no."

"What?" Oh, it hurt to talk. It hurt to breathe.

"Go back," Willodean shouted.

Sure enough, the bigger boys were yelling. ". . . getting us lost." Coy?

She was not getting them lost. Not if they went straight. She cupped her mouth to shout over her shoulder. "We can't go back. The school will be too cold."

"Better than dying out here." Was that Robert? "Let me out of this rope."

The twine at Abby's waist tugged hard enough to pull her backward. The children were trying to break free? Oh no. They mustn't separate from one another. If she could turn and comfort the children, she would, but if she did, she'd lose her bearings. Already she had to concentrate much harder than usual as to which direction was which.

She would not lose these children. Nor did she survive the past six years to die out here, like this. "You have come so far and been so brave. Only a little farther. Prepare to walk through a dip in the field."

Any grumbles were lost to the wind.

She had to lift her legs higher here — what about the younger ones? The twine about her waist tugged, pulled downward. Willodean had fallen. Abby turned and traced the twine downward to a bundle that must be Willodean. She opened her eyes a crack. "Can you stand?"

"I lost my shoe." Willodean was crying.

Abby hauled Willodean's solid weight into her arms. She tucked Willodean's stockinged foot beneath her arm. "I have you, darling."

She must keep moving forward . . . if that was the correct direction anymore. After turning to pick up Willodean, she wasn't sure if she'd pivoted back at an angle or not. Everything was white, above and below, side to side. White and so loud. She couldn't see Burt Crabtree's cottonwoods or his house. Nor could she walk straight, much less think straight anymore.

God, I came to You last night, to start anew. This isn't what I imagined You had in store for me, but You are with me. I believe it. I can't stand believing anything else.

Words floated into her mind from the Bible. Something about being placed somewhere at a moment, for a purpose, because of God's design.

Her foggy brain nudged her. It was from Esther, the woman God used to save her people. This was not the same scenario, of course. Abby did not equate her circumstances to Esther's. But the verse gave her comfort . . . if only she knew it by heart. When this was over, she'd have to seek it out in the Bible.

If she survived.

Oh, she was supposed to be counting her steps. How many paces to the house from the fence? She strained to recall her imaginary map. Thirty paces, so sixty steps? How many had she taken? Nine, maybe? So that was . . . fifty-some. Fifty-one, that's right. It shouldn't have taken her so long to execute so simple an equation, but her brain had gone soft as cornmeal mush.

And she'd forgotten to count her steps while she was subtracting. She trudged forward, gasping for breath.

Were others out in this? Had Hildie and Patty been outside hanging laundry when the blizzard hit? Had Bynum found shelter in the barn or in the house? Where was Dash? Snug in the stable with horses to help keep him warm? And Almos and Berthanne. If they died, it was all her fault.

Tears singed her face. Instinctively, she shifted Willodean and brushed at her eyes, and oh it hurt, like she scrubbed off delicate skin. Had her tears frozen her eyelids shut?

Don't think, just move. One step. Then another. Clutching Willodean, who was heavier by the moment. They had to be close to the house.

Wind blasted her back, thrusting her and Willodean forward. She twisted as she fell, so she wouldn't land atop Willodean. As she twisted, something struck her head. Hard. Pain reverberated from her forehead down to her teeth, and bright squiggles danced before her eyes. She fell to the ground.

Had she hit a tree branch? Maybe his barn or his house? If she reached out again, found it, she could trace it to the front door.

Her arms stretched, finding nothing. She tried again. Oh, they were empty. She'd been carrying something, though, hadn't she? A precious bundle? Yes, something important, although she'd forgotten what it was.

Willodean. That's what — who — she'd been carrying. What was happening to her? Her mind wasn't working right. Everything was foggy. And she couldn't find the where-withal to stand.

Do not rest. You're not finished yet.

But it was comfortable here, down on the ground. Her arms and legs were so heavy. Maybe if she rested a moment she'd have the strength to try again. Her head didn't hurt so badly anymore.

Her eyes cracked open. White, then darkness. Light. Dash's face, surrounded by a golden glow.

She must have died, out in the snow.

CHAPTER 12

"Abby, wake up. Wake up, honey." Dash's lips brushed her crimson, swollen eyelids, then her cold temple. She shivered so hard.

Her eyes opened a crack then shut again. He'd have to get her closer to the stove but — something yanked him back. A small figure flopped to the floor behind him and cried out.

"They're tied together." Burt tugged at twine connecting Willodean and Abby. "Knotted. I can't tear it. I'll get a knife from the kitchen."

That would take twenty seconds too long.

Hang propriety. Dash laid Abby on the floor and pulled up her skirt, exposing her shins. There it was, the knife gartered to her black stocking. He untied it, re-covered her legs, and snipped the twine between her and Willodean. He cut the tether between a few more children before Burt returned.

Not one of the children had said a word.

All shivered, and half of them slumped to the floor inside Burt's door. "We need blankets. Towels. Anything."

Burt didn't answer but disappeared. Dash carried Abby into the parlor off the foyer to the coal stove, where he and Burt had huddled moments before. He snatched a lap rug from a chair and laid the heavy wool over Abby's torso. "I'll be back, Abby. Don't you slip away on me now. Wake up and yell at me."

He hated to leave her, but the children needed help too. Some of the older ones walked unassisted, but he had to carry a few of the little ones to the parlor. So did Burt, who'd dropped blankets and towels on the floor to lend a hand. Dash arranged the children around the coal stove in a crescent, and not a one said anything. Not a complaint, cry, or groan. It was far more disturbing than tears. Their silence meant they were shocked to their cores.

"Come on, everyone. Snuggle up. Here's a blanket." He passed out the odd assortment of Burt's rugs, blankets, and towels.

Burt stroked his beard. "Crowded in here. Should we put some in the kitchen?"

"Not unless there's room for all in the kitchen. We need to stay together."

"I guess that's right. Conserve body heat."

Burt paused. "Glad you're here. You know more about this sort of thing than I do."

Dash didn't know much, though. He'd never felt so ill-equipped for anything in his life.

None of his skills — riding and tending horses, shooting game, chasing counterfeiters and boodle carriers — was of any use in a blizzard.

The pulsing thrum of wood on wood sounded from the foyer. Dash clambered over the children to the front door. Slender snakes of snow slithered in from the crevices around the door, which vibrated on the latch. The sound was almost scarier than the moan of the wind.

"Can we stop it?" Burt pushed at the door, as if willing it to stillness.

"It'll stop when it freezes shut." Dash shuddered from the cold here in the small foyer. "Too bad the parlor doesn't have a door. We're going to have a hard time keeping it warm."

"I figured you and I can haul the mattress from upstairs down here to block off the entrance. It's not the best solution, but it's all I can think of."

"It's better than nothing." Dash clapped Burt on the shoulder. "First let's get what we need from the kitchen. We could all use some liquid, I'd guess."

"Hot water, for starters."

"Make it warm instead. We need to thaw them out slowly. Like you do with frostbite." At the word, something twanged up Dash's leg, and he winced. Maybe not frostbite, but his nerves were coming back to life.

Burt didn't own enough mugs for everyone, but no one complained about sharing when he and Dash served six mugs full of lukewarm water. Everyone had recovered enough to sit up and sip except for Abby, who was still on the floor.

Burt led the way upstairs, and they made quick work of stripping the bed and hauling the bedclothes and mattress downstairs, blocking the parlor entry with it. They'd just finished when Abby groaned.

"Berthanne, Almos?"

He rushed to her side, caressing her cold cheek. "They're here, Abby. All your students are here at Burt Crabtree's, safe and sound."

"No we're not." Micah Story spoke through trembling lips. "They got sent home early."

"On account of the skunk." The biggest boy rubbed his forehead.

"Where are they?" Abby pushed up to her elbows. She didn't seem awake yet, like she was still in the throes of a nightmare. He hadn't noticed until now that her forehead sported a burgeoning goose egg. She'd hit her head?

Dash found her icy hands. "They're probably at home, snug by their fires." He hoped so, anyway.

"Oh." Her eyes lost the crazed look, and her chin started to tremble along with the rest of her. She must be coming back to her senses. "It's my fault."

A little girl wearing a too-large bonnet shuffled on her bottom toward Abby. "No it's not. You warned Almos what would happen if he brought Stripey to school again."

"Thank you, Oneida. But I didn't expect this storm."

Dash tucked the lap rug tighter about her. "Is that why you don't have a coat on?"

"She gave her coat to me." A taller girl started to shrug out of her blanket and work at buttons at her throat. "She can have it back now."

"Nonsense." Abby made a show of snuggling within the lap rug. "I'm fine like this."

Of course Abby gave up her coat. The girl offered a small smile and refastened the buttons.

At least the children were talking now.

Her gaze swept over the children, as if she

counted them. "I'm so glad to see you all." She staggered to her feet and embraced each child. Every one of them hugged her back.

When she'd finished, Abby glanced around the sparsely furnished room, with its threadbare chairs and the eggshell-colored drapes, which looked to have been fashioned by Burt tacking unsewn rectangles over the windows. "So we're at Mr. Crabtree's? I don't remember getting here."

"You fell against the house. The wall behind you, in fact. We heard the thump over the wind. Burt and I went out and there you all were."

Her eyes closed. "Thank God."

"Amen to that." Dash offered her a sip of lukewarm water. "It's not hot. Trying to warm you by degrees. Anyway, why'd you leave the school?"

"The roof."

"It fell in," Kyle Queen said, his hands gesticulating beneath the blanket wrapped around him. "The snow was comin' in."

"That sounds scary." Burt swigged some water.

"It was." Kyle's head swiveled to meet Burt's gaze. "But it got scarier when we went outside."

Micah shuddered. "My mama doesn't

know where I am. I'm not supposed to go anywhere without telling her first. No stranger's houses."

"I'm certain she won't mind today." Abby dropped to the floor again. "I wrote our destination on the blackboard. If anyone comes to the school, they'll know we came here."

A girl frowned. "Unless the school fills with snow."

"It probably won't get as high as the blackboard, Zaida." Abby's gaze drew his. "What are you doing here at Mr. Crabtree's, Dash?"

"I was —"

"Owwww." Kyle clutched his foot.

Dash and Burt went to the boy. "What hurts?"

"My feet."

"Let me see." Dash gently unlaced the boy's boots. He wore no socks beneath.

Abby's hand went to her mouth. "He wore them as gloves."

The foot was cold as stone and whitish yellow on the bottom, but not ashen. "I think it's superficial. The cold numbed it and it's waking up."

Burt took the boy's feet in his hands and rubbed briskly. "Your ma's the baker, isn't she?"

"Yes sir."

Burt caught the boy's gaze. "How old are you?" It was kind of Burt to help distract the lad.

"Eight, sir."

"I'm eight too," a round-cheeked boy added. "So's Micah. My name's Bud."

The rest of the children offered their ages, but Dash focused on the boys Abby investigated. Which one was Fletcher Pitch's son? Thankfully, they need not figure it out right now. The one blessing in this storm was that Pitch wouldn't be arriving in Wells for a few days. Dash doubted there'd be any way in or out of town until Saturday at least. He and Abby could relax on that front.

Well, *relax* wasn't the right word. His nerves were tighter than a violin's strings, and his toes felt like he was stepping on a dozen straight pins. "Does anyone else have tingling or pain?"

"I do." One of the bigger boys lifted his head. Josiah? The girl with the too-large bonnet raised a finger.

"What hurts?"

"My whole body," the boy said.

"How about you?" he asked the girl.

"My feet."

"I'll start with you, ma'am." She could have frostbite, which was more urgent than awakening nerves or strained muscles. "What's your name?"

"Oneida. Are you a doctor?"

"He ain't," the Knapp boy said before Dash could answer. "He's a hostler at the inn."

"That's right." Dash smiled as he examined Oneida's ice-cold toes. "I'm not even an animal doctor, but you all are about the same size as goats and ponies, so I'm pretty comfortable offering you aid."

Some of them laughed. Good. It was still far too quiet in here, considering there were sixteen children in close quarters.

Thankfully, her toes didn't look as if they required a snow rub, and upon examination, it was clear Josiah's aches were not from any injury. "Wiggle your fingers and toes, everyone, and every few minutes stretch your legs out."

"Why?" The biggest boy looked at him like he was eccentric.

"Keeps your blood moving." He added coal to the fire. "You can let Kyle's feet go now, Burt. I think they'll be fine."

"Oh. Sure." Burt's hands fell away. "Say, I don't know why I didn't think of it before, but I've got more socks upstairs. I'll fetch those."

"That'd be a help, thanks. We should

243

probably think of some victuals since we're moving the mattress. I'd hate to let our heat out more than once."

"I'll help." Abby pushed off her rug.

Dash pointed a finger. "You'll stay put."

"Listen to the goat doctor, Miss Bracey," Willodean insisted.

Abby rolled her eyes, and the children giggled again.

There were few moments of levity after that, though. After dispensing his thick wool socks to the children in need, Burt warmed several cans of beans. They all took turns eating off the shared plates, but no one took more than a few bites, not even the bigger boys.

No one was hungry. Not even Dash. The howling wind robbed their appetites.

Abby asked if Burt had any books she could read aloud, but Burt apparently wasn't much of a reader, for he didn't have so much as a farmer's almanac. Darkness fell, and before long, the children fell asleep, as only children can do, oblivious to noise. Maybe some played possum, like Burt, who made himself comfortable in an old rocking chair with a ratty blanket over him, but Willodean's breathing was even and deep as she snuggled against Abby.

Dash would probably get yelled at for the

impropriety of it, but he didn't care. He tiptoed across the crescent of children to drop beside Abby. "Are you asleep?"

"No." Her whisper was just loud enough for him to hear. "It's too loud and . . . cold."

He touched her forehead. "You're warmer than you were."

"Everything hurts, Dash. Burns."

"You weren't wearing much protection, but it wouldn't have mattered anyway in a storm like this. We need to warm up, is all."

"Why did you tell us to wiggle our fingers and toes?"

"I've heard tales of folks surviving severe cold, curled into themselves to stay warm, but then once the storm passes and they stand, it's like their hearts give out. None of us were still for that long, though, so it shouldn't be a problem. Nevertheless, I want to be careful."

With gentle slowness, she scooted away from Willodean and sat up, facing him. Her eyes looked black in the low light of the kerosene lamp they'd left burning. "Why are you here? Were you visiting Burt?"

"Not quite. I was in town, aiming for the school, following the fence line, but turns out I walked right past it and came here instead. Burt convinced me to take shelter here, much as I didn't want to. I thought

I'd thaw out a few minutes and then go to the school."

Her swollen eyes blinked. "Why were you going to the school?"

She really didn't know? His hand traced the curve of her cheek down to her chin. "For you, Abby. I had to find you before it was too late."

Abby's brain had thawed enough for her to follow conversation and subtract sixty minus nine, but she didn't understand what Dash was talking about. "Too late for what?"

"Too late to stop you from going out in the storm. I couldn't bear the thought of you out in this." He swallowed hard. "Especially not with everything that happened between us. I had to tell you how sorry I am for what I said."

He came out in this, to apologize? "Dash, no. I'm the sorry one. I said horrible things. You never should have gone out in the snow for that. If something had happened to you, I wouldn't have been able to bear it."

At the quiver in her voice, Dash pulled her into his arms. He wasn't warm, but his arms were strong, and she didn't fight the comfort she found nestled against his chest.

His fingers traced the edge of the scarf she'd wrapped over her ears and neck, trac-

246

ing where its edges met her skin. "It's all right now."

"It's not, not with Berthanne and Almos out there —"

"Maybe. You got here. It's likely they made it home too."

Lord, make it so. But that didn't mean everyone she cared about was safe. "Hildie and Patty did laundry today. And Bynum was outside too. What if they're — you know."

"I'm sure they're well, Abby."

"I've never felt like this. Like there's a sense of loss looming over me, heavy and mean as those clouds."

His dry lips pressed her temple. "Your body is in shock. Focus on the moment, where God has you in His hand. Everything is in His hands, whether you believe it or not."

She shifted, and he loosened his hold as if he expected her to pull away. But she didn't lean back. Not yet. His arms were safe, although it was different than the last time she'd been in his embrace. Back then, he smelled of soap and starch, and he'd have stolen a dozen kisses by now.

But a lot had changed in six years.

"I left my Bible in Chicago. On purpose."

"I thought so."

"I've been angry for so long. At God, and Father, and you. Last night I prayed, though. You were right, what you said about me. I'm a bitter shell."

She pulled back then. She'd given in to temptation for long enough, curling into his arms. But who knew if Burt Crabtree or any of the children were awake?

Dash let her go, tracing his hands down her arms. When he didn't speak, she licked her lips. "Maybe God brought us together again to write a better ending to our story. One where we can walk away as friends, or at least do our jobs without arguing every moment. Do you think we can, Dash?"

His gaze held hers, his pupils dark and shiny as wet ink. "I do."

It almost sounded like a vow.

"We should get some sleep. It will be a long night."

The wind answered, thunderous and long, before quieting enough for Dash to speak. "Good night, Abby."

He returned to the other side of the half circle formed around Burt's coal stove, leaving her to curl up to Willodean and listen to the wind howl. None of her students stirred, but she could see the lamplight reflected in Dash's eyes as he sat up to tend the stove.

Knowing he watched over them, she lay down again, listening to the wind.

CHAPTER 13

None of them slept well except for Willodean. Abby was up several times helping her students with cups of water, finding the slop bucket, and attempting to make them more comfortable on the hard, cold floor. Occasionally, either Burt or Dash tended to the stove. Wind still lashed the dark house when Burt tossed his blanket aside and said something to Dash about breakfast.

Abby disentangled herself from Willodean and, tucking the child back under her blanket, slunk after Burt. Dash, his lean cheeks thick with stubble, rose and followed after. She'd never seen him with a night's worth of beard before, and the sight of it did strange things to her stomach.

Foolishness. She must be hungry, that was all. Without speaking, the three adults shifted the mattress out of the way and entered the ice-cold foyer. The stark white-washed kitchen wasn't any warmer, but there were children to feed.

"I hate inconveniencing you like this, Mr. Crabtree." Abby's whisper didn't quite convey how sorry she was. "I'll make sure you're repaid to replenish your supplies."

And rather meager supplies they were too. Tins and crocks formed short stacks on the shelves by the dry sink, enough for one man for a week, but the house was full of growing children, including ravenous adolescent boys. Unless he had additional stores in the cellar, there wasn't much to eat.

He didn't meet her gaze, shy man that he was. "It's all right. And I think under these circumstances, you can call me Burt." He blocked her view to light the stove. "I've got cornmeal, but it occurs to me we're low on water."

Dash's gaze scanned the room. "Got a bucket? I can go out for some snow."

The wind's howl curled the hair at Abby's nape. "You're not going out in that."

"Just my arm. I'll stick it out the window." He pointed at the window above a tiny table for two.

Burt rubbed his unkempt hair. "Bucket is, um, in the cellar."

"I'll go." Dash stepped for the narrow door off the kitchen.

"Allow me. Stay here where . . . it's

warmer." Burt hurried through the small door.

As the sound of his footsteps descending the stairs grew fainter, Dash tilted his head. "You get the feeling Burt was a city fellow before deciding to try his hand at ranching?"

"What makes you say that?"

"He doesn't seem well versed in country life. Not a lot of provisions stocked in case of bad weather. Not to mention his house is plain."

"It's austere, but he is a bachelor."

"So am I, but I keep a tintype of my parents propped on my nightstand. His bedroom's as bare as the rest of the place."

"He must not have parents. Or he's starting fresh in the brisk Nebraska air."

Dash laughed. "Brisk is right." He shoved his hands in his coat pockets. "Oh, I forgot. This is yours. Handy little knife."

He handed her the blade she kept tied to her stocking. "Pray tell, how did you come to be in its possession?"

He opened the cornmeal tin, avoiding her gaze. "You weren't awake yet, but I needed a knife to cut the twine. I — I'm sorry, Abby. I knew you kept it just above your boot."

Oh well. He'd seen her ankles and knees a

thousand times at the swimming hole when they were children. She dropped the knife into her pocket. "I suppose modesty had to make way for urgency."

"All I cared about was untethering you all so we could warm you up. You were so cold and I thought, well, never mind." He stepped closer, reaching over her shoulder for a small jug of molasses.

"Was I that bad?"

"For a minute, I thought so." He didn't move back, but stood there holding molasses and the open tin of cornmeal, looking down at her with sorrowful eyes. Was that what Mrs. Queen had meant by his puppy-dog eyes? "Anyway, I hope you've never had to use that little knife."

She shook her head, and when the intensity of his gaze became too much, she peered down and gauged the amount of cornmeal in the tin. Enough for breakfast. "It's there if necessary, though."

"It was necessary last night. Oh, hey, Burt, didn't hear you come up the stairs." Dash set the cornmeal and molasses on the tiny worktable by the stove. "Mind if I open this window to get some snow? It'll make a mess."

Burt shrugged — hard to tell whether he minded or not. It must be difficult for a shy man to have so many strangers in his home.

Abby couldn't watch when Dash shoved the window open and let the shrill wind into the kitchen. Ignoring the noise and the blast of cold at her back, she poured what water remained in the kettle into the stove pot and set it on to boil. The stove's heat seeped through her clothes in a delightful wave, and she focused on it, rather than what was happening behind her.

"Do you have lard and flour, Burt?"

"Um, no. Why? You put it in the mush?"

The man clearly didn't cook. How did he get past thirty eating nothing but tins of beans? "I thought if I fried the mush, we could eat with our fingers, since there aren't enough bowls or utensils." She gestured eating a patty of mush with her hands.

"Oh, sure, yeah." He scratched his beard. "Well, I've got half a ham in the cellar. We can cut some fat off of that."

"You have ham?" Her stomach rumbled. "I don't wish to eat you out of house and home, but what else do you have in the cellar, if I may be so bold to ask?"

"Three potatoes."

What little food he had. Good thing Abby had years of practice with rationing food. "I'll trouble you for a fatty slice of that ham, then. We'll leave the rest of it for later, if we need it. Otherwise it will make you a fine supper."

"Here." With a thunk, Dash set the snow-filled bucket at her elbow.

She gasped. His face was bright pink, his nose redder than beetroot, his sleeve coated in white. "Dashiell Lassiter, stand here until you're warm."

"I won't argue with you."

She turned back. "Do you have coffee, Burt?"

He took down another tin. "Already ground."

Ah, the expensive stuff. "I shall let you make the coffee, then, while I see to the mush." She scooped hard, crystalline snow from the bucket and dropped the spoonful into the pot.

Burt put the coffeepot on the back burner. "I'll go get that ham."

Dash shifted closer to the stove. "I'll go back to the children as soon as I thaw out. Don't want to scare them by going back there looking like a snowman."

"Snowmen are round and sweet, Dash. You look nothing like that."

"I may not be round." He patted his flat stomach. "But I hoped I was sweet."

She pretended to consider. "Maybe after you eat some molasses."

He laughed. "I don't like molasses."

"Yes, you do."

"No, sorry."

She blinked. "But all of those cookies I used to make for you were molasses. Year after year. You should've told me."

"I may have been Dim-witted Dash, but I was never so daft that I'd tell you I didn't like your cooking."

Despite calling himself that horrible name, he was grinning, so she smacked him with a dish towel.

"Of all the despicable things." Her lips curved up as the water boiled. She gathered a handful of cornmeal and dropped it into the steaming pot. Burt had one large spoon, and she used it to beat the contents. "What I wouldn't give for a pudding stick."

"For the mush?"

"And to shake at you, for never telling me you hated my cookies."

"Just admit I'm a sweet fellow to have eaten your bad cookies."

"They weren't bad."

"They were molasses, so, they were bad."

"You are not sweet, Dash."

"Yes I am."

She tossed the dish towel at him and he burst out laughing.

Burt returned with a burlap-wrapped

hunk the size of a honeydew. "What's going on in here?"

Dash swiped a lone tear from his eye. "I don't like molasses."

"That makes no sense to me, but that's all right. I thought you were laughing on account of the wind stopping."

Abby gaped. He was right. It was quiet.

"Praise God." Dash let out a whoop.

"Now you've woken the children," she teased.

Burt chuckled. "They probably weren't asleep anyway, and no doubt they heard you laughing the same as I did."

"They'll get a good laugh out of my fried mush too." Abby added another handful of meal. "But they'll be happiest about the news we can all go home now."

Dash glanced out the window at the darkness. "We need full daylight to see what we're up against, but if it's not deep, maybe we can borrow your rig, Burt. You have a sled? Dray?"

Burt shrugged. "No. Sorry."

Dash met Abby's gaze. "With the children, we're going to need to wait for help, then."

"You're right." Abby was disappointed. Nevertheless, the children would be looking to them for clues as to how to respond to their extended confinement. "Dash, can you slice some fat off the ham and put it into that pan there? And Burt, will you please tell the children we'll eat in ten minutes?"

"Yes, ma'am."

Dash found a knife and worked at the ham. After he cut off a piece, he held the pan out for her inspection. "This enough?"

"More would be better."

"These knives are terrible. They need a good sharpening. I should've used yours."

"You hush, Dash Lassiter. That's private."

Grinning, Dash continued to saw away at the ham. It was indeed taking him a long while, but she needed extra time for the mush to cool enough to handle, anyway.

Once the grease melted somewhat, Abby molded the mush into patties and fried them. It was not the best-looking fried mush she had ever made, but the fat infused a tasty flavor to it, and everyone ate his or her share, huddled around the coal stove in Burt's parlor.

Micah wiped his lips. "Can we go home now?"

"Soon." Abby explained it was safer to stay put until help came.

No one looked happy at that, and soon after they'd finished their mush, the children grew restless. Without books, toys, or games, there were few options to keep them occupied. The girls were weary of cat's cradle, and a game of Duck Duck Goose ended with Josiah tripping over Florence's arm and knocking Burt's chair sideways. When Abby put a stop to that, the boys fashioned a ball by tying someone's gloves by the fingers until it formed a lumpy shape. The ball smacked Oneida on the side of the head, so Abby caught it. "Shall we play something quieter? Like Buzz?"

"Aw." Coy never liked the counting game when they played it in class, where the first person started with one, the second counted two, and so on until they reached seven. Sevens were replaced with the word *buzz,* as were multiples of seven. If you made a mistake, you were out, and it went until only one person was left. "I'd rather go home."

"Me too, but look," Dash said. "The sun's coming up."

The children pushed against one another to claim vantage at the parlor window. Abby stood back but could see enough. Pink tinged the gray horizon, shifting to lilac then the faintest of blues as they watched. Not a single cloud marred the sky. Soon the sun would be high enough to fully illumine the landscape, but there was sufficient light to make out large drifts piled against the barn and cottonwoods.

Dash turned to Burt. "Let's go to your barn."

Abby's stomach lurched. "Is it safe?"

"I think so. Looks like there are some drifts out there, but it's not too deep in places. Ready to climb out the window with me, Burt?"

"Why do you want to go to the barn?" Burt's brows lowered.

"Jasper and any other animals you've got. Their water's undoubtedly frozen solid, and they'll have eaten most if not all their hay. I'll lend you a hand."

"I'll go. My horse, my responsibility." He sounded perturbed.

Dash's eyes rounded. "I'm happy to do it myself —"

"No. You stay here. You're, er, guests."

At his brusque departure, Dash rubbed the back of his neck. "I didn't mean any harm, but the animals need tending. I would have done it so he didn't have to. Fact is, I'd have liked to look in on Jasper since I saw to a wound of his."

"Burt's overwhelmed by things, I guess." Like his home overrun with veritable strangers. To a bachelor accustomed to a quiet house, this must be exhausting. She turned to the children. "Come, let's play Buzz. Sit in a circle."

They'd had enough of sitting still, though. Bud and Kyle, in particular, fidgeted, and Micah and Jack were on the periphery of their peers' antics. When the game ended, the young boys rolled over one another like puppies. Abby was loath to discipline them for being energetic children, but she had to intervene before they broke furniture or hurt someone. "Boys, we are guests. No horseplay."

When Burt returned, his brows were still knit in a knot above his nose. Was he upset at the children's behavior?

"Animals all right?" Dash looked up.

"Fine."

Abby tried to meet Burt's gaze, but he still avoided looking at her. "I'm terribly sorry for the disturbance we've caused you."

"Don't be. They're bored." Burt waved his hand. "You younger boys, come here. Let's start a game of Goose."

"You have a board game?" Abby felt as if she'd been tossed a rope to cling to after falling down a well.

"No, but I have pencils and paper and a pair of scissors. We can make the board ourselves. I'm pretty good at recollecting things and drawing them once I see them."

"What an amazing gift." Abby envied it.

"I want to help," Willodean offered.

He turned in Abby's direction, his gaze on her hem. "Not a lot of room over here." In other words, he had all he could handle with Micah, Kyle, Bud, and Jack.

Dash rubbed his hands together. "Maybe the rest of us can find objects to be the game's stakes and counters. Buttons or straw or something."

"But I want to draw," Willodean protested.

Abby laid a hand on Willodean's shoulder. "How about paper dolls, since Mr. Crabtree has paper?"

"I want to do that too," Nellie said. All the girls echoed the sentiment.

As Abby assisted the girls in tracing and cutting, she kept an eye on Dash, who'd not been able to find more than matchsticks for the counters, so he'd assigned the boys to make stakes out of the girls' scrap paper.

Dash moved to the front window then turned and beckoned to her. Stepping over the children, she joined him, curious as to what the full morning light revealed of the world after the blizzard. Dash stepped aside and pulled back the rough drape so she could see.

Beneath a blue sky, the snow spread as far as she could see like white flannel encrusted with diamonds, shining in the morning sun. Drifts piled against the cottonwoods and fence, but otherwise, the snow wasn't as deep as she'd expected. Nothing moved, and nothing held color but the sky. Beautiful. But at what price?

Were the people she cared for safe? Almos and Berthanne. Hildie, Bynum, and Patty. Her students' families. Were they looking out at a similar view from their warm houses? Or were they in trouble?

Tears prickled her sore eyes.

Dash shifted toward her. "You all right?"

She couldn't speak without crying, so she offered a tremulous smile and turned back to the children. Burt had tacked four sheets of paper together to form the board. It was clearly recognizable as the game of Goose, with its numbered squares from one to sixty-three leading players on a spiral journey through hazards like the prison and inn toward the end. Parts were drawn with childish hands, but the path was expertly done, drawn by Burt's steady hand.

There were too many children to all play at once, so Abby counted them off into four groups. The first group stood in a small circle. Josiah pointed his finger into the middle. "I'll count us off. 'He had money and I had none, and that was the way the quarrel begun as O-U-T. Out!'"

"Aw," Coy said. "I'm out."

"At least you're playing before the rest of us," Zaida chided him from her spot on the floor, chin resting on her fist.

Hopefully they wouldn't need to invent many more activities for the children before help arrived. They had shelter, though. She would have to cling to her blessings. Who knew what waited for them outside? When they learned the full effect of the storm, it might be difficult to find joys amid the losses.

At lunchtime, Dash carved into Burt's ham with the blunt kitchen knife. The children ate and sipped water, but he could hear a few stomachs rumbling for more. Their hunger and boredom surely contributed to the increase in bickering in the parlor. A handful of girls quarreled about who would play the Goose game again, and the boys resumed tossing their homemade balls. One smacked Dash in the neck.

If it was just him, or him and Abby, they could leave on foot. But it was too cold to attempt walking the children to their various homes, especially when he had no idea what the roads were like. Things would be faster and safer with a rig to carry them all, which Burt did not have.

With an ear-splitting screech, Willodean

flopped to the floor like a fish.

He knelt before her, hands on her shoulders. "What is it?" Pain? Hunger? A temper tantrum? "Do you hurt, sweetheart?"

She couldn't talk for crying. Abby brushed past Dash and took her in hand, murmuring soothing sounds that hit Dash somewhere beneath his rib cage. He'd always known Abby would make a good mother. Why hadn't she married someone else and started a family by now?

Abby looked up. "I think she's spent. The wind, the cold, confinement."

And fear. Even now, its chilling breath hung in the room, an invisible sense that life at this moment was not normal. Hard enough for an adult to face terror like this, but for a little one like Willodean? She was just a little thing. Almost a baby.

Dash tugged his extra-large hankie from his waistcoat pocket. Ridiculous, how big it was, but it served him well during times of winter illness. "Here, Willodean. It's a mite big, but it used to belong to a friend of mine. Giant of a fellow, seven feet tall and broad as a bear." He comically dabbed the hankie over Willodean's face.

She sputtered, but at least she'd stopped crying. "Was he really a giant?"

"Well, this here hankie was the size of his

hand." He held up his hand beside the larger handkerchief in comparison.

"You're fibbing."

"Am I?"

Abby mouthed, "Thank you." It was obvious she was scrambling to come up with something new to occupy the students. Her brows lifted. "Let's sing."

"Sing what?" Micah, who like Kyle, Bud, and Jack had attached himself to Burt since making the game board, resumed his place by the stove.

"Anything."

Never a good singer, Dash snuck backward until Willodean tugged him into the semicircle. She pointed from him to the ground. "Sit with me."

"Yes, ma'am." He hoped he knew the words to the songs.

Abby grinned. "Let's start with patriotic tunes."

The students stopped fidgeting to sway or bob their heads, and sometimes clap. When they'd exhausted "Battle Hymn of the Republic" and the other songs they knew, they moved on to hymns and then Christmas carols. Christmas wasn't that long ago, and everyone knew verse after verse.

"What next?" Abby asked. " 'Silent Night'?"

Bang bang.

Abby gasped and a few children shrieked. Dash hopped to his feet.

"What was that? The roof again?" Zaida's voice was shrill with fear.

"Not the roof." Dash shoved the mattress aside. "Sounded like the door. Stay here where it's warmer."

Burt followed and tugged on the front door, but it didn't give. He cursed — hopefully none of the young ones heard it.

"Is someone there?" Dash leaned close to the door and yelled.

"Bynum Elmore here." His smacks echoed through the door.

A loud cheer erupted behind Dash. Abby and the children hadn't stayed in the warmer parlor but filled the foyer. Their happy smiles, especially Willodean's, warmed Dash better than the coal stove had done. He turned back to the door. "Door's frozen shut. Go to the kitchen window and I'll meet you."

Within minutes, he and Burt reopened the kitchen window and admitted Bynum Elmore and three other fathers. Willodean leapt into Bynum's arms. Bob Ford kissed his children, Elkanah Topsy gripped his boys in an embrace, and Gilbert Knapp swiped away a discreet tear when Zaida and Ches-

267

ter grabbed him about the waist.

"Where's our pa?" Vernon moved close to Florence.

Bynum lifted his head from Willodean's neck. "Waiting for you at home, I expect. I found Ford on the way to the school, and we encountered Knapp and Topsy coming from town. Thanks for leaving the note on the board for us, Miss Abby."

"Hildie and Patty? Are they —"

"Fine. Worried sick about you and Willodean."

"Thank God." Abby's relief was palpable. "Did you encounter anyone else on your way here?"

"Like who?" Bynum set Willodean down and shook Dash's hand.

"Almos and Berthanne Sweet. I had to send them . . . I sent them home early." Her face mottled.

"We'll find them." Dash rested a hand on her shoulder. Thankfully, she didn't shrink away from his touch.

"I'll help look." Her chin lifted.

"Actually, Miss Bracey, we were thinking you could come back to town." Knapp caught her gaze. "We decided my store would be a central location for folks to meet up and claim their young'uns, if you wouldn't mind."

Dash could tell she'd rather search for the Sweet children, but she nodded. "Sounds smart."

"I'll come too," Burt offered.

Abby turned to him. "Thank you for your hospitality, Burt. If you hadn't welcomed us in, I don't know what we would have done."

His cheeks reddened above his beard. "My pleasure. Glad I could get acquainted with the children I see playing every day."

It didn't take long to load everyone onto the drays the men had brought, wood boards fixed atop sled runners. The temperature was still shockingly low, but the children's spirits were high. They chattered as if they were on a sleigh ride.

Dash's mood wasn't light, however. The world looked altogether foreign. Above, sun dogs shone on either side of the sun, blinding him in their intensity. On the ground, drifts clumped as tall as a man, especially against buildings and fences, but in other areas, the snow was shallow — or non-existent. Here and there, the wind had stripped away the snow down to the bare dirt. And everywhere, the landscape was dotted with snowy brown lumps. Frozen cattle. It was enough to set anyone on edge.

It didn't help that he was hungry and tired. He'd gone days without sleep before, hunting counterfeiters and smugglers for the Secret Service, but there was something different about this experience. Maybe it also had something to do with knowing at the end of a long night following a suspect, he could return to his quarters, fill his stomach, and sleep.

Sleep would be a long time coming, however. Wells wasn't his community, and he'd never met Berthanne or Almos Sweet, but he cared for the people here, and he wouldn't rest until those children were found. They, or any others who might be lost.

And there would be losses, even if the community didn't lose a soul to this blizzard. Lost livestock and sources of income. Damage to buildings. Dash could only pray that would be the worst of it.

Main Street was eerie in its silence, but the general store was almost a shock to him, with its loud activity and warmer temperature. Dash hadn't been inside three seconds before someone pressed a hot mug of coffee into his hands. He took a moment to gulp it and a warm, flaky biscuit — oh, he'd never tasted anything better — before preparing to head out to look for the Sweet children.

Someone grabbed him from behind in a fierce bear hug.

He craned his neck. "Isaac. Why are you here?"

"Because Geraldine was fretting about Micah, so I said I'd find him, but I missed the group who went to the school. And because you, my friend, were missing." He released Dash.

My friend.

A surge of affection rushed through Dash. Isaac had become a good friend, but he couldn't forget why he was in Wells. That phony bill of Pitch's that Isaac gave him was easily explained, just like the phony bills he'd received at the general store, but the situations felt different from one another.

And he'd learned not to ignore his gut.

Nevertheless, he was more than relieved Isaac was safe. "Were you all right in the post office?"

"Sure was. I assumed you'd be at the inn, but then I got here and Knapp said you up and left when the blizzard hit. What were you thinking, running out like that? You're that lovesick that you lost your common sense?"

"Not lovesick. Regretful." He was too weary to speak anything but the truth. "Abby and I had an understanding some years ago, but I left Chicago. Didn't say goodbye, didn't explain. Just left. Bad man-

271

ners, I know."

Isaac gaped. "No, it's beyond that. I'm not the most experienced fellow when it comes to ladies, but — Dashiell, badly done."

Dash could've used his advice six years ago, rather than Abby's father's words of so-called wisdom. "I thought it would be easier that way. Clean break and all that."

Isaac shook his head like Dash was an idiot. "No wonder you came to apologize to her. And no wonder you went out in that storm looking for her."

"I'm just glad we're all well, but there are two lost children. Will you help us find them?"

"Of course. Who?" Isaac's gaze caught on something over Dash's shoulder. "I bet they're that fellow's children, since he's giving your schoolmarm what for."

Dash spun around. Abby trembled before a man with wind-chapped cheeks and quivering jowls. He couldn't hear her, but her voice rose in volume. ". . . sorrier than I can ever say. The weather was mild when they left. I didn't know the storm would hit when I sent them home."

"They didn't get home, though, thanks to you. What kind of incompetent teacher are you?"

Tears streaked down Abby's face.

Dash moved beside her, flanking both her and Mr. Sweet. "We'll find Berthanne and Almos. We're starting the search now."

"Don't forget Stripey," a small voice said at his elbow. He hadn't noticed Willodean following him.

"Who?" Bynum came up behind her and scooped her into his arms.

"The skunk, Papa."

Mr. Sweet buried his face in his palms. "He brought that skunk to school? Why'd he do something like that?"

Willodean's eyes went wide. "To feed him pork crackling, even though Miss Bracey said, 'No, Almos, don't you bring that skunk again to school,' but Almos did anyway. That's why they had to go home."

"Come on, Simeon." Elkanah Topsy gripped his neighbor around the shoulders. "We'll find them. It ain't nobody's fault."

"He's right." Dash stared down at Abby. "This is not your fault."

"But —"

"It is not your fault," he enunciated. "Do you understand?"

"Of course I don't. I should've noticed the sack earlier. I had no idea Stripey was there, much less being fed pork crackling. Mr. Sweet's right. I'm incompetent."

"I've got a suspicion that boy had help hiding that skunk from you. Willodean knew about it. You don't have eyes in the back of your head, Abby. Nor can you allow a skunk in the classroom. You had to send them home."

"I know, but —" Her shoulders sagged. "If they're out there?"

"I will find them. And in the meantime you're needed here to tend your students. Also so I can find you when I come back. Keep your head up and pray. And have faith."

He wanted to kiss away the lines of worry marring her forehead, but instead, he took a shovel from Knapp and joined the other men to begin the search out in the world of white.

CHAPTER 14

By the time dusk fell, most of Abby's students had been collected from the general store by their anxious parents. Bynum and Mr. Topsy escorted their children home before searching the school grounds for Almos and Berthanne, while Mr. Sweet, Dash, Isaac, and others searched around the Sweet farm. Both groups would comb their way toward each other until they met in the middle. All that remained under Abby's care now were the Knapp children, of course, and Vernon and Florence Johnstone.

Bad news had arrived a few hours ago. Florence and Vernon's father, Harvey Johnstone, was on foot between town and home when the blizzard hit. By the time he reached his door, one of his feet was waxy purple, according to Mrs. Queen. She'd heard the news from the doctor's wife, who believed the limb would probably have to be amputated.

At that horrifying thought, Abby's prayers grew even more feverish for Berthanne and Almos. Were they alive? Would they lose fingers and toes, or worse?

Stop it, Abigail. Prayer is the greatest weapon in your arsenal. Hadn't Dash told her to keep the faith?

She'd try. She needed God's help, but she'd try.

Mrs. Knapp had graciously offered to keep Florence and Vernon so their mother could care for Harvey, and as a light snow began to fall at three o'clock, Abby, the three Knapps, and the Johnstone children left the store for the adjoining residence to start supper. The large kitchen smelled of simmering ham bone and was richly decorated in a rosy pink hue with frill-trimmed white curtains. Mrs. Knapp bustled about, pulling bowls from shelves and fussing with the stove. "Oneida, start the corn bread."

Oneida clapped. "May we have honey?"

"We may. Chester and Vernon, I need three onions and three potatoes from the cellar for the soup. Florence, go with them and look for a pint jar of carrots."

"What can I do?" Abby donned the frilly apron Mrs. Knapp handed to her.

"Why don't you slice those vegetables the

children bring up while I start the corn bread?"

Mrs. Knapp's knives were far sharper than Mr. Crabtree's. Abby made quick work of peeling and slicing, praying all the while because every minute that passed was another minute Berthanne and Almos could be out in the cold, frightened, or worse.

"That onion's giving you tears, eh?" Mrs. Knapp dumped the jar of carrots into the soup pot.

"I suppose so." She shouldn't admit the real reason tears were falling. She didn't want to scare the children any more than they had been.

Oneida peered up at Abby's face. "Miss Bracey's eyes have been red like that since the storm."

Mrs. Knapp joined her daughter in scrutinizing Abby. "They are inflamed."

"They'll heal, I'm sure." Abby scraped the potatoes into the pot.

"So will that knot on your head, but let's put a compress on it and your eyes while the corn bread bakes."

They sat around the table together waiting for supper to cook, Abby with a delightfully warm compress over her eyes while Mrs. Knapp read Psalms to them. One was especially comforting, about God being present in times of trouble. Abby would have to memorize it later. Then they ate the salty, flavorful soup and sweet corn bread. The hour was early, but dusk fell and the children's lids were heavy.

"None of us slept last night," Abby explained.

"Here either." Mrs. Knapp's eyes took on a haunted look. "Come to bed, children. Florence, you can wear one of my gowns. It'll be a bit large, but it'll do."

Once the children settled for the night, Abby sat up with Mrs. Knapp in the snug parlor, assisting with the mending by the light of two pretty cut-glass kerosene lamps. Her glance kept stealing to the window. "It's full dark now. I wonder where the men are."

Mrs. Knapp didn't look up from sewing on a button. "They'll be here soon, I'm sure."

And who else would be with them? "The only person we've heard any news about today is Harvey Johnstone. Do you know if anyone else is missing, aside from Berthanne and Almos?"

Saying their names hurt.

"I don't rightly know. All the schoolchildren's families seem to be accounted for, but beyond that, some folks may be holing up at home. It might take a few days to know who's well and who isn't. In the meantime, we'll keep the lamps burning for the menfolk. They'll appreciate that hot soup."

"It smells wonderful."

"My Gilbert loves a good ham-bone stock." Mrs. Knapp kept up a steady stream of chatter on her husband's favorite foods, which didn't require much participation from Abby beyond the odd "mm-hmm" or smile. Abby darned a hole in one of Chester's stockings and prayed for those out in the cold. And for Dash.

He'd been wonderful at Burt Crabtree's, helpful, hardworking, and gentle with the children. She'd always known he'd be a good father, and she used to imagine him playing with their own little ones someday.

That old familiar pain speared her from her stomach up into her chest. At least she wasn't angry at Dash now. Just hurt and sad enough she wanted to go hide in the kitchen to shed a few more tears, offering the excuse she needed to stir the soup.

You're tired. Bone weary, and her body ached from ears to toes from the cold and exertion. But Abby had a feeling that her lack of anger had nothing to do with fatigue. God was helping her. Healing her. Sadness was part of the process toward that fuller healing. She had never allowed herself to grieve Dash leaving, much as she struggled to grieve for her parents, considering how complicated their passings were, thanks to Fletcher Pitch.

Hmm. She hadn't thought of Pitch all day. At least he couldn't get into Wells in the next few days. Roads were blocked, and she'd overheard the telegraph wires were down too.

A scrape and thump drew her attention. "Is that the men?"

"I believe so." Mrs. Knapp's mending fell on the floor as she rushed out. Abby followed suit.

Mr. Knapp, Isaac Flowers, and oh, there was Dash behind them, dusted in white from his eyebrows to his boots.

The moment his gaze met hers, she knew. They had not found Berthanne and Almos.

"Had to stop looking," Isaac said, shaking snow from his hat. "Got too dark."

"Good news is we didn't find any bodies," Mr. Knapp added as his wife kissed his cheek.

That didn't make Abby feel any better.

Mrs. Knapp extricated herself from her husband's arms. "We have hot soup."

Isaac held up a hand. "Thanks, ma'am, but I promised Geraldine I'd let her know what we found."

Dash tugged off his gloves. "I'll take some of that soup, if you don't mind."

"Miss Bracey and the children helped with it." As Isaac departed, Mrs. Knapp led the way into the kitchen and ladled two bowls before a childish cry pierced the evening quiet. "Chester's having one of his nightmares. I'd better see to him."

"I'll go too. Days like this makes a man want to hold his children any chance he gets." Mr. Knapp tugged the napkin from his collar and joined his wife. The sound of their footsteps faded as they mounted the stairs.

Abby was keenly aware she was alone with Dash. The hair on her arms and nape stood at attention. Being around Dash again had been, well, confusing, to say the least. His departure from her life six years ago set her on one path, and his return had nudged her onto another, one that returned her to God's fold.

She should say something. Had to say something, now, while they had a moment of privacy.

"Are you cold?"

She clamped her jaw shut. They had a minute alone and *that* was what she asked? Of course he was cold.

"Better now, but the temperature is so far below zero, I couldn't even guess." He sampled his soup. "Ah, I can feel that all the way down my gullet. Want some?"

"No, I ate earlier."

"You look exhausted."

"So do you." Lines ridged his eyes.

"Wouldn't hurt me to get a few hours of sleep. I need to get up before dawn to tend the horses at the inn and be ready to search again at first light." His face took on a troubled look, but he shook it off. "I know you're worried about Berthanne and Almos. We all are. But you need to rest too, and do your best to trust God's got them in His hand. He's got you too." His hand reached across the Knapps' table to rest atop hers.

It was a gesture of comfort, just as his hug had been last night, and his touch on her shoulder this morning. But this was different somehow. Tiny flickers sparked up her fingertips.

She couldn't deny having feelings for him. Did love like she had for Dash actually ever die? Maybe, for some people. But not for her. It had always been there, ignored and aching in a corner of her heart.

That didn't mean she could let him into her heart again, though. Or that she *should*. He hadn't loved her then, so he wouldn't love her now. But she still wanted to know why he left. She needed to know, so she could finally put this in the past where it belonged and move forward with her life.

Maybe she was so tired that she didn't care about what would happen when Mr. and Mrs. Knapp returned downstairs, but she had to know the answer. Tonight.

"Why did you leave six years ago, Dash? Why did you go without telling me goodbye?"

Dash fiddled with the fraying edges of the leather-covered Bible resting on the table. Telling her the truth wouldn't do any good. It would only bring her more pain.

But it might also help them both heal from what he'd done. If she understood, perhaps she would believe that it had nothing to do with her . . . even though it had everything to do with her.

He met her gaze. "I left to keep you safe."

"What do you mean, *safe*?" She shrank back. "Were you working for the Secret Service then?" She whispered, although poor Chester's crying surely prevented his parents from overhearing their conversation.

"No, not until three and a half years ago. Before that I was an investigator."

"In Chicago?"

He shook his head. "I went to Kansas City to look for work and stumbled into a robbery investigation. I helped the police, and the sergeant took a liking to me and hired me as an investigator. I found some counterfeit money, turned it in, and that's how I came to the attention of the Service, but — we were talking about something else. Me leaving to keep you safe. What I meant is your life with me wouldn't have been secure."

"I don't understand how I was in any jeopardy. This makes no sense."

How to say this? He could grasp no other way than straight out. "A man like me, starting a business, we'd face hardship. You'd go without. I wouldn't have been able to provide for you in a manner befitting your expectations."

"The only thing I expected was a life with the man I loved. I told you as much."

"But you didn't know what it would be like. You'd never known hunger."

She snorted. "I have now, and I would have far preferred experiencing it with a loved one than by myself. Why didn't you discuss this with me? You had no business assuming things for me."

"I . . . didn't assume, Abby." He expelled

a long breath. He'd hoped she'd never learn the truth. But what else could he do? "Your father would have cut you off without anything. Not just financially, but altogether. He disliked me that much."

Her head shook. "That's not true. He warmed to you, remember? So much so that he offered you that position at the bank. But you abandoned that too."

"It wasn't quite like that." He squeezed her fingers. "He gave me the job because he knew I couldn't do it, Abby."

"Nonsense. You said you were doing fine."

"I lied to spare you, and because I intended to make it work."

"But Father said you had a future at the bank."

"Me? Working with numbers? Factoring interest rates at top speed for impatient customers? No, Abby. I was doomed to failure."

"You were supposed to be talking to people about loans, not working numbers."

"That's not how it happened." He puffed out another long breath, one that carried a lifetime of disappointment with it. "You know what a dimwit I am."

Her eyes narrowed. "Numbers and letters aren't everything, Dash. You know about caring for horses and how to tell counterfeit dollars from real ones. I don't know a thing about those. Does that make me a dimwit?"

He had to smile. "No, but my problem is different. You know that, Abby."

"Maybe if you'd talked to Father, he would have offered you a different position."

"I tried. That's when he told me what your life would be like, married to me. And that if we wed, he'd shut his doors to you."

"He said that?" Her head dipped.

"I'm sorry, but yes. I despised him for it, but at the same time, I knew he was right. You deserved a husband who could provide for you and wouldn't cost you your family. So I promised him I'd keep you safe, knowing the only way to achieve that was to leave you alone. He told me a clean break was best, to just go, and he'd explain things to you."

Her eyes blazed. "So that's why you didn't tell me. But you should have."

"You loved your father. I couldn't turn you against him."

"I loved you too. Which is why I dressed in your favorite pink dress and waited for you so we could tell my parents we wanted a June wedding." She stared at the table-cloth. "I waited so long I feared you'd been in an accident, and at that point Father told me you'd quit your job and left town — and he assumed you'd told me. I suppose that last bit was a lie to make you look worse in my eyes."

Guilt stabbed him in the gut. "I'm so sorry."

"The irony of it all is it didn't work. What Father wanted? My 'security'? He left us despondent, rejected and alone. If I'd married you, I doubt I would have experienced any of those things."

Maybe not. "I still would have failed you, you know. I can scarcely read or write."

Her chin lifted. "Well then, it's a good thing I'm a teacher. I'm trained in instruction."

What was she saying? "You want to teach me?"

"I'm *going* to teach you, Dash, once Berthanne and Almos are located and we've helped our neighbors. It's not as if we can watch for our friend right now. Nor can I teach. My schoolhouse is in shambles."

"About that. I thought I'd help repair the roof."

She rolled her eyes. "You have two other jobs to occupy you. You don't need a third."

"I think I have time to do more than one thing."

"Even learn how to read?"

He met her smiling gaze in the flickering

lamplight. "Even that, I suppose."

He finished his soup, still holding her hand. He tingled down to his toes, and he was certain it had nothing to do with frost-bite.

CHAPTER 15

By nine the next morning, Bynum called at the Knapps' for Abby and brought her back to the farm. It was hardly the smooth, flat ride from town Abby had grown accustomed to. The snow wasn't even, and some places were icy.

Bynum pulled the wagon to a stop in front of the porch, and the front door squeaked on its hinge as Hildie rushed out. "Oh mercy, I'm glad you're home."

"Me too." The Knapps' parlor sofa was a vast improvement over Burt Crabtree's floor, but her aching hips would be glad to be in her own bed tonight. More than that, however, she was relieved to see Hildie.

"Thank you for protecting our Willodean during the storm. I don't know what I would've done if —"

Abby embraced her hostess — gently, of course, so as not to hurt the baby. "I was so worried about you, Hildie. You and Patty and Bynum. The wind blew in so fast."

Hildie pulled back. "I was taking down the sheets. The first gust about blew Patty away." She smiled as if it was a joke, but Abby could only imagine Hildie's fear at trying to rescue her little one in that storm.

Abby stomped snow from her boots before going inside. "Did you sustain damage?"

"Bynum's Jerseys." Hildie's eyes moistened.

Those sweet calves and the mamas! "Oh no. Bynum loved those cows."

Hildie pulled a hankie from her sleeve. "It's hard, but we'll start again."

"And I will help however I can. I meant what I said the night before the storm. I'm here and I intend to be a blessing, not a burden. I'm — I'm sorry I was so distant for a while."

"I shouldn't have pried."

"You weren't prying. You were showing compassion."

Hildie's mouth stretched into a genuine smile. "I wouldn't be showing much compassion on your cold bones if I kept you standing on this porch any longer. Come inside."

The kettle whistled in the kitchen. "That'll be hot water for tea, but you'll want to freshen up first, I expect."

"Yes, thank you." After living in the same clothes for two days — had it only been two? It felt like a lifetime — Abby was eager to wash her face and change. Hildie poured some of the hot water into her floral teapot before dumping the remaining contents into a pitcher. Abby carried it up to her room, accompanied by Willodean, who held a soft towel and the floral soap Hildie saved for Sundays.

It felt like luxury, washing with warm water and fragrant soap. She took extra care everywhere the snow had touched with its needling fingers: her hands, her face, oh, how wonderful it was to press a warm cloth against her eyes. They felt better today, but they were still tender. So was the knot on her head. Abby donned her thickest pair of woolen stockings and tucked her knife into the drawer with her underthings. She wouldn't need to protect herself against Fletcher Pitch today.

Once she'd dressed, she hurried downstairs. Hildie had a teacup ready for her. "Something to invigorate the body and warm our hands."

"I'll take a cup," Willodean said from her spot at the table sorting dried beans.

"Me too," Patty added. She helped with

291

the sorting, but her beans formed blotchy shapes.

Hildie shook her head. "You girls may have cider."

Abby found the cider jug and poured portions into two clean jam jars, all the while lifting silent prayers for Berthanne and Almos. *May the men find them quickly today, Lord. Guide their steps, sharpen their vision. Forgive me for sending them out . . . Lord, may it not have been to their deaths.*

"What's wrong?" Hildie took the cider cups and offered them to the girls.

"Just praying for Almos and Berthanne."

"We all are." Her smile didn't reach her eyes. "Drink your juice, girls."

Willodean slurped a sip. "We had tea at school, Mama, but Miss Bracey said you wouldn't mind."

"I don't. I imagine it warmed you up inside."

"A little, but not much. We didn't drink tea at Mr. Crabtree's. Just water. We also ate beans and fried mush but no green vegetables because Mr. Crabtree didn't have any."

"Maybe he didn't have enough to share."

"No, he really didn't have any." Abby shook her head. "I don't think he cooks beyond tins of beans and ham. He had cornmeal but no lard or butter."

Hildie examined the girls' progress with the lima beans. "We'll have to invite him to supper to thank him for keeping you all safe."

"That would be kind." Abby sat beside Patty and watched her chubby fingers create shapes with the beans.

This was such a comfort, this quiet, gentle time together in a warm kitchen. No investigation into which of her students, Micah or Kyle, was Fletcher Pitch's son. No thoughts of Pitch at all, just agreeable company and the absence of strife. At times over the past two days, she hadn't known if she would experience such homey pleasures again, or if she'd have a chance to make things truly right.

Hildie sat down by Willodean. "Why are you smiling, Abby?"

Was she smiling? "I'm grateful for the moment, is all. It's a wonderful thing, to be back with friends."

Hildie met Abby's gaze and held it for long, wordless seconds before she smiled. "It is indeed, my friend."

Willodean looked up. "Friends are good."

"You're my best fwend," Patty said, patting Willodean's arm.

Hildie and Abby exchanged a warm smile.

The girls finished their cider and pranced to the parlor to find the cat. Abby poured water atop the lima beans. "Speaking of friends, I'm eager to visit Mr. Yates."

Hildie's mouth twisted. "He's your *friend*?"

"Perhaps not in the traditional sense, but yes." Maybe she should use this opportunity to confide in Hildie. Not everything, of course. But something. Her heart raced like a rabbit's as she resumed her seat. "We have a lot in common."

"Is he from Chicago?"

"I don't think so. I meant in our pasts."

Someone knocked on the front door. Abby and Hildie exchanged glances. They hadn't heard horses. They hurried to the entry, and Hildie swung the door open. Dash stood on the porch, eyes wide, hat in hand.

"We've found them. Berthanne and Almos."

"Found them," Abby repeated, her voice a whisper. "Are they . . . oh Dash, are they alive?"

Had Dash forgotten to say? "Yes, sorry. Not a cold finger or toe. Or a whisker, as far as Stripey is concerned. They found shelter at a neighbors' house."

"Whose?" Hildie beckoned him inside.

"The Reinharts'. Haven't met them yet, but they're an older couple to the north of the Sweet farm," he said.

"The Reinharts aren't on the way home from school for those two." Hildie's brow furrowed. "Did the storm confuse them?"

"Doesn't sound like it. They'd taken a roundabout route to kill time so their folks wouldn't know they were sent home early."

Abby's pulse pounded in her chest, pushing sweet relief through her veins. "Thank God."

Hildie blew out a breath. "Amen to that. Care for tea? It's hot, but I can brew coffee if you prefer."

"Tea's fine." Anything to warm his bones.

Hildie hung Dash's coat on the tree and led them into the kitchen. Willodean and Patty came too, and Willodean pointed at the chair closest to the stove for him. Grinning his thanks, Dash took a seat, allowing the heat to warm him. "Thank you."

Abby poured him a cup of tea and sat beside him. "Why didn't anyone find the children yesterday?"

"The Reinharts had some high drifts to contend with."

"I heard you say Stripey lived." Willodean leaned on his chair.

"Yes, and while I don't think they were

thrilled by their four-legged guest, he stayed in the cellar and didn't spray anything."

The little girls found that hilarious. Not so much the big ones, but they smiled. His gaze met Abby's as she swiped a tear. "What is it, Abby?"

"God's good."

"Yes, He is."

Hildie set out a chipped plate of cookies. "Where's my husband?"

"He went to search for someone's cow, and he said he'll be home shortly." Dash reached for a cookie. Its sugar sweetness made a perfect complement to the tea.

"No molasses in these," Abby said.

"I can tell." He grinned.

Hildie looked between them, biting her lip. "You must stay for lunch, Mr. Lassiter. We've hardly had a chance to get acquainted."

Should he? Dash looked to Abby for permission. Both knew this was about more than a neighborly lunch. For Abby and Dash, this would be the first normal thing they'd done together since deciding to move toward peace. She nodded.

"I'd love lunch. The inn's not expecting me back until afternoon."

Abby pushed back her tea. "In the meantime, Dash, would you like to, er, study?"

"I'd love to, *er, study,* if Mrs. Elmore doesn't mind."

Hildie burst into laughter. "Depends on what you mean by study."

"Oh bother, I didn't mean anything like that." Abby's cheeks enflamed.

Dash should rescue her from her embarrassment, even though it brought the most endearing flush to her cheeks. "She's trying to spare me from humiliation, Mrs. Elmore. You see, I'm not a good reader."

"I'm not either. I prefer my ladies' journals to Abby's thick books any day."

"I'm afraid I wouldn't do well with your journals, either." Dash shrugged. "I'm hopeless."

"Nothing's hopeless. I'm proof of that." Abby rose. "I'll be right back."

"You really can't read?" Willodean's head tilted at an adorable angle.

"Not well. My writing's pretty bad too."

"Hostlers don't need reading and writing, Willodean," Hildie said.

But Secret Service operatives did, and while Dash figured he wouldn't leave here today reading or writing, at least he'd have some time with Abby.

She returned with a slate and a primer. He hated those things. Memories of painful recitations made his palms sweat. He wasn't a boy anymore, though. He'd proven he could meet all sorts of challenges, with God's help. He could give this another go too.

She scooted in her chair. "Ready?"

He'd never be ready, but he nodded.

She opened a book. "Read this to me."

It was a book for babies, with big font and a picture of a calf. Dash swallowed his pride. Deep breath.

"Take your time," Abby said.

"It's a cow, Mr. Lassiter." Willodean climbed onto his legs.

"Moo." Patty giggled.

He tweaked their curls. "Thanks for the help, ladies."

Hildie leveled Willodean with a look. "Come, let's find the cat."

Willodean settled deeper into Dash's lap. "Patchy Polly's sleeping in the parlor, Mama. I wanna stay here."

"No." Hildie crooked her finger.

Mumbling, Willodean crawled off Dash's lap and trudged out of the room with her mother and Patty.

The Elmore females may have left the kitchen, but Dash's shame hung thick in the air. "This is useless, Abby."

"Pfft. How did your father teach you to shoot a rifle?"

"What does that have to do with any-thing?"

"Everything. So, did he hand you the rifle and tell you to figure it out?"

He rubbed his forehead. "You know he didn't."

"Remind me again. You were shooting game birds. And . . ." She motioned for him to finish the story.

"I missed every target, so he told me to slow down. Not to look ahead of the bird but at the bird. And once I hit one, he said I'd done well but had to keep practicing."

"And it worked, because you became an excellent shot." She leaned closer to whisper. "How did you come to be able to distinguish genuine currency from counter-feit? Especially Pitch's?"

He'd told her it was the feel of the paper, hadn't he? Ah. She hadn't forgotten but wanted him to focus on things he could do well, not what he couldn't do. "Some bad bills are thinner paper than the govern-ment's. His is the tiniest bit thicker, such high quality others don't notice at first touch. Some see imperfections in counter-feits, but I feel a difference in the paper."

"I can't do that." She stabbed her index finger into the tabletop. "I got four dollars from Mr. Flowers and they felt the same to me."

Her suspicious mind! "It was one dollar, Abby. That doesn't make him a —"

"My point is," she interrupted, "I couldn't tell a difference, but you can." She sat back, looking satisfied. "You have many talents, Dash. Things that come easy, like horses and feeling paper. Other things require more effort, like shooting. Or reading. So, as your father said, slow down. Don't look ahead of the bird — or the word, as it were. Let's practice."

All right, then. "This word's easy. *Here. Here a is, um, yo*— I think it's *young com.* Cow. Not *com.*" He puffed out a breath. "Abby, it's a tangle of weeds to me."

"I know. Try the next line."

"The — I know it says calf because of the picture."

"Copy the word for me." She extended the slate.

He did it, and she pointed at the last letter. "That's backwards."

Argh. "I didn't mean it to be."

"I think I know what this is. Your *m*'s and *w*'s, and other letters being backwards."

"Isn't it called stupidity?" He laughed at himself.

"No, as I've told you a million and one

times. It's called word blindness."

"My vision's fine." He thought, anyway.

"I didn't give it the name. Some doctor did, in an article I read. He says some people read words out of order or confuse letters that look similar, like *m* and *w*. Or *b* and *d*. Or letters seem to move around on the page."

That didn't happen for him, but the swapping letters? Sounded right. "What does he say to do about it?"

She sighed. "Not much."

Dash burst into laughter. "Wonderful." He swiped a tear from his eye.

Abby laughed too. "But *I* say we can do something, or at least try. When you learned to shoot game, your father had you slow down. Let's try that, focusing on one letter at a time. Then one word at a time. When you finish a word, ask if it makes sense, just like you did with *cow*. You've always compensated for your reading struggles, memorizing math facts and Bible verses. I think you can compensate when it comes to reading too."

"That sounds like a slow process, Abby. But let's try." He'd take any sort of improvement.

Her grin was all the reward he needed. It sent a flash of something hot through his bones, skull to toes —

Uh-oh. He cared for her, didn't he? Still. Maybe he'd imagined his response. Nope. His arm prickled when her arm brushed his to erase the slate.

She covered up most of the cow poem with a small piece of paper. "All right, start here."

The picture was a clue, but he tried anyway. "The calf ju–jumps."

Hildie poked into the kitchen. "Bynum's back. Coming up the drive."

Abby tapped the page. "Let's finish this before he comes in."

Dash's head ached by the time he read *The calf eats grass,* but by then Bynum was inside and he and Hildie stood conversing in the entry.

"I didn't even know he was missing." Hildie's voice carried.

"No one did."

Closing the book, Dash sent up a prayer. His suspicions were confirmed by the look on Bynum's face.

They'd found someone. Lost someone.

Abby went still. "Did you find the cow?"

Bynum ruffled his hair. "Yep. And Maynard Yates."

Abby's face paled. "Wh–what?"

"At the cemetery, at his wife's grave,

curled into a ball." Bynum took a cup of tea from Hildie. "Strangest thing. His coat was off and he'd torn away his collar, like folks do when they're gasping for air. Maybe it was that snow dust choking him."

"Or it could have been delusion." Dash shrugged. "I've heard some people act hot when they're freezing."

Abby's fist covered her mouth. "Poor Mr. Yates."

Bynum's eyes went wide. "I'm sorry. I should've been more delicate sharing the news, even if it's about someone nobody will miss much."

"That's not it." Hildie came around Abby and gripped her shaking shoulders. "She says they're friends."

Bynum's shocked expression surely mirrored Dash's. She'd danced with Yates, said he had a soft interior, but more went on between them than he'd guessed. He tipped his head at Bynum. "Is anyone seeing to the body?"

Bynum nodded. "His horses too, but Mayor Carpenter asked if you'd see to them from now until something's decided."

"Of course." Poor animals. And poor Mr. Yates. Dash returned to the table and dropped to a squat in front of Abby. "I'll make sure Yates is laid to rest properly, all right?"

She nodded, hiccuping. "I want to help . . . clean out his house or plan his service or . . . something, if I can. I don't think there will be anyone else to do it."

He'd grant her anything he could. "I'll speak to the pastor. See if he had family anywhere."

Hildie met his gaze. "Let me talk to her for a spell. You all go look in on the girls."

Dash hated to leave. Wanted to be there for Abby. But Bynum was waiting, and Abby had curled into Hildie's side.

He sent up a prayer as he went.

Abby's eyes burned. Her throat thickened with a painful lump as tears spattered her blouse. "I thought we had more time."

"I'm so sorry." Hildie's fingers brushed Abby's hair in soothing strokes, much like Mother used to do. "I remember you dancing with him. Is that when you first became, er, friends?"

"No. Not until the night before the storm." She pulled a hankie from her sleeve and swiped her nose and cheeks. "Before that, well, you know he insinuated I couldn't cook, so I made him cookies."

"Those molasses cookies were for him?"

Hildie's fingers went still. "I thought they were for Dash."

"Turns out Dash hates molasses."

"Oh."

"And I wouldn't have made Dash cookies anyway. I was still so angry." Abby's throat softened. "That's what Mr. Yates and I had in common. Our anger. Unwillingness to forgive. I recognized it in him the night of the mayor's birthday." Abby swiped her eyes. "You see, a few years ago, my father died."

Hildie shifted to sit beside Abby. "I figured he'd passed. Him and your ma, since you don't talk about them."

"His death was . . . sudden. And what was worse was, well, we learned he'd been involved in crime."

Hildie gasped. She'd called her friend here in this very kitchen, but she could well change her mind now. Would she judge Abby by her father's actions? Would she reject her as so many others had done?

Abby owed it to Hildie and any chance they had of a friendship to continue. If Hildie turned her back on Abby because of it, it would hurt. But Abby had to try anyway.

She probably shouldn't get into details, considering she was here to hunt for

Fletcher Pitch's boy. Nor could she divulge anything about Pitch. But the rest, she could share. "We were shocked, hurt, entertaining questions for which there were no answers. And then, all of our friends abandoned us." She couldn't include how humiliating it had been when no one welcomed her to sit with them. "When I saw Mr. Yates at the birthday party, the same thing happened to him. No one spoke to him. That's why I approached him, because I know how it feels to have folks not want to be around you."

Hildie's face darkened. "But in your situation, it wasn't your fault. Folks were horrible to you on account of your father. Yates, however, brought his isolation on himself by being a grumpy ol' coot."

"That didn't mean he wasn't hurting. I suspect his pain made him lash out all the more, because that's what I've done. I pushed you away, Hildie. You offered friendship and I was afraid to take it because I didn't want you to reject me. Confiding in others, well, it hasn't served me well in the past."

Hildie enveloped her in a hug, awkward with the baby between them, but warm and bracing. "I'm glad you're telling me now. About everything."

Not quite everything. Hopefully Hildie would be as generous and understanding when Abby eventually revealed she was here to find the son of a counterfeiter.

But for today, it felt good to have a friend. Abby held Hildie a little tighter.

CHAPTER 16

Once Abby's tears dried, she and Hildie joined the men in the parlor. Abby explained her final conversation with Mr. Yates. She did not mention specifics about Dash, but she could tell from the way his lips pressed into a thin line that he knew he was the cause of a portion of her grief.

"So you see," she continued, "when Mr. Yates and I parted, I told him I'd read the Bible that evening. He said he might do the same. I think he may have, because of where he was found. At his wife's grave. He told me he'd have to talk to her — he meant he'd speak to her grave, which he'd never done."

"What on earth did that woman do to upset him so much? I always thought she was as sweet as bee's breath," Hildie mused.

"Maggie was polite, to be sure," Bynum agreed. "And Maynard was not. But I never paid any mind as to why."

"I'm not condoning his actions, truly."

Abby rubbed her arms. "He was rude to me and, presumably, to everyone else. But I can understand how pain can make a person sourer by the day."

"I can too, now." Dash's voice was quiet.

"There were better ways to handle things, though." Bynum stood.

Abby's path to that truth was long and tortuous. She'd have to do better from here on out, looking to God instead of her circumstances.

Hildie smiled sadly. "Mr. Yates might have become a new man, had he time."

"Since he was at his wife's grave, I think maybe he was a new man. New in Christ." Dash met Abby's gaze.

Bynum clapped Dash's shoulder. "Hate to say this, but I'm expected back in town. I said I'd dig out some remaining drifts."

Dash nodded. "I'll go with you."

"After lunch. Mr. Lassiter said he'd stay." Hildie rose, then inhaled sharply and bent over.

Abby's arm went around her friend's shoulder. "Is it the baby?"

"Yes, but don't anyone get excited. See, it's all better now." Hildie straightened. "Let's eat."

Bynum frowned. "I don't know, Hildie. Your time is close. I'd better stay home."

"And I'd better go." Dash slipped a finger beneath his collar.

Hildie rolled her eyes. "It is not my time; it's hunger pains. This baby must have the appetite of a plow horse, because I might eat your portion too, Bynum, if you want to stand there arguing with me." She took Abby's arm and tugged her toward the kitchen. "You two fellas coming or not?"

"Coming, ma'am." Bynum chuckled. "Can't argue with a hungry woman."

Abby turned back and grinned. "Sounds wise."

Dash held up both hands. "Then you won't get any arguments from me. About anything."

"Oh?" She walked backward so she could look at him. "If that's the case, let's talk about that awful scarf of yours."

"My scarf isn't awful."

"It's ratty. I'll make you a new one."

"But I like this one," he said.

"Don't argue, Dash, remember?" Bynum teased.

"All right, then. A new scarf it is." Dash's gaze followed after Abby as she led the way to the kitchen. The past few days, things between them had definitely moved beyond businesslike.

And he liked it far more than he should.

■ ■ ■ ■

Dash spent the rest of Saturday digging out waist-high snowdrifts before tending Maynard Yates's horses and those at the inn. Despite the work, he didn't grow warm enough to perspire. The blizzard might be over, but a thick blanket of cold trailed in its wake, progressing southward with tortoise-like slowness.

So far, the only loss in Wells was Maynard Yates, which was one too many, to Dash, but plenty of folks suffered injuries, from lacerations to frostbite. Word was Mr. Johnstone's leg had to be amputated below the knee.

But the stories from outlying areas were worse, one tragedy after another — blocked trains full of shivering passengers desperate for rescue, men and women perishing feet from their front stoops, and worst of all, the schoolchildren who never made it home on Thursday.

Lord, I don't understand such loss. The world is full of fear and suffering due to the cruelty of nature . . . and men.

Men like Fletcher Pitch. No, Dash mustn't forget why he was in Nebraska in the first place. The blizzard hadn't changed that.

It wouldn't shake his faith, either. Gathered among fellow believers in church on Sunday morning, Dash was once again reminded that despite the sadness and struggles in the world, it was also a place full of hope and joy. He'd seen neighbors helping neighbors. Compassion and kindness. Reunions among family members. Reconciliations, like his strange one with Abby. He caught her eye across the aisle and they shared a smile. Who'd have thought that would ever happen again?

After the final hymn, he sidled beside her and greeted the Elmore family. "How are you faring?"

"Counting our blessings instead of our troubles," Hildie said. "I'd hoped to see more folks in church, though."

"It's still so cold, I'm sure a lot of people had no choice but to stay home." Abby glanced over Dash's shoulder. "Pardon me, but I see Mayor Carpenter. I'd like to ask him about the school repairs."

An impromptu meeting broke out in the narthex over repairs to the schoolhouse roof. Mayor Carpenter listened thoughtfully, finger to his cheek. "I'd like to see children resume school next week, if possible. By then, the trains will be running, and life will return to a semblance of normalcy."

"Not quite normal," Abby whispered to Dash as the mayor stepped away, her breath warm on his cheek. "Open roads means our friend can get into town."

"We'll be waiting for him." He resisted the urge to touch her.

"Miss Abby, ready?" Bynum interrupted. By the way he kept stealing glances at Hildie, it was obvious he was concerned about her. She looked fine to Dash, except for the finest of lines around her mouth.

"I am. Good day, Dash."

"Good day."

Abby smiled as she left. He'd have liked more time to talk to her, ask if this church service was different for her now that she'd turned back to the Lord. Unlike the other women, she didn't carry a Bible in her arms. He'd have to change that somehow.

The next day, after seeing to the few horses at the inn, Dash crossed to the livery. What fine horses, healthy and cared-for animals. He whistled to them as he fed them and mucked out their stables. The last stall, number six, belonged to a mare with a broad blaze on her head, white as the moon. How beautiful she was, sleek and strong and — what was the Bible verse? Fearfully and wonderfully made.

Since Hildie mentioned counting her blessings yesterday, he'd determined to watch for evidence of God's creative touch, despite the hardships caused by the blizzard around him. Right now Dash could see God's care in the mare's thick eyelashes and sweet, gentle snuffing against his shoulder.

Dash patted her neck. "What's your name, anyhow? Maybe it's written down somewhere, not that I could read it if it was, but I'll look anyway. You finish your oats, now." He'd added a few extra drops of molasses today. The horses loved it. Maybe that was why he didn't. Molasses cookies always reminded him of horse food.

After Dash hauled the manure out back, he searched Yates's desk for clues about the horses or any extended family. Yates kept a ledger on rentals, but the handwriting was so tiny Dash's head spun. He tried Abby's reading trick, covering the majority of the page so he could only see one word at a time, but it was useless. Even Abby would require a magnifying glass.

The door slid open, admitting weak morning sun and a rush of brisk air.

"Isaac," Dash greeted.

His friend glanced around the space. "I haven't been in here before. Cleaner than I expected. The way everyone talked about Yates, I expected cobwebs and dust."

"He kept a tidy place. So tidy I can't find any paperwork."

"Maybe he didn't like clutter. Anyway, I just saw Sheriff Grayson. He said you can go ahead and look in the house for anything to indicate any living kin, if you wouldn't mind. He'd do it, but he's headed out to help search for some missing girls in the next town over."

"Missing girls." Dash's chest tightened. The blizzard's effects were far reaching and cruel, and still not entirely over with. Dash lifted a prayer. "Does the sheriff need help?"

"A few men went with him. Come on, I'll help you look through Yates's house."

The house was adjacent, but no door connected the two buildings, so Dash and Isaac went outside and around the corner to the front stoop. A hip-high drift piled against the house; he'd have to dig it out later. Dash let them inside, into an entry hall, cold and silent as a tomb — but far more rich in decor than Dash would have expected, with a polished oak credenza and framed samplers on the forest-papered walls. Likewise, the parlor was well appointed and vibrant with color. The rugs and furnishings weren't new, by any means, but they were bright,

315

and the drapes had a springlike look to them, with all those pink flowers. They'd clearly been chosen by Yates's wife.

"No photographs to guide us to his relations." Isaac loosened his fine woolen scarf. "I'll take a look-see at the desk."

"I'll try the kitchen." Dash found a stone-cold coffeepot by the stove, clean dishes by the dry sink, and a Bible open to Luke on the scarred table. Nothing unusual, except for the Bible, which Abby had said she'd encouraged him to read. He'd clearly done so before he went to the cemetery to visit his wife's grave.

Hopefully he'd made his peace with God too. Seemed likely, according to what Abby had said.

Perhaps the Bible had a genealogy in it. He'd show it to someone who could read better than he could.

Isaac returned, shrugging. "No correspondence, newspaper clippings, nothing. Didn't see anything in his bedroom either."

"Are there any other rooms?"

"An empty one. Not a stick of furniture in it. It makes being a bachelor look downright depressing."

"God calls some people to singleness, you know."

"I thought I was one of them." Isaac

fingered the scar on the table.

"You *thought*?"

"I think — well, meeting Geraldine has challenged that assumption. See, I had a gal. About ten years ago. But she left me a note that said she was in love with someone else. That's why I gave you such a hard time about leaving Miss Bracey, I suppose. I know a fair piece about what that feels like."

Isaac hadn't meant it as a sting, but Dash felt it all the same. "I wronged Abby, and we've talked. I can never undo what I did, but I think she might forgive me someday. I'm still trying to forgive myself."

They'd said more about their feelings in two minutes than they had in the entirety of their time as flatmates, and Isaac clearly wasn't comfortable with it. Tightening his scarf, he moved to the door. "Need to get back to the post office, but I'll treat you to supper at the café tonight."

Dash waved goodbye and tucked the Bible under his coat. He gave the place one last look, but Isaac was correct. No old letters, no tintypes, no journals, no evidence of any relations. What would happen to Yates's horses and livery? Or this house? It was a snug little place, perfect for a small family.

A frigid gust stung his ears and nose when he strode out to Main Street. He should give the Bible to the mayor before he returned to the inn. Frank and Sy could use his help clearing the drifts against the house.

Mayor Carpenter exited the café, saving Dash the need to visit his office beside town hall. "Just the man I was hoping to find."

"What a happy coincidence. I need to talk to you too. Something about you has come to my attention. You aren't really a hostler, are you?"

Dash froze, and not because of the icy temperature. *Answer a question with a question.* "Sir?"

The mayor chuckled. "I have a proposition for you. Come with me."

CHAPTER 17

Abby snuck off the sofa an inch at a time so as not to awaken Willodean and Patty. They'd fallen asleep beneath the shelter of her arms while she read to them from *Mark, the Match Boy.* Patty's lips puckered around her thumb, whereas Willodean's mouth opened wide. Neither usually napped in the morning, but the past four days had been exhausting. Abby could easily curl up for a rest herself.

Instead she covered the girls with a white crocheted blanket before tiptoeing to the kitchen. It was so quiet, maybe Hildie had fallen asleep too.

Instead, Hildie paced the kitchen rug, hand at the side of her protruding stomach.

"Hunger pains again?"

"No." Hildie stopped walking, grimaced, and held her breath until she turned red.

The baby was coming. Abby's heart stopped, then sped off like a six-horse team.

"Sit down."

"Standing's better," Hildie answered through gritted teeth.

"I'll fetch the doctor."

"Bynum said he's out making house calls. Frostbite and such. But there's a — ohhhh." She gripped the back of a chair.

"Then I'll go get Bynum." Wherever he was. He was helping someone. With something. Every thought fled.

Hildie's head shook, back and forth like a horse's. "The girls need you."

"They're asleep."

"For now."

"But you need help and I don't know how to do it, Hildie."

Hildie couldn't talk for a while after that. Her stomach grew taut under her dress. What on earth? At least Abby had one of her questions answered. It did indeed hurt to have a baby.

Like a gift, a knock rapped on the front door. *Thank You, Lord.* "I'll ask whoever it is to fetch Bynum and the doctor for us." Hildie didn't respond, just clutched the chair back. Abby hiked her skirt to her knees and ran to the front door.

Baskets over their arms, a woman and boy stood on the porch, noses and mouths wrapped in scarves. Abby would recognize their eyes anywhere, though. "Geraldine, Micah. Come in, please." She waved them in and shut the door.

Geraldine tugged her scarf down to her chin. "We brought you some treats to thank you for all you did to protect Micah and the other children. Food, but I also sewed you an apron. I'll make baskets for Mr. Lassiter and Mr. Crabtree too, but without the aprons. I've never met Mr. Crabtree, but every man can use a handkerchief, can't he?" Her smile fell. "You don't want an apron."

"Yes. No. Baby." Abby rubbed her forehead. "Hildie's having the baby. Right now, I think."

Micah whistled. Geraldine set her basket on the little table by the coat tree. "Sounds like we'd best be on our way, then."

Micah looked up at his mother. "You said I could play with Willodean and Patty."

"This is an inconvenient time for them, Micah."

"Not at all. Your visit is well timed indeed," Abby protested. "I don't know what to do. The girls and I are alone."

"You need the doctor?"

"And Bynum, but Hildie doesn't want me to leave. Now that you're here, though, I have a better idea. You're a mother. Would you assist Hildie while I get help? Micah can keep occupied with the girls." It was a perfect solution. Geraldine had experience in these sorts of matters, and Abby had none. Abby reached for her bonnet on the coat tree peg.

Geraldine gripped Micah's shoulder to hold him back. "Oh, I think she'd be far more comfortable with you here than me."

"I think she'd be more comfortable with someone who knows what to do." Abby wound her scarf around her neck and ears, but it didn't muffle the sound of Hildie's groan in the kitchen. "I'll return as quickly as I can, I promise."

Geraldine froze, as if she'd been left outside during the blizzard. "I . . . I don't — it was a long time ago. I hardly remember it, so it will be far better for her if you stay. I shall ensure the doctor is found and sent here at once. Come, Micah."

"Aw." Micah sounded just like Coy. "I wanted to play."

Geraldine opened the door and pulled him outside with her, shutting the door herself.

"But —" Abby stared at the door. "I don't know what to do."

Hildie let out another low groan. Lord, have mercy.

"Miss Bracey? Is Mama sick?"

She spun. Willodean stood in the threshold, rubbing her eye.

"No, sweetheart. The baby's coming. I need your help with Patty. Will you stay with her in the parlor so I may care for your mama?"

Willodean nodded. "We'll play with Patchy Polly."

"Good idea. Thank you, big girl. What a helper."

Abby paused before entering the kitchen to take a breath and whisper a prayer. It seemed she was about to learn more than she ever expected about childbirth.

At least Geraldine had been true to her word. Within the hour, Bynum had returned, a curly-haired woman in tow. He gave Abby the briefest of glances. "Doctor's still out, but Edna Sweet here is a midwife. I'm going to get the horses out of the cold and be right back."

Almos and Berthanne's mother was a midwife? She'd no idea, and frankly, midwifery wasn't paramount on Abby's mind when she saw the woman. It wasn't the proper time, but Abby's heart raced again. "How . . . how are Almos and Berthanne?"

"Oh, they're well." Mrs. Sweet shrugged

out of her voluminous coat.

"After the storm? They're really all right?"

She'd stayed away, after the way Mr. Sweet had shouted at her. She assumed the Sweets hated her for sending their children out before the blizzard.

She didn't know she'd shed a tear until Mrs. Sweet swiped it from her cheek. "They were smart enough to go to the first house they found. The Reinharts spoiled them to death, feeding them cocoa and cookies. My children want to go back and visit, although the skunk is not welcome, according to Mrs. Reinhart." She laughed.

"I was so worried. If something had happened, it would have been my fault."

"What foolishness is this? Nobody knew about that storm. One minute we had that breeze from the south. The next minute, well, none of us will soon forget it."

"Can you forgive me, though?"

"There's nothing to forgive. But if it makes you feel better, then yes. Now, I'd best tend to Hildie."

"Of course. She's in bed now."

"She should be walking," Mrs. Sweet muttered as she mounted the stairs.

"She was," Abby called after her.

Relief didn't fill Abby — it was more like a plug had been pulled, sapping her strength. Help had arrived, but also, Mrs. Sweet had forgiven her for sending the children into the storm.

Forgiveness was easy for everyone but her, it seemed. Dash had apologized and explained his actions of six years ago, which was more than she ever hoped to receive from him, but the wound of his rejection still stung. Would it heal, if she forgave him? Maybe she could forgive him for being young and listening to her father — someone else she needed to forgive.

You forgive me, Lord. Your Word says so. I want to be forgiving, because I want to obey You. Show me how.

The only answer was the cheery sound of the girls giggling in the parlor. Why didn't God answer her? Why did He leave her alone to figure things out?

Maybe He hadn't, though. The girls' merriment was a sound of life. Soon there would be another little cry coming from upstairs, a new baby, full of promise and hope. More evidence that God was active in the lives of His people. She mustn't give up so easily.

Bynum returned, pausing to greet the girls before hurrying upstairs. Abby fed the girls lunch and made sandwiches for Bynum and Mrs. Sweet. Nothing for Hildie, as instructed. Then she started supper simmering on the stove and played dolls with the girls on the parlor floor. They all looked up at the sound of footsteps descending the staircase.

Bynum entered the room, shaking his head. "Nothing yet."

Really? It was coming on late afternoon now. How long did these things take? "Care for some coffee?"

"That'd be most welcome."

"I'll bring it up to you and Mrs. Sweet, then." She stood, stretching out the kinks in her back while he patted the girls on the head and then returned upstairs.

As she put the pot on the stove, an unfamiliar horse pulled up outside the window. She recognized the rider, though. Dash was here, and in an all-fired hurry. She opened the door before he could knock.

"What's wrong?" he asked instead of saying hello.

"Nothing. Why?"

"I heard a doctor was needed here."

"Yes." She ushered him into the foyer, which had seen more traffic today than in her entire stay at the Elmores' thus far. "Hildie's ready for the baby."

The tense line of his shoulders eased. "Oh. I won't stay, then, but I brought you a gift." He unfastened his coat and reached inside, withdrawing a black leather book. "Yates's Bible. It was open on the table. You know what that means."

"Mr. Yates read it. Thank you, Dash. That is indeed a gift."

One of the most precious she had ever received.

Why didn't Abby take it from him? Dash extended his arm farther and gave the Bible a little bounce on his palm. "That's not why I brought it. See, I told Mayor Carpenter and some other folks about your friendship with Mr. Yates. Not the details, of course. Just that you'd reached out to him and it seems like he responded — to you and to the Lord. The mayor looked at the front of this to see if it had a genealogy in it, but there wasn't anything. We don't know how to find his kin. So, barring the arrival of any relations, we all agreed you should keep this."

She took a half step backward. "Oh, I couldn't."

"Who else should have it? The only friends he had were horses. I rode one here, by the way. Sweetheart of a mare. Wish I could figure out what he named her."

Willodean danced out of the parlor.

"Hello, Mr. Lassiter."

"Hello, Willodean."

Patty tugged her thumb from her mouth with a pop. "Hewwo."

"Good afternoon to you too."

"We're hungry, Miss Bracey." Willodean's arms folded, and Patty nodded.

"I'll get supper on, then. Play a little longer and then we'll eat. Dash, come with me while I warm things."

He followed Abby into the kitchen, sniffing the tantalizing aromas of beef and onions. "Pot roast?"

"Beef soup with barley." She set the old Bible atop the table.

"Can I help you?"

"No, this is easy." She bustled around the stove, cracking a brown egg into a bowl and mixing in milk and cornmeal. "I'm so glad you found that Bible open. I suppose since he's gone, I'm not breaking his confidence telling you this, but his wife — Maggie — hurt him. She's been gone a few years. I saw her stone in the cemetery, and their baby's stone. Eugene. He died twenty-five years ago. Isn't that sad? Mr. Yates's brother, also named Eugene, is buried close by too."

"Do you know what happened between Maggie and Maynard?"

"No. He said no one knew the truth but

took her side anyway."

"And he never got over it whatever it was."

She poured batter into the pan, her face downcast. "Just like me."

"Not like you."

"I was well on my way, though."

That familiar stab of guilt pierced Dash's gut. If he could change the past, he would, but all he could do was restate his apology. He'd apologize a thousand times if necessary. "I'm sorry for leaving, Abby."

"Thank you, Dash, but I know you are. You've already apologized. I think I'm ready to leave our . . . situation in the past. Father manipulated you, and while it still hurts, I'm not going to hold it against you anymore. Does that mean I'm on my way to forgiving you?"

"I think so. I know it'll take time."

She popped the corn bread into the oven and sat across from him. "Did I really not accept you for who you were, like you said? I thought I did, but I must have done something to make you say that. Make you feel that."

He'd regretted saying that to her, but they were being honest, weren't they? "When your father offered me the bank job, you were ecstatic. I felt like you were so happy, you'd wanted it all along. For me to fit into your father's life, not the life I wanted."

"I told you not to take the job, remember? I was happy my father was showing an interest in you. That's all."

He'd muddled things in his mind, looked for ways to justify what he'd done. But she had indeed encouraged him to pursue his dream. "You're right. I ask your forgiveness for that too."

She shook her head. "I was naive. Blind to my father's cunning. I'm sorry for that."

"I forgive you, Abby. It's all right."

"Thank you." Her eyes flashed with moisture. "That feels . . . nice. Being forgiven."

"It does, doesn't it?"

"I'm glad things are clear between us. It's like a burden's been taken out of my hands." She stretched her arms across the table to demonstrate, knocking the Bible to the floor between them, spine up, pages spread. A yellowed piece of paper skittered out. "What's that?"

Dash picked it up. "I don't know. The mayor and I didn't see that. Maybe you'd better read it." If he tried, it would take all night.

"Just a minute." She stood, gripped a towel, and lifted the soup pot lid to stir the contents. Then she resumed her seat. "All right, let's see. Oh, it's a letter."

"To whom?"

"Mr. Yates. 'Dear Maynard,' it says. Dated nearly twenty-three years ago." She turned the page over. "From Maggie, his wife. I'm not sure I should read this."

"It could tell us if he has any other relations."

"Valid point. Here we are, then. 'Dear Maynard, some things are easier to write down than speak face-to-face. That might account for my silence of late, so I'll just say it here. You know I loved your brother Eugene. You did me a kindness, marrying me when he died and left me in a delicate state.' "

"Of grief?" Abby rubbed the bridge of her nose.

Dash didn't have the best of feelings about where the letter was going next. "Maybe."

" 'When you claimed little Gene as your own —' " Abby flushed pink from mortification. "Oh. *That* sort of delicate state. Perhaps I should stop."

"It's all right, Abby. Go on."

She cleared her throat. " 'When you claimed little Gene as your own I knew you loved me, but then baby Gene died, and you lost the last of your people in the world. I'm sorry the birth was so hard I couldn't give you a child of your own to love. If I had, you'd have more people, someone to love you back, because I can't be your people. My heart died with Eugene. I've got no love left to give. I'll never ask you for anything but for you to lie me beside him in death. Until then, I will give you a good house and stay as your wife, Maggie.'"

What a punch to the solar plexus this must have been. "Huh."

"He told me she never loved him. He was right." Abby's fingers went to her lips. "I guess she thought she was doing the right thing, with this letter. Just like you did by leaving. I'm not saying that to dredge things up for the hundredth time. Just saying he and I, well, were kindred that way."

"I'm sorry." He'd be sorry until death.

"I know. I'm sorry too." Abby folded the page and returned it to the Bible. "But it's over now. I hope he's at peace."

Dash prayed so.

A high-pitched cry of aggravation pierced the air. Too high to be Patty or Willodean. Abby's wide gaze met his. "The baby."

He stood. "I should go."

Willodean and Patty rushed into the kitchen, though, grabbing his hands. "Did you hear the baby?" Willodean jumped up and down, shaking his arm.

"We sure did." There it went again, in fact.

332

"You've got a new brother or sister." Abby's face shone with joy. "Isn't that wonderful?"

"I'm gonna kiss it wight here." Patty pointed at her nose. "Seven times."

Heavy, slow footsteps sounded on the stairs. Little girls clutching his hands, Dash hurried with them into the foyer. Bynum's shoes came into view, then his legs, and then all of him, grinning and carrying a bundle smaller than a loaf of bread. "Meet your brother, Stuart."

Abby hauled Patty into her arms to give her a better view of the bundle, so Dash did the same with Willodean. Bynum craned up his arm so they could better see the tiny, red face, capped with a shock of dark hair. The rest of little Stuart was bundled in a yellow blanket, except for his fists, which rested under his chin.

Patty stroked the blanket over him. "He's so pwetty."

"Boys aren't pretty, Patty," Willodean scolded.

"Stuart is," Abby countered. "All babies are beautiful, but Stuart is especially so. How's Hildie?"

"Perfect." Bynum's smile was like nothing Dash had ever seen, a concoction of relief and amazement. It must be the look of a father.

Dash hadn't thought about babies much when he planned to marry Abby, although he knew they'd come along someday. Since leaving Chicago, he hadn't thought about babies at all. Now, faced with one in the flesh, he couldn't think of anything else. Would he have a family someday? Could he, as an operative? Several of his fellow Secret Service members did, but near-constant travel around vast divisions kept them away from home most of the time.

He shifted Willodean's weight in his arms. How old was she? School age, so six? Seven? Not that long since she was Stuart's size. People who said children grow too fast weren't kidding. He wouldn't want to miss a minute of it, with his own children.

If he ever had any.

"You all can come up to see your mama in fifteen, twenty minutes." Bynum kissed his daughters' hair. "I'll take Stuart up now, but I had to show him off."

"Bye, Stuart." Patty waved. Abby lowered her to the floor.

Dash pretended to drop Willodean before "catching" her, something his father had done with him. She squealed, so he did it again, three more times before putting her on her feet.

"My turn." Patty reached up.

He hoisted her up, then feigned dropping her. "Oops! Oh, oops again, Patty, my apologies, oh no, I've dropped you again."

She giggled in his ear.

Abby smiled at the display. "All right, ladies. Clean up the parlor, and I'll have supper on for you in a few minutes. Care for a bowl of soup, Dash?"

"No, I'd better get back to town before full dark, but I'll help you first, if you like."

"Sure." She led the way into the kitchen. "Do you mind getting the corn bread out?"

"Not at all." He took the thick towel she offered and removed the bread, setting it atop the stove.

As Abby reached for bowls, her skirts swished about her slender ankles — *stop looking at that, Dash.* He kept his gaze fixed on her face as she took the lid off the soup pot. "What a day. I was alone with Hildie and the girls when Hildie started having pains. I've never been so happy to see anyone in my life as I was when Mrs. Sweet came. Except for when Geraldine Story arrived with Micah to give me an apron and some muffins — don't tell, but she'll be baking some treats for you and Burt Crabtree too, for keeping Micah safe in the blizzard."

"Unnecessary, but I'll enjoy the goodies."

"I was hoping Mrs. Story would stay with Hildie while I left to look for the doctor." She ladled spoonfuls into two bowls. "I asked her to stay and lend aid, but she said she didn't remember anything about Micah's birth and left. I was shocked and so disappointed, truth be told."

Huh. "Maybe she didn't want Micah here."

"Still seems like she could've offered me a morsel of advice, though. But not one word, Dash. Not even to get towels or tell Hildie to walk around instead of going to bed. It was like she didn't know any more about birthing a baby than I do, and she's a —"

Abby stared at a blank spot on the wall.

"A what, Abby?"

"A mother." She turned around. "Isn't she?"

"What sort of question is that? Of course she is."

"I didn't mean it like that. She's Micah's mother, yes. But what if Geraldine doesn't remember Micah's birth because she wasn't present for it?"

"You mean he's adopted?"

Her face didn't change. "By his aunt. I

think Geraldine is Katherine Hoover. Micah is the son of Fletcher Pitch."

CHAPTER 18

Abby's pulse thrummed in her ears as she set the bowls on the table. "I'll feed the girls and then we can go. We've got to talk to Geraldine and ask her for that tintype before Pitch comes to town."

She didn't bother calling him *our friend* instead of his name. The baby started squalling upstairs and it was a wonder Dash could hear her, but she could tell he did, because his eyes narrowed, his expression the same as when he focused on each individual letter during their reading lesson.

"It's a compelling notion, I grant you."

"Of course it's compelling."

"I wish we had something more substantial, though. There's still Mrs. Queen."

Pfft. "How substantial are some of your leads when you're investigating subjects? I imagine you rely on your instinct, and my instinct is telling me Geraldine is Katherine."

"All right, but we need to wait until tomorrow. It's getting dark."

"Well, you're going home now, and you live in town. You go see her." Disappointment pinched her stomach. "I wish I could go with you, though."

"You've reminded me about propriety, and I don't know how suitable it'd be for me to call on her in the evening. Might give folks the wrong impression, especially Isaac, and I'm not ready to tell him everything yet. There's no harm in waiting until tomorrow when you can come with me. If you're, er, not needed here." He glanced at the ceiling.

Poor Stuart must be getting a bath or a change or something else intolerable, to make him scream like that. "I've promised to help, but I can get away for a short time."

"Good. I can come for you with one of Yates's horses at, say, nine?"

That gave her ample time to cook, serve and clean up breakfast, and set lunch on the stove. "Perfect."

"See you then, Abby." Dash's grin set her heart hooping through her rib cage.

Oh dear. That particular response to his smile hadn't happened to her in over six years. Maybe she was just happy about finally figuring out who Fletcher Pitch's boy was — poor little Micah, such a sweet lamb. He didn't deserve this.

But her thoughts returned to Dash like a persistent moth dancing around a lit candlewick.

She'd best be careful, or she'd be burned again. And this time she knew better.

After seeing to his chores Tuesday morning, Dash saddled Yates's two riding mares and called for Abby at the Elmores'. She was waiting for him on the porch, bundled from her crown to her toes against the cold. He hopped off his mount. "The Elmores don't mind you leaving?"

She shook her head. "I think they'll be glad for a few hours of family time. Hildie also asked me to stop by the general store, if you don't mind."

"We'll see to that errand on our way back." He held out a hand. "Ready?"

"Yes, although it's been awhile since I've ridden." She planted her hand on his palm, set her boot in the stirrup, and climbed into the saddle.

"Sorry I don't have a sidesaddle to offer you. Yates didn't own any. Not much call for that around here, I guess." He mounted his horse again and clicked with his tongue. Abby followed suit and they were on their way. The road was still icy in spots, requiring his concentration, but Dash had a hard time focusing with Abby beside him.

She stifled a yawn. "Pardon me. I was up all night."

"Baby keep you awake?"

"Not really. I only heard him cry once. He's a darling, Dash. But you know that, because you saw him."

Dash grinned. "I saw his face and part of his fingers, but yeah, I guess he was nice."

"You're a horrible tease." She sighed. "But anyway, I was thinking of Micah. He's the dearest child. Poor little boy, to have Pitch as a father. What will become of him?"

"I don't know. A case can be made that Geraldine kidnapped him. But, you could also argue that she was the guardian chosen by Micah's mother. He doesn't have any other relatives that I know of. I don't know who'll care for him when this is over."

Silence fell as she sorted out the information. "That's sad," she said after a while.

"It is, but my job has taught me to keep moving forward. I have to trust God to sort out the details."

"I haven't done much of that, as you know."

"Every day's a good day to start." They shared a grin.

"So who am I riding?" Abby patted the bay mare's neck. "She's pretty."

"Number Five."

"I beg your pardon?"

"Yates didn't keep a record of their names. They're all in numbered stalls, and that's how he referred to them in his ledger, so that's what I've been calling them. This one's Number Six."

"How unoriginal of you, Dash." Abby laughed.

"Maybe those are their names. She responds to it, don't you, Six? I'd hate to confuse the horses by changing their names now."

She bent down toward her mount's head. "He's always been stubborn like this, Five. I'm sorry."

"Four's a little ornery, but he's a pretty one. Three's the strongest, I think, but I'd have to hitch him to something to be sure. Yates had a good eye for horseflesh."

"Are they to be sold?"

"I'm not sure. The mayor's talking to some lawyers. That's not all. He approached me and said he could tell I was more than a hostler. I thought he'd found out about the Secret Service somehow, but he'd decided I seem like I'd rather be my own boss and asked me if I wanted to take over the livery."

"Really? What a compliment. But of course, you can't. You have a job."

"I couldn't tell him that, though, so I told him I'd think while lawyers ensured Yates doesn't have any kin. But waiting on news reminds me. Word came in this morning. A young woman in Holt County was discovered Sunday night, hiding from the storm in a haystack, too weak to move."

Her mouth gaped. "Three days after the blizzard? That poor woman."

"She's the schoolteacher, Abby."

Her head bowed. "Will she live, do you think?"

"I don't know." Dash faced forward, eyes on the horizon. "But I do know, it could've been you caught out in the storm."

"It could've been you too."

Her catching voice made him turn to look at her. "But it wasn't."

She fixed her gaze on her hands. "We have much to be thankful for."

"We do."

They turned west on the road toward town, past Burt Crabtree's quiet property. The school beside it, however, was abuzz with activity. Several horses were hitched to the rail on the west side, and a wagon of supplies stood out front. Men bustled around the school's perimeter while others sat atop the roof. He grinned at Abby. "Surprise."

"They're fixing the roof today? Land sakes, that's wonderful." She waved her arm. "Thank you," she called.

A few men, like Mayor Carpenter, looked up from their tasks and returned her wave. And was that wave from Burt Crabtree? Hard to tell from this distance, but the fellow had a beard.

"We're hoping school can resume next Monday. I told the others I'll help later today."

"May we stop? I'd love to see their progress so far."

He chuckled. "I doubt they've done much more than lay tar paper, but I'm glad you're excited. However, we've got an important errand first. Geraldine, remember?"

"Oh yes." She sobered. "I forgot for a moment. Maybe on the way back?"

"It'd be my pleasure to return you to your schoolhouse, Abby."

"My schoolhouse." She looked wistful. "I shall miss it at the end of the term. Miss the students. Oh, there's one now. Hello, Kyle."

The boy was almost unrecognizable in his multiple layers of outerwear. He lifted his arm to wave but couldn't quite reach shoulder height, for all of the clothes he wore. "Hello." His voice was muffled behind his scarf.

Abby pulled her horse to a stop. "What are you doing out here alone?"

"Micah and I went to look at the work on the school."

"Where is Micah now?" Dash circled Six around the lad.

"I dunno. He saw a friend."

"One of the boys from school?"

Kyle's attempt at a shrug through his many layers was almost comical. "It was a man. Might've been the postmaster. He didn't invite me, which Mama says is a rude thing to do to your friends."

"She's right, and it was also dangerous. I don't like you boys being out where there are so many snowdrifts, without a friend," Abby said. "You could get hurt."

Maybe Isaac was planning something special, some way to get closer to Geraldine, and wanted to involve her son. But Dash would have to have a word with his friend tonight about taking a boy from his friend. "I tell you what, Kyle. Let us see you home."

He reached down and told Kyle how to position his arm so Dash could pull him up behind him on Six's back. "Put your hands around my middle. Good. Ready? Let's go."

He clucked his tongue and Six started off at a slow, steady gait.

Abby kept up an animated conversation with Kyle, her voice so light that Dash was surprised to glance at her and see a worried crease between her eyes. Perhaps she was concerned about Micah discarding Kyle, but she didn't show any other signs of distress until they'd deposited Kyle at the café.

"Let's go to the dressmaker's," Dash said.

"Wait." Abby's eyes narrowed and the crease between them deepened. "Micah separating from Kyle doesn't sit well with me. It got me thinking. What if Micah isn't with a friend? What if he's been . . . well, been taken?"

"By who? You think Pitch managed to get to Wells in the past few days despite the blizzard?" Because that didn't sound plausible. The trains had been stuck, hadn't they? And no one had arrived in Wells on horseback, on foot, or in a carriage. If Pitch had just now arrived and come for Micah, wouldn't one of the men working on the schoolhouse have noticed something suspicious, like Micah crying out for help or resisting a strange man? Dash shook his head. "If he was kidnapped, it couldn't have been by Pitch, because I don't see how anyone new

346

could've come into town since Thursday, Abby."

"No. I think . . . oh Dash, what if Fletcher Pitch isn't *coming* to Wells? What if he's already here? What if he's been here all along?"

Dash's thoughts scattered like spilled marbles, and he scrambled to capture them back. "That's not possible, Abby. Pitch didn't know about Wells until a day before the informant told me, right before I came here for you, and he said outright he couldn't leave just yet."

"Are you sure? Could the informant have lied? Or been lied to? Fletcher Pitch is a clever man. It could have been a ruse."

Dash thought back. In mid-November, he was about to move here and take some job, any job, as cover while he investigated which eight-year-old boy in town was Pitch's son. The schoolteacher's health-related departure gave his superiors the idea to bring a teacher into the investigation. Sensing no immediate hurry, they waited until the start of the new term to bring Abby down. It wasn't until the first of January that Dash's informant told him Pitch had just found the town where his son was and would be going to find him. The informant received the news via telegram, in response to a letter he'd sent weeks before.

It could have been sent from anywhere, of course. Even Nebraska, perhaps from a town near Wells where Pitch might periodically go to receive forwarded correspondence. Dash rubbed his forehead. What precisely had Pitch said? The informant had wanted something from him, and Pitch had replied: *Not available. Traveling to my son once I finish business here. When I saw the name of the town where he abides, I knew.*

Dash repeated it in his mind. *Not available.* Maybe Pitch wasn't finishing business, as he'd said, but was using it as an excuse to explain his absence. Maybe he'd moved his operation to Nebraska weeks, months earlier without telling the informant. Or he'd traveled back and forth between Nebraska and Kansas City for a time.

"I hope you're wrong, Abby, but yes, now that you mention it, it's possible Pitch is here."

"More than possible. He's selling postage and probably committing mail fraud to ship out his counterfeit currency."

"Isaac Flowers." His roommate. His friend.

"Pitch's latest false name." Her eyes sparked like flint. "It has to be him. He gave you that bad dollar, remember? One of his own making? He's new to town too. Arrived in the early fall. He's had months to study the boys to determine which is his. And he sure seems to have taken an interest in Geraldine and Micah."

Dash's stomach soured. There had to be another explanation for Isaac's actions. "Micah likes stamp collecting." Dash dropped from Six's back and tethered her and Five's reins to the post outside the seamstress shop. "And he's enamored of Geraldine."

"Perhaps his affections are a pretense so he can get closer to Micah."

"I don't think it's a pretense." Dash reached for her. She released the reins and slid off the saddle into the circle of his arms. "He gets a moony look on his face when he talks about her."

"Maybe he's a good actor." She craned her neck to look up at him.

Not that good. "What about the tintype, though? She'd recognize him, surely."

She frowned. "I forgot about that. Maybe she lost it and doesn't remember what he looks like. Maybe he doesn't look the same anymore because of that mustache he grew."

"Or maybe Isaac isn't Pitch." He hadn't let go of her. He really should, but she fit just right in the circle of his hands. Staring down at her clouded his thinking, though, so he let go and stepped back. His thoughts cleared up at once. "He did say he was left by a woman around ten years ago. He never got over it."

"Just like Pitch."

"Isaac could've brought him home on his horse while Kyle's back was turned, watching the men work on the schoolhouse. Let's go inside and check."

"All right. But I still say he's Pitch."

Isaac was his friend, though. He didn't want to believe Isaac was Pitch. But Isaac had given him that dollar, and there was more of Pitch's money circulating through town. He'd received two more of those dollars at the general store. Pitch could be shoving his own money, little by little, in Wells.

And then there was the matter of Isaac's prosperity. He was wealthy, with fine clothes and secretive habits.

Dash's stomach sank to his boot heels.

The dressmaker's shop smelled like those perfumey sachets his mother had liked, and fringe dripped from everything, from the curtains to the frocks for sale. Geraldine stood behind the counter shuffling papers. "What a surprise. We haven't had any customers since the storm."

"I'm afraid we're not here to shop, Mrs. Story." Dash removed his hat. "Do you have a few minutes to speak in private?"

Her face paled. "Mrs. Leary's taking a late breakfast at the café. Micah's off with Kyle, watching the men work on the school-house."

"Actually, Kyle is at the café. Micah went off with Isaac, according to Kyle."

"Oh." Her frame relaxed. "Thank you for telling me, but I thought something like that would be happening. Isaac wants Micah's permission to court me. Isn't that thought-ful?"

"It is. So you know for a fact Isaac went to be with Micah?"

"Yes." Her brow furrowed.

"Then Micah will be home shortly, I'm certain," Dash insisted.

Abby didn't look convinced, though, as she laid a hand on the woman's arm. "We need to discuss something else with you."

"You're scaring me. What's this about?"

"I — haven't been truthful with you. I didn't come to Wells just to teach. I came on the behest of the Secret Service."

Dash withdrew his commission book from his pocket, opening it to reveal his badge. "We're desperately looking for a woman named Katherine Hoover. Is that you?"

"Me? No." Geraldine's eye twitched, just as it had at the schoolhouse when Dash wondered if it indicated she lied. Then she jerked her arm, twisting to run, but Abby clutched her. "Geraldine, please. Fletcher Pitch is probably in Wells. We need your help before it's too late."

"Here? No, I — you're Secret Service?" Her eyes were like a wounded deer's.

"Yes, and I've been hunting Pitch for a long time," Dash said.

"He wants Micah." Her voice rose in pitch. "I need to get him home."

Dash returned his badge to his pocket. "I'll bring him back, I promise, but I ask you not to run again when we return. We can protect you, and with your help, we can prosecute Pitch. Will you stay?"

She stared at him, breathing hard. "It was you, looking for me in Missouri?"

"Yes."

"I thought it was *him.* I thought — never mind. I won't go anywhere without Micah, so no, I won't be leaving. Is your name really Lassiter?"

"It is."

Abby looked apologetic. "I'm Abby Bracey. I didn't lie about that."

"So it seems we were honest with each

other about something, at least." Geraldine stared at Dash. "You've got to find Micah."

"I will. Abby, stay with her." *Don't let her leave.*

She understood. He could tell because the last thing he saw before the door shut was the resolute set of her jaw.

CHAPTER 19

Abby poured two cups of tea into delicate china cups and offered one to Geraldine. "Should I call you Geraldine or Katherine?"

"I haven't been Katherine in a long time. I don't think I'd answer to it anymore." Geraldine looked as if she might faint into the depths of the parlor couch.

Abby shifted closer and slipped a supportive arm around Geraldine. "Pitch'll be in jail soon."

"He'll get out of it somehow, and we'll always be looking over our shoulders." Geraldine rubbed her eyes. "I promised Nancy I'd protect Micah with my life, but during the storm, I didn't know where he was, how he was. The waiting about ate me alive. I felt so helpless."

"Nancy? That's your sister's name?"

Geraldine nodded. "I failed her, though, by spilling our secret. I told a friend why I was running away after Nancy died. That's how you found me, isn't it?"

"It started Dash on the path, yes."

"I should've known not to come to Wells."

"Why?" Abby sipped her tea.

"Wells was my father's name. Wells Hoover. I saw it on the map and couldn't resist its pull — but that was foolish, because Fletcher would have known my father's name too." She glanced up from her tea. "I fibbed to you about a friend inviting us to join her in Nebraska."

"I understand." Abby set down her cup with a soft plink. "What did Nancy tell you about Fletcher?"

"Most of what I know comes from the letters she sent me during their courtship and early marriage, how they met and all that. She waited tables at a restaurant he frequented, harboring no idea of his arrangement with the restaurant owner to pass along his counterfeit bills. All she could see was his winsome smile."

"He sounds refined."

"On the contrary, he was shy. Awkward. Stepped on her feet when they danced, fumbled for the right words. He wasn't the sort of man who plied her with compliments or candies, so when he drew a picture to let her know how he felt, my sister knew he meant it."

"I've never thought of a man stepping on your toes as endearing, but I suppose if he's not accustomed to dancing but makes the effort, it could make a good impression." Abby certainly hadn't held it against poor Burt Crabtree at the mayor's birthday party.

Her mouth went dry.

"He drew her a picture?"

"He's an excellent artist, which makes sense, since he's an engraver. She said he had an amazing memory and could draw anything after only seeing it once."

Like a Goose game board?

Burt, who was so helpful during the blizzard.

Burt, who didn't know much about horses, which he'd need to run a successful ranch. Whose house was sparsely furnished, his pantry near bare, his knives dull . . . because he hadn't really been setting up a home, because he had no plans to stay in Nebraska. All he ever did was repair a fence.

And watch the school.

Geraldine talked on. "That was in the beginning, of course, before Nancy realized who she'd married. That he wasn't just a counterfeiter. He killed two men."

"More since then." Abby willed her heart to slow to a steady pace. "Dash believes you have a tintype. Fletcher and Nancy's wed-

356

ding portrait. Did you keep it or destroy it?"

"Oh, that." Geraldine stood. "I kept it so one day Micah could know what his mother looked like. His father too, I suppose. I still don't know what I'll tell him about Fletcher. I'll fetch it, since I'm sure you'd like to see it."

Geraldine retreated into one of the bedrooms. She returned a few minutes later with a muslin-wrapped packet that fit on her palm. Resuming her seat, she handed it to Abby, who untied the ribbon around it.

The thin metal plate affixed to a brown mounting board was small enough she could tuck it into a pocket. Micah had inherited the bride's intelligent eyes. Her husband was handsome, clean shaven, and his eyes smiled even if his mouth was set in a serious line.

Her skin crawled, like spiders crept over her. "You haven't seen this man anywhere? Maybe looking a little different, after ten years, like with a beard."

"No, never."

How was that possible? Abby revisited events in her mind. Hildie said Burt kept to himself, which was true. He didn't attend church. But wouldn't their paths have crossed in town?

He left the mayor's party before Geraldine and Micah arrived, and the day after the blizzard, he left the Knapps' store before Geraldine came to collect Micah. Perhaps they truly had missed one another all this time.

"Keep this safe." She passed back the tintype.

"Of course. Will it help convict him?"

"It'll help identify him, but it won't prove he counterfeited anything. Or murdered anyone." For that, a different type of evidence was required. Did the Secret Service have definitive proof against Pitch, something that would sway a jury? Abby's stomach clenched with fear that they didn't. Pitch had been so careful to hide his face, change his name and tactics. Even Dash's informant knew little of Pitch. So how could they prove he was the so-called Artist who ran a counterfeiting ring and killed numerous people, including her father?

Lord, I know vengeance is Yours, but I'd like to see him receive justice for killing Father.

Burt was among the group of men occupied with repairing the schoolhouse, wasn't he? This was the perfect time to find evidence — if she hurried. "There's something I must do. Would you like someone to stay with you?"

"I want to be here when Micah returns but . . . I don't want to be alone, either. I need a few things from the general store. There are always a lot of people there, so I'll do that. If you can wait a moment for me to leave a note for Mrs. Leary? She can direct Dash and Micah to me there." Geraldine bent over the desk by the window and pulled a few sheaves of writing paper toward herself. A few scratches of the pen, and she plugged the ink bottle. "Done. I'll fetch my coat. One moment, please."

The moment Geraldine slipped into her room, Abby rushed to the desk. She didn't wish to frighten Geraldine by telling her about Burt Crabtree — Pitch — especially when he was at the school and of no immediate threat to her or Micah. But he would be a threat quite soon, and she couldn't allow the opportunity to search his property pass by. If she waited, there might never be another chance.

Abby scrawled a few lines on a blank sheet, but the note was messy from her haste. And wet. She didn't have time to blot it. Blowing on the damp ink, she turned her back.

With a rustle of fabric, Geraldine reappeared. "Ready."

Abby shoved the note into her pocket. She

waited while Geraldine left her brief note for her employer on the shop counter, locked the door behind her, and started toward the general store. "Why are you walking with me?"

"I want to ensure you arrive in one piece, is all."

"You're trained, like your operative?"

"Not quite. But I'm not defenseless." Her knife was where it belonged, tied snug to her calf.

The general store bustled with activity, but once Geraldine found a group of women to join, Abby caught Mr. Knapp's attention. She held out the folded note. "This is for Dash Lassiter. It's imperative that he read it the moment he arrives."

"Which will be?"

"Soon, I think."

His head tipped to the side. "I'm not the post office, you know."

At his mention of the post office, guilt prickled her skin. She'd been wrong about Isaac, but there wasn't time to address it now.

"It's important, Mr. Knapp. Important and private. I trust you to see he gets it."

He stuffed the note in his apron pocket. "No one's dying, are they?"

Not yet. "Thanks, Mr. Knapp."

Halfway to Burt Crabtree's, she remembered Dash's word blindness. How could she have forgotten, even for a moment? She'd shared ideas with him on how to approach reading, but they hadn't had time to practice. How foolish she'd been.

She didn't have time to go back, though. All she could do was pray and trust the Lord would help him read it, or that he would show it to someone he trusted. She mounted the horse Dash had brought her to ride. "Well, Number Five, it's up to you and me now."

"Isaac, hey, come here a minute." Dash had years of practice sounding calm when he felt anything but. His attempt at a measured tone seemed to work yet again, because Isaac grinned as he descended one of the ladders propped against the back of the schoolhouse.

"Ready to lend a hand?"

"Not quite." *God, Isaac is my friend. Thinking he might be Fletcher Pitch? It's eating me up. But I have a job to do. Help me do it to the best of my ability.*

"I need to talk to you." He led Isaac behind the school, away from the horses. If Isaac was Pitch and he ran, Dash would catch up before he reached the horses or the road. Fletcher Pitch would not get away today.

"I wanted to talk to you too." Isaac swiped perspiration from his brow. "I may need your room back. Not in the next few weeks or anything, but I've asked Micah Story for permission to court his mother. Thought it would be a nice touch, him being the man in her life and all. He said yes, and if all goes well, I hope to marry her."

"You asked him today?"

"Yeah. He came out here with his friend Kyle to watch us work."

"But he's not with you now?"

Dash's question managed to swipe the grin off Isaac's face. "I went back to work, he returned to town."

"Actually, he didn't."

"Where is he?" Isaac craned his neck and looked around.

"We don't know."

Isaac's head jerked back. "What? What do you mean, *we*?"

Was this the reaction of a concerned friend or a faked response by a guilty party? Time to change tactics . . . and positions, in case he needed to subdue Isaac. "Are you sure you didn't take him somewhere? On a walk or —"

"Why are you asking that? In that tone

like you . . . like you don't even know me? I didn't do anything but tell him goodbye."

Dash nodded as if he completely believed it. "What'd you do as soon as he left?"

"I went back up on the roof, where I've been ever since. You can ask any of these fellas. Dash, I don't like you interrogating me, especially if Micah didn't go back with Kyle. He could be missing or hurt. There are snowdrifts and ice patches. We've got to look for him." A note of panic rang through his speech.

He could fake his concern, but he couldn't fake witnesses to account for him having been on the roof all this time.

"We'll look. I have to ask first: Do you know a woman named Katherine Hoover?" His arms tensed if Isaac — maybe Fletcher — ran or fought. Dash had done this too many times not to be prepared.

"I know Hoovers in Sewickley, Pennsylvania. They're my mother's kin. Those who you mean? I don't remember a Katherine, though. What does that have to do with anything?"

Dash scarcely listened to the words. He watched Isaac's eyes, the direction of his gaze, the muscles in his jaw. Isaac gave no indication he lied. He did not know the name of Katherine Hoover.

"What about Fletcher Pitch?"

Isaac's hands lifted in impatience. "Who are these folks? Did they complain about me being here instead of the post office? Because if Micah's lost or hurt, it'll be a lot longer before I get back to work."

Relief flooded Dash's veins.

"Never mind, they're not important. Let's go find Micah now, though he could be back in town, for all I know. I think we should drop by the seamstress shop, and if he hasn't returned, we'll get some help to join the search." Dash clapped an arm around Isaac and drew him around to where the horses waited. "I've got a lot to tell you in a short amount of time but here's a start." He tugged his commission book from his pocket and, since they were hidden from the men by the horses, flashed his badge at Isaac.

Isaac's eyebrows lifted, disappearing beneath his hat brim. "You're a sheriff?"

Dash couldn't help but smile. "Not quite. United States Secret Service, Treasury Department."

"Why'd you take a job as a hostler, then?"

Dash climbed into Six's saddle. "Long story, but it starts with Abby."

Passing the school, it was hard for Abby to

tell which man was which, up there on the roof. She waved nevertheless, praying she looked like the grateful schoolmarm on her way back to the Elmores' place.

Someone waved back. Hopefully not Burt Crabtree. It'd be horrible if he saw her sneak into his house.

She looked straight ahead, focusing on the road as she passed Burt Crabtree's house. Then she doubled back and urged Five over a low-lying beam of Burt's Virginia rail fence. Five landed knee-deep in a snowdrift, jostling Abby, but she held on to the reins. "That's a girl," she whispered. "I'll give you something sweet back at Mr. Yates's. All right, here. We can stop."

Five turned her head as if to ask why Abby had chosen such an unpalatable spot as this, a patch between the cottonwoods behind the barn. It offered a sheltered spot to tether Five, though, and it was hidden from the house as well as the road.

The snow was six inches deep between here and the house. It sucked at her boots and dampened her skirts, increasing the difficulty of her march with every step. Her toes burned, but soon this would be over, and she'd be snug and warm, with evidence against Pitch that would make him sorry he'd ever come to Wells, Nebraska. Or poked the likes of her by killing her father.

She pressed on, rounding the barn to the side of the house. Movement shifted in the kitchen window — he was here? Not at the schoolhouse? She froze — she'd make up a story. Say she'd come to thank him for his hospitality — *Thank You, Lord, that Geraldine didn't bring him muffins yet, or she would have had the worst surprise of her life.*

But Burt passed the window again, slowly, his head bent down as if he was reading something. Sure didn't seem like he'd seen her. She wouldn't loiter, though. A few steps and she slipped inside the barn.

It didn't smell like any barn she'd ever been in. Oh, there was the faint smell of horse — singular. No others. Jasper was his name, wasn't it? Burt only had one horse? Who would believe he intended to ranch with one horse?

This barn also smelled clean, like window washing day. Light poured through the two large south-facing windows, illuminating a dustless desk — no, not a desk. A drafting table? She'd never paid attention to what they looked like before, but she'd seen one years ago. One of Father's friends was an architect, and his table was wide, deep, with no drawers. This was similar, but a bag lay on top.

There was no cincture for her to open. She poked it. It yielded to her touch like sand.

The only other thing on the table was a weathered wood box. Abby fumbled with the latch. Inside were tools she couldn't identify, but their metal points might well be used for engraving. A soft red cloth encased a heavy magnifying glass. Would these be enough evidence to convict him?

There had to be something else around here. Her gaze scanned the floor, landing on a roll of tracing paper, of all things, and a crate beneath the table. It looked like it could be heavy, so she knelt before it to examine the contents.

Metal plates. Many, many metal plates. Some plain, some etched with vignettes like the pictures she recognized on bills. Some were two by three inches, some smaller, but all were exquisite, expertly detailed. Abby had no idea how it was accomplished, but she was certain these small engravings somehow came together to form a plate for printing bogus currency.

Now this, this was evidence.

She couldn't carry it all, but she could take a few in her pockets. That wouldn't be considered tampering with evidence, would it, if she used it to lead Dash here?

There. Ready. Now all she had to do was sneak out and get to Five.

Scritch. That sure hadn't sounded like a mouse. Abby turned. Nothing there, nothing anywhere —

Achoo!

She jumped, clutching her throat. She wasn't alone. The noise was high-pitched — no horse or man sneeze. "Hello?"

Out of the dark corner crawled a small boy.

Oh Lord, Burt — Pitch — knows! He knows Micah is his boy. She rushed to enfold him in her arms. "Micah, I'm so glad to see you."

He didn't reciprocate. "Don't say you saw me, please, or I'll get into the worst kind of trouble."

"With your mother?"

"And Mr. Crabtree. He said I needed to wait here and not tell anyone or my surprise won't happen."

"What kind of surprise?"

"I don't know. Maybe I get to ride Jasper, but Mr. Crabtree says it's special because I'm the smartest, best boy he's ever seen."

With a click of the latch, the barn door opened. Burt Crabtree paused in the threshold, eyes narrow. "What do we have here?"

Micah spun around. "I'm sorry, Mr. Crabtree. I didn't tell her I was here. She just found me."

"She did, eh?"

"Yessir. Do I still get my surprise?"

"Of course." He withdrew something from his coat pocket that flashed in the light. A knife, and not one of the dull ones from his kitchen.

"What's that for?" Micah's voice was high with fear.

"Don't worry, Micah." Fletcher Pitch licked his lips and grinned. "I have a little surprise for Miss Bracey too."

CHAPTER 20

Dash didn't bother to stomp the snow from his boots before charging into the general store. There wasn't a second to waste.

Isaac rushed past him, his gaze frantic as he searched among the women gathered in the sewing section. His shoulders slumped in obvious relief. "There she is."

"I don't see Abby, though. Or Micah." Dash swept his gaze across the floor, looking for the child's feet.

"I'll ask Geraldine if Micah came back."

"Ask about Abby too."

"Hey." Knapp bustled around the counter. "You're tracking dirty snow all over my store."

"I'll mop it later. Something important's come up."

"That's what Miss Bracey said." Knapp withdrew a paper from his apron pocket. "She left this for you."

"Where'd she go?"

"It's probably in the note." He took a half step back. "I have customers to see to."

"Of course." Dash carried the note to the window by the checkerboard table. She'd been sloppy folding it — and writing it. Blotches of smeared ink obscured the scrawling penmanship. Just looking at it made Dash's throat tighten. He needed Isaac to read it for him. Isaac knew almost everything now. He turned to beckon his friend.

Isaac was in the far corner of the store, blocking Geraldine from the others' view. To anyone else, it might appear they were having a romantic conversation, but from Dash's vantage, he could see Geraldine's tears and Isaac's comforting touch on her hands.

He couldn't interrupt that, but he needed help. He was stupid, Dim-witted Dash, a lost cause —

That wasn't true. Abby said word blindness had nothing to do with intelligence. Reading and writing would take him longer, that was all. And take practice. He'd do some of that practicing now, and if he couldn't do it, he'd disturb Isaac.

Dash set the page on the table and stared at it. He had no paper to use to cover the words he wasn't reading, so he used his gloves. It might look funny, but it worked.

He could recognize his name fine. The next word was *I,* so that was easy too. What followed was difficult, with an ink blot over it.

A. M. I am. He worked out the next word. *Pibing.* But *pibing* didn't make sense. That *b* must be a *d.* Piding? *Riding.* That made sense.

I am riding to Burt — the next word must be Crabtree's. He skipped it. " 'I am riding to Burt Crabtree's to . . . enormous ink blotch.' Ugh, Abby, why didn't you blot the page? Not even Isaac will be able to read this. 'I am riding to Burt Crabtree's to something something. Saw the t-i-n —' "

Tintype. Dash was across the store in a heartbeat. "Geraldine, I need that tintype. Abby says it's Burt Crabtree."

"Burt?" Isaac's jaw went slack.

Fingers trembling, Geraldine fumbled with her purse clasp. "She didn't say anything, just that I shouldn't be alone and she had something to do." She shoved a fabric-wrapped rectangle at him.

He wasn't delicate, shoving the material aside. Dear God.

"Have you seen Burt, Isaac? He was working on the school, wasn't he?"

"He left before you came to get me." Isaac

stared at the tintype. "That's him, all right."

So Burt left the school. And he guessed what Abby's errand was. She'd gone straight to him.

Dash had no choice. He marched to the center of the room and pulled his commission book from his pocket. "Folks, listen up. I've got an announcement, and I can use all the help I can get."

Abby stepped backward, tripping over her hem but managing to steady herself against the drafting table. She couldn't escape, but that didn't mean she couldn't lure Pitch deeper into the barn. There. Far enough. *Shout from your diaphragm.*

"Run, Micah, run! Fast as you can to get help. He's a bad ma—"

Pitch spun, chasing Micah outside, giving Abby time to try the window. It was locked, but she — *ow.* Pitch gripped her arm, hard as a tourniquet, swinging her around. At least it looked like Micah had escaped. Good boy. Pitch gripped her so they were nose to nose. She had no choice but to inhale his stale coffee breath.

"That wasn't helpful of you. I want my boy back."

"And I want my father back, but neither of us are getting what we want."

"Your father?"

"Charles Bracey. You slit his throat on the bank steps in Chicago four years ago."

"Ah, you are related to him. I never forget a name. Or a face. But I figured the odds were pretty slim that we'd both be here starting fresh, as it were. Now I see we both hid our true reasons for coming to Wells."

"Your fresh start wasn't convincing. No provisions, and your knives are dull as hot butter."

"This one's not, though." He swung her around so her bustle pressed into his stomach, pinning her arms. She kicked backward, but cold pressed into the lace trim at her neck, near her ear. It pierced her skin, sending shafts of pain through her body.

"If you don't move, the knife won't nick anything crucial. But if you keep kicking at me, I can't promise you won't get split the same way as your father."

What choice did she have but to fall still?

Still didn't mean compliant, though. She scanned the barn, looking for a weapon, anything within reach. If she could bend down to her calf for her knife —

Oh Lord, show me how. Show me when.

Instead words came to her mouth. "We know you're here, Fletcher Pitch. They might not know who you are yet, but they know Micah's your boy, and you'll never get him. Ever."

The knife pressed deeper. "I should just kill you right here, but you were good to my boy. And you could prove useful."

"How could I ever be useful to the likes of you?"

"I need to think it through first, how to get them to take my offer."

"What offer?"

"Micah for you."

"No one will agree to that."

"Lassiter would. Love makes a man do just about anything."

"He doesn't love me."

"Come on, now, Abby. For a teacher, you sure are a dunce. Lassiter can't take his eyes off of you."

It wasn't true. Dash felt guilty, that's all —

"We're going for a ride." He dragged her to the horse stalls, and she stumbled to the ground. He gripped her wrists together, and before she had the presence of mind to kick, he bound her hands together. The knife skimmed from her neck, cutting farther down. "Just a reminder what'll happen if you fight me again."

Blood darkened her coat. "I'm bleeding."

"Of course you are. Stanch it if you want." He reached up her sleeve. "Don't all women keep handkerchiefs up here? Eureka." He stuffed the hankie in her fingers, and she bent her elbows to press her bound hands to the wound. Then he took two hankies from his pocket to help curtail the blood flow — no, not to help her. He pried her jaw apart and shoved them into her mouth, so deeply she gagged.

She was still half retching when Pitch hauled her atop his horse.

"This is Jasper," he told her in a pleasant tone, as if they were conversing about the café menu. "He had a bursa, but I got him seen to. By your fella, in fact. I can't bear the mistreatment and suffering of animals."

Only humans, apparently.

Pitch opened the barn door, obstructed from the schoolhouse by the farmhouse. None of the men working on the roof could see them as Pitch led her and the horse out into the crisp cold. Then he scrambled behind her on the saddle and wrapped his arms around her.

Jasper trotted around the back of the barn and into the cottonwoods. A little farther, and they reached the road.

Dash would have no idea where she was or how long she'd been gone. Unless . . .

Pitch muttered something about the fork. When they took it, a narrow path more than a road, she loosened her fingers and let the handkerchief at her neck fall to the ground.

CHAPTER 21

Dash rode Six hard all the way to the school, where he dismounted in under a second. "Isaac, you know what to do."

They'd worked out a plan, and there could be no mistakes now. Isaac, Knapp, and a few other men garnered the attention of those working on the roof while Dash and the Miller brothers, Frank and Sy, slipped around the back into the open field behind the school. If they stayed north of the house, Burt — Pitch — shouldn't be able to see them coming.

Slowly, slowly, they climbed over the rail fence marking the boundary between Burt Crabtree's and the school, continuing on to the rear of the house. Dash gestured for them to get down and mouthed a countdown to them. *Thirty, twenty-nine.*

They nodded, remembering what they'd volunteered to do. They now had twenty-eight seconds to get into position.

Dash scrambled, ducking, around to the front porch. Shame there weren't more men — law enforcement would help, but the sheriff was off assisting a widow with a broken window. Knapp had left Sheriff Grayson a note.

Three, two, one.

Dash didn't try to be quiet anymore, mounting the porch steps and kicking the front door. Its feeble lock gave way to his boot. The back door broke open with a crash too. The Miller brothers were inside.

No one in the parlor. Dash took the stairs two at a time, leaning to one side so he'd be harder to shoot if Pitch had a yearning to lean over the banister and kill him. Sy and Frank were behind him; he could hear their boots. The entire downstairs must be vacant.

He took the first room. Looked under the unmade bed, behind the chest of drawers. Nothing. "He ain't here," Frank yelled from the second bedroom.

"Or here."

They met in the hall. "We should check the cellar."

"I did," Frank said, his face greenish. "Found a body. Had a deed to the house in his coat pocket. I think he was the real Burt Crabtree. Do you suppose this Pitch fella, well, you know?"

"I do." A snarl curled Dash's lips. No wonder "Burt" hadn't wanted him to go down in the cellar with him.

They'd seek justice for the true Burt, but in the meantime they had a job to do. "The barn, then. It doesn't have windows facing this direction, so he may not know we've been in the house, but we shouldn't count on it. Oh, I forgot." The Millers suffered from hay fever. "You don't need to go any farther with me."

"I said I'd help," Sy insisted. "Killer, barn full of hay, and all."

Frank nodded. "The others should be here any moment too."

Armed with hammers and whatever other tools they'd been using on the roof. *Lord, let it be enough.*

When would Dash learn it was never enough, in his own strength? *I need Your help to read a letter, and I need it to apprehend Pitch.*

God had sent him help in these men. He nodded at them. "Then keep your heads down, boys."

They hurried outside. Dash shoved the barn door open, sliding to the side to find cover in case Pitch was hiding with a gun. The Miller brothers hid behind a pair of barrels. Sy plugged his nose to avoid sneez-

380

ing, managing to hold it back.

Dash heard nothing, not even a snuffle from the brothers or the horse. He craned his neck and looked to the stalls. They were empty. "He's gone."

"Are you sure?"

"Not a hundred percent, so cover me, if you'd be so kind." Dash abandoned his concealed nook and poked into the corners, behind barrels and sacks, before he called them out and allowed himself to investigate the worktable by the window.

Sy gave in to his sneeze.

"What's all that stuff?" Frank pointed to the spilled box on the ground.

Dash pointed at the metal plates. "Dies. Engravings. And these are his tools." Burins of different sizes and shapes, chisels, calipers, dumped on the floor.

"That's how you counterfeit? With those little things?"

"Part of it. It's a many-step process. As far as we're concerned right now, it's evidence. Gather it, will you? Put it in a box, a crate, anything you can find, and get it back to the sheriff's office."

While Frank gathered the evidence, Sy tugged a handkerchief from his coat pocket and wiped his nose. "What are you gonna do? Hey, where are you going?"

"To look for Abby and Micah."

"I'm coming too." Sy stuffed the hankie in his pocket. "Frank don't need me to take this to the sheriff." Clearly he wanted to protect his little brother.

"Where're you going, though?" Frank dropped a handful of burins into a box. "They could be anywhere."

"They might've left a trail in the snow."

Isaac burst into the barn, followed by a group of half a dozen men: Knapp, Topsy, Mayor Carpenter, and a few others Dash had seen but never spoken to. A regular posse, all ready to assist. "Where are they? Where's Micah?"

"Gone." Dash explained their findings. "I'm heading out. Pitch is dangerous, so no one need come with me." They'd been warned more than once, but Dash had to be certain they knew what they were in for if they came with him.

"You best believe I'm with you." Isaac was at his side. "I'm not going back without Micah."

"And the rest of us ain't letting that crook take our children," a farmer said.

The mayor lifted his chin. "I don't cotton to criminals abiding here. I say it's past time this Pitch learned his lesson."

Dash looked each in the eye, finding

resolution and purpose there. He couldn't have asked for better companions. "Say your prayers, men, and keep your wits about you."

Horse tracks — from one horse, probably Jasper — led Dash and the others through the near-foot of snow behind the barn to the road. No surprise there, because the blizzard wind had scraped this section clear of snow. No tracks to follow.

Isaac grunted. "Pitch could've gone any direction. How do we know where to start? We'll have to split up."

"No." Dash stared at the ground, hunting for the slightest sign. "He didn't go past the schoolhouse, because no one saw him, which means he went north, at least for a while."

Topsy rode abreast of Dash. "One horse or two, going single file?"

"He only had the one, I think. Nice horse, but he wouldn't win any races, especially not with the additional weight of Abby and Micah in the saddle." Not to mention the awkwardness of the arrangement, three people astride.

"Not Micah. Look." Topsy pointed.

Two figures on a single horse had turned the corner from the road that led to the

Elmores' place.

"Micah!" Isaac sank his heels into his horse's flanks and sped off.

Dash followed after, a thousand questions competing for supremacy on his tongue.

Isaac dismounted and ran to pull Micah off the horse, whirling the boy in a circle. "Your ma and I were so worried."

"I didn't know what to do."

"So he ran to our place," Bynum explained.

"That was smart, Micah." Dash kept his voice even despite his heart hammering in his throat. "Can you tell us what happened? It's very important."

"I went to the schoolhouse with Kyle. Mr. Flowers was there and he asked me to help him plan a special supper for Mama. But then Mr. Crabtree told me he had a surprise for me in his barn. He's so nice to me, I said yes. I thought I was gonna ride his horse."

Dash nodded with encouragement. "What next, son?"

He looked at his feet. "I don't want to get Miss Bracey in trouble."

"You won't. She was there for work."

"I don't think so, sir. She was *snooping.*"

Good for her. "It's good that she did, in this case."

384

"Oh." Micah's brows knit in confusion. "I hid from her because I didn't want to miss my surprise. Mr. Crabtree told me it had to be a secret and he'd be right back. But then I sneezed and she saw me and she said we needed to leave, and then Mr. Crabtree came. He didn't look right."

"What do you mean?"

"He just didn't look nice anymore. He had a knife. Miss Bracey told me to run, so I did what she said. I forgot to think where I was going, though, and I got lost."

"Ended up at our place," Bynum added. "Told me what happened, and I'm confused as can be about the whole mess, but I thought I'd better get him back to his mother and find the sheriff before I paid Burt Crabtree a visit."

Dash met his gaze. "Sheriff's busy. And Crabtree's gone. With Abby. We have something he wants." He didn't dare say Micah's name aloud, but the men seemed to understand, even Bynum, who didn't yet know the truth about Abby, Dash, and Fletcher Pitch. Pitch would undoubtedly offer to trade Micah for Abby.

"Does he expect us to wait around until he sends a note or something?" Topsy scratched his jaw.

"Maybe." Dash had no intention of waiting around, though. He may have lost the element of surprise, but he wouldn't let Pitch get away. And if that blackguard laid a finger on Abby —

His gaze landed on a fragment of snow ten or so yards away, where a path split off the main road. Why was there snow there, on an otherwise dirt trail? He guided Six toward it.

"What is it?" Bynum followed.

"Not sure."

It wasn't snow. It was a handkerchief, soaked in the middle with blood, its edges clean and white, like it had been folded and pressed against a wound. He dismounted and picked it up.

He'd seen it before, with the *A* stitched in the corner. Held it at the handkerchief dance.

Fury tightened his stomach and fisted his fingers. "They went this way."

"You sure?" Bynum dismounted beside him.

"They left a trail after all." He held up the hankie.

Bynum sucked in a breath. "I'm coming with you."

"You sure? You've got Hildie and little ones to consider."

"Abby's part of my household, Dash. My

family. I want to get her home. Hildie'd be the first to tell me yes."

All right, then. He looked up at the others. "Where does this path lead?"

"Nowhere." Mayor Carpenter shook his head. "At the end of it some pioneer built a sod house and gave up one winter. Still owns the property, but nobody lives there."

"Sounds like a good place to hide and think." Dash mounted Six. "No one needs to come with me."

Isaac shook his head. "No way is Micah coming to that. He needs to go home."

"Agreed. Take him back."

"I'd rather help bring this monster in." Isaac twisted in the saddle. "Is anyone else heading back?"

"Sy." Dash nodded at him. "You're going back."

"Naw I'm not. I'm old enough."

"I need a man I can trust to get Micah back to his mother, and then tell the sheriff where we're going. Tell them everything you've seen, and don't argue with me. We're wasting time."

With a ragged breath, he nodded. "Come on, Micah. Wanna gallop?"

"Not that fast," Isaac cautioned as they left. Micah whooped.

"Let's go." Dash waved his arm and led

the charge, clutching the bloodstained handkerchief in his hand.

Pitch had done this to Abby. *Dear Lord, protect her. And protect Pitch from me when I get ahold of him.*

Pitch squeezed Abby to him like he was wringing out a dishrag. Did he want her to suffocate? *Try to breathe. Focus on something.* Like using the wits God had given her, finding landmarks on the path. Two bare cottonwoods. A stump. If she managed to escape —

"Whoa." Pitch tugged Jasper's reins.

It was an old sod cabin, long abandoned, by the sunk-in looks of it. Come spring, flowers would probably grow on the roof. It might actually look charming then, instead of like a decomposing onion.

Pitch alighted from Jasper's back and tied the reins to a broken post beneath a dilapidated shelter that had once been a chicken coop, maybe. "Get down."

It ached, holding on to the saddle horn with bound hands, then swinging herself down. When her feet touched ground, she leaned her head against Jasper's side to catch her breath.

"Enough of that." He grabbed her arm and pulled her around the sod house to a wood door held in place with fraying leather straps. Before going inside, he held her jaw and tugged it open to pinch out the handkerchiefs he'd stuffed there. She resisted the urge to bite him, but she didn't want the gags again.

Her mouth was dry, which reminded her —

"Jasper's wheezing. He needs a drink."

"Don't we all."

Clearly he didn't mean water. "I thought you didn't approve of mistreating animals?"

"You ever stop talking?" He shoved her inside the dark soddy.

At least it was warmer in here. Not by much, without a stove, but it was out of the wind. A faint odor of stagnant water permeated the stale air. "Who lived here?"

He pushed her onto her bustled bottom against the wall behind the door and pulled an upended crate to the window where he could sit. "It's empty, is all I care. I've spent a lot of time exploring the area in case a need arose."

"Sure took you long enough to identify Micah."

"Because I was careful, Abby. A wise man bides his time. Didn't anyone ever tell you that?"

"The blizzard worked well to your advantage, didn't it? You had time to get to know the boys without arousing suspicion."

"The blizzard had help, where the school's concerned." His grin was impish. "I loosened a section of the schoolhouse roof several weeks back. Figured once we had a good storm, the roof wouldn't hold and the students would have to come my way. Of course, if the blizzard had hit two hours later, everyone would've been home already. But the risk paid off."

"You sabotaged the school, endangered the lives of every one of those children, for a chance to talk to the boys?" If her hands weren't tied, Lord help her, she'd grab her knife and put it to good use.

But they were tied, and she couldn't get to her knife without him seeing it. Maybe if he focused hard enough outside, watching for the men, she could at least unfasten the ribbons holding it to her stocking.

"I make opportunities, Abby. That's how I get by."

"You could've gotten by any number of different ways, as talented as you are. You could've been a famous artist, or engraved for the government."

His derisive laugh made her stomach burn. "No wonder Dash likes you. Such spunk. Were you like that in Chicago, when you were together? The banker's daughter and the hostler? Micah's mother liked to read stories like that, rich lady and the servant."

His gaze fixed outside the window, so she shifted position. The rustle drew his immediate attention, but she hadn't done anything beyond getting more comfortable where her bustle was concerned. And positioning her right leg where all she had to do was lift her skirt and grab her knife.

"You want to know how I knew Micah was my boy Junior? Not his looks or his build. He must take after a grandparent on Nancy's side or something, but I saw all I needed to in my parlor, when the wind was lashing the house. When he's scared, he gets a look just like his mother used to. That's how I knew he was mine."

"You must have seen that look from Micah's mother a lot. She had to have been afraid of you, to run from you."

"I could've made her understand, but she didn't give me a chance. It wasn't fair. I may be a lot of things, but I am fair."

"Not to the federal government, flooding the market with your phony bills. Not to the families of the people you've killed."

"Your father deserved it. He went back on his word. I can't allow people to do that."

"You must know what you do is wrong, else you wouldn't change your name and hide."

"How'd *you* find all this out, Abby?" He changed the subject. "How'd you know where Micah was?"

She gulped. Half the truth would suffice. "The Secret Service paid me to come teach here. I was supposed to wire an operative when I identified your son."

"And now they'll know what I look like. Micah and I will have to remain hidden from here on out, but that's all right. How's your neck? You're not stanching the blood anymore."

"The hankie got full. May I use part of my, er, underthings as a bandage?"

He thought a moment. "Go ahead."

"Turn away, then. I won't have you ogling me."

"Yes, ma'am." Chuckling, he shifted and stared out the window.

She'd have to be careful. And fast. She reached beneath her skirts and found the seam of her cotton slip. Tugging at it would be easier if her hands weren't bound, but she'd die before asking Pitch for assistance. She yanked and stitches ripped. Then, so hasty her fingers fumbled, she loosened the ties around the knife so she could rub the rope against the blade —

"Finished?"

"No, but I do not require your help."

"Ten seconds, Abby."

She ripped more of her slip to cover the sound, then rubbed the rope against the edge of the knife for a few seconds. No use. Bundling the strip of her slip, she reached up to press it into her neck.

Pitch was watching her when she finished. "I'm working out a plan, how to trade you for Micah. If all goes well, you'll be back at the Elmores' in a night or two. Depends on how easily I can get a message to Lassiter and make arrangements."

"I'll be home, and you'll have Micah?"

"Of course. A woman shouldn't take a boy from his father, Abby." Pitch watched her, his stare cold and unblinking as a snake's. "That's kidnapping."

"So's this."

His laugh caused her skin to break into goose pimples. It would be a long, frightening night if he kept watching her like that.

A twig snapped outside the sod house — or an icicle broke. Something made noise, and Pitch stood and glimpsed out the side of the window. "Don't see nobody. Must be the horse. Keep your mouth shut, anyway."

He inched to the door and opened it a crack.

A resounding boom sounded in Abby's ears. Pitch flew backward, landing faceup, his eyes wide.

CHAPTER 22

The door opened with a violent crash. Bodies filled the sod house, men — oh, it was Dash, grim expression flattening his lips, rifle in his hands. His sweeping gaze took in Abby but didn't linger as he moved to stand over Pitch. He glanced at the blood soaking the top half of Pitch's pant leg.

Pitch blinked. "Huh. Not only did you find me, but you actually hit me, hostler. Impressive."

"I'm not a hostler. I'm an operative for the United States Secret Service."

Pitch's smile was disarming. Perhaps that's why Abby screamed when he swept one leg beneath Dash's feet, sending him to his knees. He knocked the rifle from Dash's grip and pummeled him in the face.

Abby reached to her calf and worked the ropes against the knife. No use, but she could untie the knife. She clutched it with her bound hands and scrambled to her feet.

Someone — Isaac — shoved Abby outside, into someone's arms. Bynum. Glad as she was to see him, his weren't the arms she wanted.

Bynum's eyes softened at the sight of her neck. "Let's get you where it's safe, Miss Abby."

"No, Bynum. Dash —"

"It's decided. We each have a job, and mine is to get you away from here."

"I can't. Not yet." She wriggled from his gentle hold and hurried back into the sod house.

Dash and several other men aimed guns at Pitch, but Pitch held a pistol at Isaac's head.

Dash cocked his pistol. "Drop the weapon, Pitch."

"Like killing a postmaster is going to add any jail time?" He licked his lips. "Drop your weapons, all of you, or his brains'll be —"

"Enough." Nodding at the others to do the same, Dash lowered his pistol to the floor. "You aren't the shy violet you pretend to be, are you?"

Pitch grinned. "Now tell your friends outside to toss their weapons in here and then lie down in the snow, or I kill Flowers and then your Abby, who stupidly rushed in after you."

Had she made things worse? Abby hugged herself.

"Do what he says," Dash yelled outside. His hands rose in the air.

One by one, the men outside came to the threshold and tossed weapons inside. Knives, hunting rifles, shotguns, and — were those hammers and a saw? "Lie in the snow on your stomachs, hands over your heads." Pitch watched to ensure they obeyed. When he was satisfied, he jutted his chin at Dash. "Now you fellas. Get out."

Mr. Topsy and someone she didn't know filed out of the sod house, leaving Dash last. Surely he had a plan. But so did she.

"Dash! I'm sorry," she said in her best fake blubber.

He glanced at her, tender-eyed, before she held out the knife, hilt first. His sad eyes widened and he reached, but Pitch stretched out for it too.

It left Abby's hands, but into whose, she wasn't sure. Pitch and Dash tussled, too close together for her to assist. Isaac dashed back inside, gathering the rifle and turning it on its end, ready to hit Pitch with the butt, but Pitch and Dash rolled over one another, kicking, grappling, wrestling for the knife. Dash punched Pitch in the jaw once, twice, thrice before Pitch kneed him, flipping him onto his back.

The knife was between them as they thrashed. *Dear Lord, help.*

"Don't do it, Pitch." Dash's voice was strangled. Was he begging for his life?

No. Something else, because Pitch went still and fell atop Dash.

Abby gripped Pitch's shoulder and tugged, but he was too heavy for her. Isaac hauled him off, revealing the knife lodged at a steep angle in Pitch's gut.

Scrambling to his knees, Dash yanked his scarf from his neck and plunged the blue yarn into Pitch's stomach. "Isaac, we need the doctor, now."

"Don't think it'll make much difference," Isaac said.

"It was an accident. I had the upper hand, but he kept fighting — I warned him. I've gotta keep him alive to serve his time." Dash pushed with both hands, but blood soaked the scarf, pooling on the floor. The color drained from Pitch's face.

Abby couldn't move, much less breathe. Four years of agony, grief, pain, all stemming from the actions of this man, culminated in this moment. For so long, she'd wanted to see Pitch brought to justice, feel the satisfaction of knowing he would pay for what he'd done to her and so many others. Yet now, knowing full well he would have killed her and every man here, those things fell away, replaced by a need so great, she fell to her knees in his line of sight.

She felt the weight of Dash's gaze. "You got something to say, you better say it now."

Lord, give me words. "Look at me, Pitch."

His blue gaze was cold as ice.

"You think I'm going to tell you how much I hate you, but I'm not. I wanted to tell you . . . we have something in common. Our hearts."

A muscle clenched in his jaw.

"I'm pretty sure yours has been an open wound, just like mine, since our true loves left us. Dash and Nancy. Fairness is important to you, right? Well, it wasn't fair, what they did, leaving without a word, as if everything we'd been through didn't count for anything. As if we'd imagined those moments of tenderness. My dreams died. I expect yours did too. How do you heal from a betrayal like that?"

He stared into her eyes, his breath gurgling, but he didn't try to speak. Just as well. She'd rather he listened.

"I didn't want to forgive Dash, ever, but I did for two reasons. One, hate turned me into a person I didn't like. Two, I'd forgotten that God chose to forgive me even though I didn't deserve it. I couldn't earn it. All I could do was ask for it, and it was there. He helped me forgive Dash and my father, for getting involved with you. And now, I forgive you too, because I refuse to waste another minute of my life drowning in bitterness."

Pitch leaned his head back, exposing his throat like the pain was more than he could bear. His gaze bore into hers, however. Hateful. Unrepentant. But he was still listening.

"One other thing. Dash left me because he thought it was best for me. Nancy left you because it was best for Micah. Because you've done awful, awful things. You still have time, but soon, you're either going to meet the county judge or meet your Maker. The judge won't be lenient, but God's willing to forgive you. The choice is yours."

Folks mumbled, something about the likes of Pitch not belonging in heaven. But Abby didn't belong there either. Not on her own merit. Only God's grace saved her. Nothing else.

Pitch didn't answer. Just wheezed.

She rose and joined Bynum outside. Things were between God and Pitch now.

■ ■ ■ ■

Dash fought the blood pumping out of Pitch's stomach until the doctor arrived with Sheriff Grayson. His arms ached, but his efforts might not have been worth it. "Will he make it, Doc?"

"Too soon to say." The doctor glanced up. "He lost a lot of blood."

"Lassiter." The sheriff drew him outside, where it was colder but the air didn't reek of blood. "Guess the world knows you're not a hostler now."

"The secret's out." Dash leaned against the sod wall, resting his head.

The sheriff nudged Dash's face to the side, where Pitch had landed a good punch. "Ought to have the doctor look at that."

"Abby's more important." Dash's gaze met hers. She sat on the crate several yards from the house, three men tending her like hens. Bynum packed snow into a handkerchief to numb the pain in her neck, and Knapp stood by with his loose necktie, probably to wind over it like a bandage. Topsy stood by with furrowed brow, instructing them what to do.

The sheriff spit in the snow. "She'll turn out well enough."

"Mr. Lassiter." Mayor Carpenter approached, hand extended to shake. At seeing Dash's bloody fingers, he offered a clean handkerchief instead. "Job well done. There are a few things I'd like to discuss with you later, if you don't mind."

"Sure." Probably legalities. He didn't care. He just wanted to get to Abby.

"A celebration is in order. The blizzard is past and our community is safe again. Tomorrow at two, town hall for cake. I'll order it from the café."

"I'll be there," the sheriff said as the mayor went off, sharing the news of the celebration with the others. He glanced at Dash. "I can tell your attention is elsewhere. Go be with your woman."

Dash didn't need any more of an invitation. He held her gaze as he crunched over the snow.

Bynum patted Abby's hand. "I'm gonna check with the doctor, see when he can take a look at you, Abby. Later, back at the house? You aren't bleeding much anymore."

"Sounds good. Thanks."

Bynum and the others slipped away. Dash dropped to his haunches so they were face-to-face. His thumb grazed her jawline. "I'm sorry I didn't get to you in time."

"But you did. Perfectly."

"Not soon enough." He stared at the knot of Knapp's necktie at her throat.

She reached to take his chin and guide his gaze back to hers. "I'm fine. Micah's fine, isn't he? That's all that matters."

Her touch soothed and stirred him at the same time, and he wished he could rest his cheek in her palm. Take her hands. Carry her home in his arms.

But he'd hurt her before. He wouldn't do it again by taking liberties in front of a dozen men. He lowered his hand but couldn't let go of her altogether. His fingers took hers.

Her gaze lowered to his neck, unadorned but for his shirt collar. "You can't say no to a new scarf now. I'll knit a green one. Unless you prefer store-bought."

"Oh no. Knapp doesn't have anything I'd like as much as a new green scarf from you."

Bynum waved at him. They must be ready to move Pitch out onto the wagon. Best to get Abby out of the way first. "Come on. Let's get you back to the Elmores' place."

"I won't argue." She winced when she stood. "My neck throbs something awful."

"If the doctor offers you something for the pain, take it. Here, Bynum will hand you up to me." He mounted Six and then reached down. Bynum hoisted her by the waist. Dash lifted her sideways across the saddle, half on his lap, securing her with his arms. "Comfortable enough? Warm enough?"

She snuggled into his chest. "Yes to both."

That made two of them. Ignoring Bynum's amused grin, Dash nudged Six forward.

As she snuggled closer into him, leaning her temple against his collarbone and tucking her head under his chin, Dash's heart forgot to beat. *Lord, I still love her. I didn't want to have feelings for her again — if they ever stopped. I haven't looked at another woman since. But —*

"I'm sleepy, Dash."

"Just rest, sweetheart."

"But Five. She's still at Burt Crabtree's. In the cottonwoods behind the barn."

"We'll get her, then."

She was quiet, her breathing even as Six carried them back on the path. He hated to wake her, but he had to retrieve Five from Burt's property. She didn't protest, though, just snuggled back into his chest as he backtracked to the Elmores' place, Five's reins in hand.

Hildie met him at the door, eyes red-rimmed. "Abby?"

"She's all right." As he spoke, Abby stirred.

"Is Bynum —"

"Fine. He'll be here soon. Micah's safe too, but Abby was injured. Doc will be here when he can, but he's tending Pi— Burt Crabtree. He's not who he seemed, and he's the one who hurt Abby."

She flinched. "Carry her upstairs. I'll warm some broth for her."

"Hi, Willodean, Patty," he greeted, passing them.

"I'll show you Miss Bracey's room." Willodean marched ahead, followed by Patty. It made the going slower, but Abby smiled.

The girls climbed on Abby's bed. "Here."

"Thank you, Willodean. Why don't we make room for her now?" They scooted off so Dash could set Abby on the bed. "Go ask your mama for bandages, please."

Abby sank against her pillow as they left. "It's done now, isn't it?"

He poured a half glass of water from the pitcher at her side table and handed it to her. "Just about. You were so brave. And telling him about God? I love you — your spirit, doing that."

"I didn't say anything that wasn't true. He's just a man, Dash. A man with a broken heart. There are a lot of us out there, I

405

guess. But we need to know there's hope." She took a sip.

Voices rose from downstairs. Bynum and the doctor. Dash stepped back to give them room.

Abby pushed herself up. "Is he dead?"

"No. Not sure what'll happen tonight, though. In the meantime, Miss Bracey, let's see to your neck. Gentlemen, excuse us, please."

Dash couldn't help but kiss her forehead before he left. He followed Bynum downstairs to the kitchen, where Hildie held a tiny bundle of a baby.

She scowled at him. "You look like you could use the doctor too, Dash."

"It's nothing. Where are the girls?" Dash glanced in the hall.

"In the parlor, dressing Patchy Polly in a baby gown." Hildie's gaze hardened as he pulled out his commission book. "What's that?"

"I'd like to talk to you. Explain a few things."

He lacked the stamina to break it gently. Facts were best, anyway. While he and Abby hadn't lied about their past relationship, they hadn't been honest about why they'd come to Wells. Everything had to do with Fletcher Pitch, whom they knew as Burt

Crabtree.

When he finished, Hildie dashed tears from her eyes. Bynum stared at his hands.

"I've disappointed you, I know. And for that, I'm sorry. If you can't tolerate having Abby in the house because we withheld the truth from you, I'll —"

"We'll discuss it later." Hildie rose and busied herself at the stove.

Bynum glanced at Dash then shrugged.

Exhausted and uncertain, Dash left. He couldn't very well stay. He rode Six at a sedate pace, past Burt Crabtree's place and the school with the half-repaired roof. He'd wire his superiors and then struggle his way through a more detailed report tonight. Maybe Isaac could help him write it, if he wasn't with Geraldine and Micah.

What would happen after that? He might be instructed to transport Pitch to prison. Or if Pitch died, Dash might be expected back in Kansas City on the first train. Maybe even Washington.

That wasn't the real issue making his head ache, pounding against his skull with every beat of his pulse. The real issue was what he was going to do when Abby returned to Chicago and he had to live the rest of his life without her.

CHAPTER 23

At half past one the next afternoon, Abby glanced at her reflection in the small parlor mirror before allowing Dash to drape her coat over her shoulders like a cloak. Hildie had graciously loaned her a loose dress to accommodate her bandaged throat. Mother would have despaired of Abby's frumpy appearance, but more eyes would be drawn to the bandage on her neck than her saggy frock.

Dash was handsome as ever, despite the scab on his lip and the bruise blossoming on his jaw. Those were marks of his bravery. The rest of him looked good too, from his dark blue suit to his fresh-shaved cheeks, emphasizing the strong jut of his chin and the planes of his cheekbones. She'd rather look at him than at herself in a mirror anytime.

Once outside, he assisted her into the wagon he'd brought. "Borrowed it from

Yates's. These fellas here are One and Two, the horses from the first two stalls." He unfolded a heavy lap robe and tucked her in, from her legs up to her chin, like she was an infant.

She tugged it down a fraction. "It was kind of you to come all the way out here. I could have gone to the celebration with Bynum and Hildie." They'd left ten minutes ago. "I think she's brave going. Stuart is only a few days old."

"I don't imagine they'll stay long, but it's important to celebrate when God answers prayers and good things happen."

"I suppose that's true. Micah was found and a villain was thwarted. It's a wonderful thing for the community, and the truth is I've come to love Wells. For the first time in years, I feel as if I belong somewhere. Like I have friends. But . . . I'm not sure I still have any, after yesterday. I might not be welcome anymore. You might not be either."

"Because we've been lying to folks?"

She turned away to stare at the white horizon. "When the truth about me came out in Chicago, I lost all my friends."

"The truth about your father, not you."

"Then this situation is worse, because I'm the one who deceived everyone."

"Hiding information on behalf of the

409

federal government isn't the same as fibbing, Abby. You were tasked with an important job. And I think, given the chance, you'd do it again. Even knowing you had to work with me."

She laughed, which he'd surely intended. "I suppose."

"I know you're worried. You're in pain too. How couldn't you be?"

"It's superficial." But the wound in her neck throbbed and the cold didn't help, because of the way her muscles tensed. "I'm more concerned about Hildie. We scarcely talked last night, and this morning the baby needed her. At lunch I apologized because I was supposed to be helping with the baby, and instead I've caused all this trouble, and she said nonsense, but she's got to be upset. There wasn't time to properly talk after that, either. She helped me into this dress of hers and they left for town hall."

"I wondered where you got that dress. It's pink, which you don't wear too often."

Not since Dash left her, since he'd loved how her pink frocks made her cheeks look rosy. The memory used to ache, but it didn't any longer. "Maybe there's no harm in adding something pink to my wardrobe again."

"I know you're worried, but let's see how this goes, all right? The mayor wants us there. Invited us specifically. Well, me, but he meant you too. And he knew the truth when he did it."

They'd turned the corner and were passing Burt Crabtree's place — the barn that held so many secrets, the house that looked cold and sad without smoke rising from its chimney. Seeing them wasn't as bad as she'd expected. "The land will sell quickly, won't it? To a new owner who hopefully isn't a criminal."

"It's a good piece of property, to be sure."

"What's going to become of Jasper?"

"He's with Yates's horses at the livery. In stall Number Seven."

She smiled. "He'll be glad for the improved company."

Dash shifted on the wagon seat. "It was hard to miss that 'Burt' didn't know much about horses, but I gave him the benefit of the doubt."

"That's not a bad thing."

"It might be, if you're in the Secret Service."

She wanted to ask him what that meant, but he turned right at the church and there they were, yards from town hall. Abby took a deep breath, drawing cold air all the way down to her diaphragm. She didn't want to do this. She'd be stared at, so she'd grab a cup of punch for something to do and then wonder if she should join a group of ladies. Would they let her sit with them?

I'm not alone, though. You're with me, aren't You, Lord? Thank You for being my companion and strength.

Dash set the wagon's brake. "Ready?"

Good thing he didn't wait for her answer. He came around, plucked the lap robe from her, and oh! She hadn't expected him to take her by the waist and set her on the ground. The whoosh of movement robbed her of breath — or maybe that had something to do with the way he held her close to his chest. "You all right?"

She couldn't find her voice, so she nodded.

He took her arm and led her into the vestibule. Mrs. Carpenter and Mrs. Knapp stood inside, deep in conversation, but they looked up as Dash and Abby entered.

"Why, hello," Mrs. Knapp greeted.

"How are you, Miss Bracey?" Mrs. Carpenter glanced at the bandage.

"Well enough, ma'am, thank you."

Dash led Abby through the vestibule. "That wasn't so bad, was it?"

"I suppose not." They'd been courteous, if not effusive. How would the others treat her?

"Ah, there they are." Mayor Carpenter met them in the threshold. "Help yourselves to the baked goods, please. Mrs. Queen baked the cake, and other townsfolk contributed their finest offerings. Try my wife's prune compote."

"Thank you, sir." Dash shook his hand.

"Oh, and Lassiter, about that matter we discussed. A minute, if you would?"

"Of course." Dash offered Abby an encouraging nod and departed, leaving her alone.

Folks stared. Stopped talking. Bynum, holding little Stuart. Hildie, talking to Sara Queen. All her students and their parents.

Abby's heart rattled in her rib cage. She'd known it would be like this once people found out she'd hidden the truth from them. She turned around to find the punch bowl.

Movement in her periphery caught her attention. Geraldine — Katherine Hoover — came alongside Abby, lower lip clamped between her teeth. "Miss Bracey?"

Before Abby could answer, Geraldine enfolded her in a gentle hug. "Thank you for saving Micah."

"I — didn't. He went to the Elmores'."

"Because you told him to run." Geraldine's voice shook with tears. She wasn't

413

angry? Abby's eyes closed, and she leaned into Geraldine's embrace. "Because," Geraldine continued, "you cared enough to help put an end to Fletcher Pitch's reign of terror."

"Because you protected all of our children during the storm. Thank you." It was Mrs. Queen's voice. Abby opened her eyes. She hadn't realized other women had gathered around her and Geraldine.

"Because you are brave. And a good teacher." Hildie touched Abby's cheek.

"Because you love our children," Mrs. Sweet said. "Enough to discipline them if they need it, and enough to pray for them."

"And get to know them," Mrs. Queen added.

Abby pulled from Geraldine's hug. "I wanted to know you — truly, all of you — but that wasn't the only reason I asked to meet with each of your families, you know. I came to Wells to locate Fletcher Pitch's son."

"We know." Mrs. Queen smiled.

"But . . . I lied."

"So did I." Geraldine shrugged. "They understand why I did it. We understand why you couldn't be completely forthright with us too. You and your charming former beau."

"Maybe again?" Mrs. Queen's eyes twinkled.

"Poor Abby is in no condition to be teased. She's weak as a day-old kitten. How about some sugar biscuits and Sara's cake?" Hildie pointed at the table.

"I'll go with you to hold your plate," Geraldine said.

Abby hesitated. "You're too kind."

These women had no idea how much their friendship meant to her. God knew, though. And He confirmed it when Hildie smiled.

"And then come back and sit down. I've saved you a place next to me."

The cake and coffee warmed Dash, but not nearly as much as the attention some of the women bestowed on Abby. They didn't reject her, as she feared.

Bynum sidled up to him, cradling little Stuart, who was wrapped in a blue crocheted blanket. "Your face looks worse today, but the rest of you looks like one happy man."

"Pitch can't hurt anybody else now, although I wish he'd survived the night."

"His death was an accident. I'm just glad he didn't take anyone else with him." Bynum shook his head. "Last night, Hildie was beside herself with worry for Abby. She's

415

part of our family now." He met Dash's gaze. "She'll be staying with us."

"Do you suppose the womenfolk have told her yet that they want her to stay on as teacher?"

"They're smiling a lot. I'd say yes. I hope they're also telling her the town's adults have agreed to protect Micah from the truth that Fletcher Pitch was his father. They'll let Geraldine tell him when he's old enough to understand." Bynum's gaze caught on a small figure darting beneath the cake table. "Patty — I've got to — here, take Stuart."

Dash found himself awkwardly holding the baby in his palms. He was lighter than a sack of sugar. Warmer and cuter too. Dash slid one hand up the baby's back, the way Bynum had done. There. That was better. Now Stuart's head tucked into the crook of Dash's elbow and his tiny spine rested on Dash's forearm. Miniature feet strained against Dash's belly, but the little fellow was only stretching. No yowls. Now that they were both a little more comfortable, Dash's shoulders relaxed. Holding a wee one was pretty pleasurable, all told.

He took turns watching Stuart's dark, unfocused eyes and Abby interacting with her students and their parents. Everyone smiled, and a few shed tears, especially

Geraldine, but Isaac was nearby to lend his handkerchief if necessary, at least until he spied Dash with Stuart.

"Getting ideas, Dash?" He approached, jutting his chin at the baby.

"Maybe. How about you?"

Isaac flushed. "One thing at a time."

"One thing at a time," Dash agreed. Although things had a way of happening faster than a person planned, sometimes.

The mayor beckoned Dash to the front of the room.

"Excuse me, Isaac." Where was Bynum? Still wrestling Patty. "Stuart, you're coming with me." Dash strode, baby and all, to the front of the hall, stopping in the exact spot where Abby had stood when she addressed the parents of her students, what seemed ages ago.

"May I have your attention, please?"

Hildie's mouth formed an O and she stood up. "Sorry, I'll take the baby."

"He's fine. Relax, Hildie." She sat down as those gathered laughed. Once the room quieted, Dash looked out at them all. "I'm a man of few words. Not much for reading them or speaking them, but I can't leave today without thanking you for your assistance. Fletcher Pitch is — was — one of the most dangerous, slippery criminals the

Secret Service has pursued in its almost twenty-three years of existence. Catching him was my job, but when I asked you for help, you all said yes, to a number. Some prayed. Others joined me, risking your lives. For that, and for helping save Micah and Abby, I thank you."

Folks clapped. Others nodded acknowledgment. Dash smiled, humbled by the display, but he wasn't quite finished. "Two more things to tell you. One, a funeral for Maynard Yates will be held Friday afternoon at the church. I hope to see many of you there. And last of all, Miss Bracey and I will be taking our leave from the party now, so I'll have to hand Stuart off to somebody —"

Mrs. Leary, owner of the seamstress shop, was at his arm in an instant. "I'll take him."

He held on too long, waiting to be sure the baby was secure with her before lowering his arms. "Thanks, ma'am."

"Anything for you." She winked.

He approached Abby, whose brows knit. "What's wrong? We're not leaving, *leaving*, are we? I signed a contract for the term."

Her friends laughed. Dash tucked her arm into the crook of his elbow. "No. You need rest, is all. The mayor's going to tell them about Pitch and such."

"He died," she said as they made their way out of the hall. "Sara told me."

"At least he died with a choice for eternity, thanks to you."

He led her out onto the cold street, but not to the wagon. "Where are we going?"

"You recall that 'and such' I mentioned that the mayor's going to tell folks about? I'm going to tell you in the livery."

She eyed him askance. "Why?"

"It's quieter. Warmer than the street. And I thought you might like to see Five."

"Sounds like our childhood, talking in the stable."

"A little bit." He slid open the livery door.

She paused at the stack of crates beside the desk, which was cluttered with paper and small items. "What's all this? These were from Burt Crabtree's barn — Pitch's barn. You know what I mean." She held up a slender steel tool.

"The sheriff and I decided to store the evidence here. These are all Pitch's engraving tools. You're holding a burin." Dash pointed. "That tracing paper is used to make a screen to diffuse light when engravers work. It's quite interesting how they form the screens, at an angle — anyway, this little bag here is a cushion, filled with sand so it weighs down the metal when they're engraving it, so it stays still. You already saw his engravings, I think."

"He was gifted at it. Pity he didn't make an honest job of it."

"I think he enjoyed his, er, illegal activities as much, if not more, than the engraving, though. At any rate, these will go to Washington on the next train."

"And you? Are you going on the next train too?"

"It's my job to accompany the evidence, yes."

She turned away. "Oh, there's Five. Hello, girl."

Dash sidled beside her, perpendicular to her shoulder. His right hand cradled her cheek — soft, fuller now than when they'd met again last month in Chicago and she looked as if she hadn't eaten well in months. Gently, he turned her face toward his. "I'm going to Washington, but I'm coming back."

"Why?" Her voice was a whisper.

"Because this is where you are." He met her gaze. "I need a new place to live, since Isaac's pretty sure he'll be a married man by spring, so I'm going to move into Yates's house. Not permanently. The town owns the property, but they'll let me live rent-free until the house is ready."

"The house?"

"It's time I pursued the two dreams I had my whole life, for as long as I can remember. I'm going to buy a parcel of land here and breed horses. I'm going to start with Three there. He's mine now — they all are. Even Jasper. Low cost to me, courtesy of the town."

Her lips parted. "Seven horses?"

"It was a right generous gift of them, to be sure. But I'm investing in Wells, buying property and starting a business. Which reminds me, the best plot I've seen is Pitch's. I have to raze the house and barn, though."

"Bad memories?"

"That. And I'd like something a little bigger. With a wide porch. Cozy parlor. Larger kitchen, with a modern stove."

"His was horrible," she agreed. "Sounds like a good dream, Dash."

"We'll be neighbors, though. Me at the house, you at the school. Can you tolerate it?"

"I suppose." She smiled. "You mentioned two dreams, though. What's the second?"

His pulse thrummed in his chest. "You."

He shifted, coming around to face her. Slowly, so slowly she had ample time to protest, he drew closer, holding her gaze until her eyelashes fluttered closed. He touched his lips to hers, lightly, briefly, pulling back to measure her response.

"H–how can you do that?" Her eyes stayed closed.

His hand fell, along with his hopes. "I'm sorry —"

"After all I said to you, after how I treated you, how can you like me?"

"What?" Understanding crept into his brain. "*Like* you? I've loved you my whole life, Abby. There could never be another for me. I thought I was loving you by leaving you, but all I did was cause you years of pain. If you can manage to like me again, even a little, I'd like to spend more time with you."

Her lips twitched. "You do still need additional instruction with your reading."

"We need to practice that, don't we?" His thumb brushed her cheek. Then her lips.

She melted against him. "I was angry at you for a long time, but I never stopped loving you, Dash."

Then he'd never let her go again. If she was willing.

"I'd never ask you to give up teaching, but if you'd care to court, I'll wait as long as it takes. Does your contract expire in May?"

"Oh yes, I did agree to no beaux, didn't I?

For the moment, I'd forgotten the matter entirely."

He felt a little smug at that. "So can you — could you — consider staying in Wells? After your contract is up and you're allowed to have a beau?"

"Yes, Dash." She smoothed his lapels, resting her hands against his chest. "I will gladly stay here after my contract ends, knowing you'll be here too. You are where my heart is."

"The month of May will be here before we know it, but just once more before then, may I kiss you?" His lips brushed the curve where her cheek met her chin. Then her jaw, just under her ear. Then her cheekbone.

Her lips parted into a smile. "I think this once won't hurt."

There was no talking after that for some time.

By the time he finished kissing her, kissing her as he always wished he could but never dared, sweet and long and full of promises, he knew he'd been wrong. It would be a very long wait until May, indeed.

EPILOGUE

May

A whisper of warm breeze trailed through the open schoolhouse windows and stirred the stray hairs at Abby's nape. Hildie was right. Wells was beautiful in the spring. Beyond the border of the school, green fields of corn, oats, and alfalfa swayed among budding wildflowers, and the cotton-woods blossomed white. Lilting songs of birds twittered, beckoning Abby and the students outside. *Come play, come play.*

Alas, there was a lesson to finish. "Here she is," Abby said. "The *Mayflower.* Berth-anne, Coy, Bartholomew, Josiah, you'll need this for your graduation exam on Friday."

Zaida, a future teacher if Abby had ever taught one, raised her hand. "The rest of us need to learn it too though."

"Absolutely. It's an important part of our country's history."

Micah raised his hand. "I like the picture.

May I copy it?"

Sweet Micah seemed to be flourishing despite the winter's events. Someday he'd learn Fletcher Pitch was his father, but for now, he was sheltered in the knowledge that Geraldine was his mother's sister and loved him as her own since his mother's death. Now that Geraldine had been cleared of kidnapping charges, she and Isaac — who'd inherited a great deal of money from his family, which explained his wealth, and was messy with his belongings, which is why he'd kept his door resolutely shut — had begun planning their wedding in two weeks' time. Micah was excited to have a father at last and move above the post office.

"I would love for you to use your talents to copy this later. For now, I'll tell you about it. The *Mayflower* was an English ship that carried the first English Puritans to America in 1620. There were just over a hundred passengers, in addition to the crew. Yes, Willodean?"

"Your people were on that boat?"

"Indeed." Abby lectured on some of the tribulations endured by the *Mayflower* passengers. "History offers us many examples of people who face trials but persevere. This year, we've had a few of our own, haven't we? Like the blizzard."

425

"Like Pa losing his leg," Robert said.

"And that bad man taking you," Kyle added.

"And losing Mr. Yates." Abby paused a moment to compose herself. Later, she'd have to visit his grave in the church cemetery, where he'd been laid to rest beside his wife. It would have shocked Maynard Yates to no end to see the whole town turn out for his funeral, and she hoped he'd be pleased at how well Dash was caring for his horses, One through Six.

Abby met the gazes of her students. "I hope we can all draw strength from God's Word, but also through the example of those who've gone before us. And now, that's the end of our school day. Only three more days until our final day of the year together. Don't forget to invite your parents to the end-of-year program Saturday, where Florence will sing a solo and we'll bid our graduates farewell. Class dismissed."

Almos whooped. "Stripey'll be glad to see me."

The skunk still lived in the Sweets' barn. "Are you sure he doesn't want to return to the wild?"

"He has the choice to leave the barn every day, ma'am, but he likes us." Almos shrugged.

"And we get to visit him," Coy added.

"I can't argue with a skunk." Abby bid her students farewell. When they'd all left except for Willodean, she erased the blackboard with a rag. "Willodean, will you close the windows, please?"

"Sure, Miss Bracey. Hello, Mr. Lassiter."

Abby spun and grinned. "Dash, how was your day?"

"We made excellent progress." He'd worked up a sweat, building the new barn on his property next door, which he'd purchased after quitting the Secret Service — and the inn, of course. And what a barn it would be, when completed. Horse stalls and ample storage inside, and outside, large paddocks and training areas. Every day after school, he visited Abby and Willodean, swapping tales about their days and peppering her with questions about porch swings and stoves.

The second window smacked shut. "May I go pick flowers, Miss Bracey?"

"Of course. Don't go far, though. We'll walk home in a minute."

"A minute of your time is all I need," Dash said when Willodean danced out the door. A smile pulling at his lips, he came to stand before her, so close she had to crane her neck to meet his gaze. Her head spun at his nearness, and then her leg bones turned to aspic when he cradled her jaw in his large, gentle hands.

"Would you like me to kiss you?" His words fluttered warm on her cheeks.

"We mustn't. My contract, remember? No beau."

"I think everyone knows I'm your beau, whether I kiss you or not."

They'd done an admirable job of keeping things friendly between them, and not a single person had found anything in their behavior to reproach. Nevertheless, she had not been offered another teaching contract for the fall term. Abby didn't take it as a reflection of her abilities, but rather as the town's expectation that she would not be eligible any longer.

And they were right. She was ready for her beau.

"It's time, then?"

He pressed a kiss against her hairline. "I want to marry you, Abby."

It seemed she wouldn't have a beau after all, then. She was to have a husband, which was even better.

She pulled back, looking up into eyes she'd loved for half her life. She yearned to run her fingers through his damp, unkempt hair and then tug him down for another kiss. *God of grace, how do I thank You enough for bringing us back together? What did I ever do to deserve this man?*

Not a thing. God gave good gifts, which made it all the sweeter.

He stared at her lips. "I know it's only been a few months since the blizzard —"

"Yes," she said.

"Not going to let a man ask, are you?"

Her heart pattered in an erratic rhythm. "I thought you *were* asking."

He removed a ring from his pocket, gold set with a ruby that flashed like fire. "All the words I planned have fled my tongue. I'm not one for flowery speech, anyway. All I can say is my heart is yours, and always has been. Will you live with me and be my love? Will you be my wife, Abigail?"

That was his plain speech? It rendered her weak in the knees. "Yes, Dashiell. My brilliant, brave, patient, kind love."

"Miss Bracey," Willodean called, tugging Abby back to the world.

She had to blink a few times. "Yes, Willodean?"

"I'm making a wreath for your hair."

"I shall wear it with pride," she answered. It was a suitable response regarding the wreath and the ring, which Dash now placed on her finger. He kissed her hand then her lips.

Their winter had passed. Spring had arrived, bright and fresh and warm, promising a glorious summer.

Hand in hand, they left the schoolhouse and stepped out into the sunshine.

HISTORICAL NOTE

The terrible blizzard of January 12, 1888, struck with sudden, violent force over the plains states and territories on a day so mild, people worked outdoors in their shirtsleeves and children left their coats at home when they went to school. Just as many of these children were leaving class for the day, the storm hit with a roar many described as sounding like a train or a hurricane, and strong winds and powdery snow reduced visibility to zero. Of the 235 people who perished, 213 of them were children, which is why the event has been called the Children's Blizzard or the Schoolchildren's Blizzard.

Great strength and courage was shown by hundreds of unnamed men, women, and children during the blizzard, but one particular story inspired Abby's escape from the schoolhouse. Minnie Freeman of Ord, Nebraska, decided to keep her sixteen pupils inside the sod schoolhouse when the storm hit. However, when the sod roof blew off, Minnie had no option but to lead her students half a mile though the snow to her house. Some accounts claim Minnie tied the children together with rope, although others dispute the fact. Either way, none of her students were lost. Abby's use of twine and her grim determination borrowed heavily from Minnie's story.

While some teachers and students who braved the storm survived, others were unable to find their way even over short distances due to the lack of visibility. Others found shelter wherever they could. In the story, I made reference to schoolteacher Etta Shattuck, who survived seventy-eight hours by hiding in a haystack. Unfortunately, Etta succumbed to infection a month later, at age nineteen.

I couldn't help but be affected by the stories of heroism, compassion, and loss I encountered during my research. To read true accounts, David Laskin's *The Children's Blizzard* is a gripping, heart-rending read.

While Nebraska wasn't a hub of counterfeiting in the nineteenth century, every state saw its share of folks making, selling, buying, and using bogus currency. In fact, counterfeit currency is estimated to have accounted for a third to a half of all money in American circulation in 1865. While today the Secret Service is part of the Department of Homeland Security, and agents are more familiar to us as protectors of the president, this particular role didn't come into being for several years after *The Blizzard Bride* ends. The Secret Service was originally formed as part of the Treasury Department to fight counterfeiting, and President Abraham Lincoln signed the bill creating the Secret Service on the very day he was killed. In one year, the Secret Service eradicated over two hundred counterfeiting operations. Within two years, the Secret Service's role expanded to include fraud investigations, such as smuggling, mail robbery, and land fraud.

In Dash's day, Secret Service operatives worked long hours over large territories, or divisions. They tended to be men of good character with excellent detective skills. They also had to write numerous reports for their superiors, which wasn't easy for Dash. Although an estimated 5 to 10 percent of the population has dyslexia — including mathematicians, actors, and athletes — historically, reading difficulties were often attributed to poor intelligence or laziness. By 1878, however, perspective was shifting. A German neurologist named Adolph Kussmaul created the term "word blindness" to describe the reading problems he noted, and German ophthalmologist Rudolf Berlin was the first to use the word *dyslexia* in 1887, from the Greek meaning "difficulty with words." There is no single experience of dyslexia, but it can include difficulties with reading, writing, and pronunciation.

I am grateful to those who have shared their experiences with dyslexia with me, either personally, as parents, or as educators, especially Belle Calhoune, Virginia Copeland, Carrie Fancett Pagels, Tracey Ray, Janine Roche, and Cheryl Salas.

ACKNOWLEDGMENTS

While writing is a solitary endeavor, I couldn't have written this book without an overwhelming amount of support, prayer, and assistance. I'd like to take a moment to thank a few people who've given of their time to help me with this story.

I must begin by thanking my editors, Rebecca Germany, who took a chance on me, and Ellen Tarver, who made the manuscript shine. Thanks also to my wonderful agent, Tamela Hancock Murray. Dinner's on me!

Debra E. Marvin, you are a lighthouse, shining wisdom and a good dose of humor my way. Thank you for brainstorming, reading, and offering ways to improve everything I write, including this story. I'm so glad God brought you into my life.

Shannon McNear, thank you for your help and encouragement! I'm honored to be included in this series with you and Kimberley, Michelle, MaryLu, and Kathleen. I fan girl over each of you! Keli Gwyn, Suzanne Wagner, Jennifer Uhlarik, and members of Trinity Anglican Church, I thank God for your friendship and prayers during this season.

Thanks are also due to the members of Susanne's Soap Box, my team of influencers, who are all brilliant, beautiful, and sweet. Thank you for your help and hard work, ladies!

Karl (my Prince Charming), Hannah, and Matthew, thank you for loving and supporting me through the dust bunnies, repetitive Crock-Pot meals, and occasional freak-out sessions. I don't deserve any of you, but I love you with all my heart.

Thanks to Mom and Dad, for more than I can list here, but I'm grateful for the listening ears and loud cheers.

And most of all to Jesus, who never fails and never abandons.

BIBLIOGRAPHY

Johnson, David R. *Illegal Tender: Counterfeiting and the Secret Service in Nineteenth-Century America.* Washington, DC: Smithsonian Institution Press, 1995.

Kalman, Bobbie. *Early Pleasures & Pastimes.* New York: Crabtree, 1992.

Laskin, David. *The Children's Blizzard.* New York: Harper Perennial, 2004.

McCabe, Bob. *Counterfeiting and Technology: A History of the Long Struggle Between Paper-Money Counterfeiters and Security Printing.* Atlanta, GA: Whitman Publishing, 2016.

Melanson, Philip H., and Peter F. Stevens. *The Secret Service: The Hidden History of an Enigmatic Agency.* New York: Caroll & Graf, 2002.

Mihm, Steven. *A Nation of Counterfeiters: Capitalists, Con Men, and the Making of the United States.* Cambridge, MA: Harvard

University Press, 2007.

Waitt, George O. *Three Years with Counter-feiters, Smugglers, and Boodle Carriers; with Accurate Portraits of Prominent Members of the Detective Force in the Secret Service.* Boston: Jackson, Dale & Col, 1878. www.mayoclinic.org/diseases-conditions/dyslexia/symptoms-causes/syc-20353552

ABOUT THE AUTHOR

Susanne Dietze began writing love stories in high school, casting her friends in the starring roles. Today, she's the RITA® nominated, award-winning author of numerous romances with Timeless Heart. A pastor's wife and mom of two, she loves fancy-schmancy tea parties, the beach, and curling up on the couch with a costume drama. To learn more, visit her website, www.susannedietze.com, and sign up for her newsletter: http://eepurl.com/bRldfv.

The employees of Thorndike Press hope you have enjoyed this Large Print book. All our Thorndike, Wheeler, and Kennebec Large Print titles are designed for easy reading, and all our books are made to last. Other Thorndike Press Large Print books are available at your library, through selected bookstores, or directly from us.

For information about titles, please call:
(800) 223-1244

or visit our website at:
gale.com/thorndike

To share your comments, please write:
Publisher
Thorndike Press
10 Water St., Suite 310
Waterville, ME 04901